To: Pat — My dear friend

Thanks for all the years of friendship! The support and kind words from you always gives me inspiration!

Love you so much!

D. Coyne

2011

Praise for
TREADING WATER ON RIPPLE CREEK FARM

Here is a slice of real life from days gone by when family was close, the land was cherished, and God was real. In today's desiccated culture of faux relationships, Ripple Creek Farm offers a way to go back home on the way to the future.

—TIMOTHY GEORGE is the founding dean of Beeson Divinity School of Samford University in Birmingham, Alabama and is general editor of the *Reformation Commentary on Scripture*.

A page-turning story, adventure, heart, reality, and delightful detail, B. Coyne swept me into this coming-of-age story and I mentally 'lived' those years on Ripple Creek. A wonderful book, set in the Depression and WWII era, B. beautifully-describes growing up on a farm with a big loving family. She shares family's joys and struggles, and the deep faith in God that keeps them surviving and together. Enjoyable to read, I felt like I had visited that farm! I highly recommend this book. I can see special opportunities to read this book as a family and discuss its story. Great job!

—DENISE GEORGE is author of 25 books and more than 1,500 articles, and is co-founder of "Bootcamp for Christian Writers," a write-to publish seminar.

"This is an inspiring book – it is based around the struggles of a relatively poor farming family to survive during the Great Depression/WWII era. Although the times it recounts are hard it is written in a gentle and flowing way, such that it is easy to read and hard to put down! In essence it is a testament to a time in which acceptance of life, with all its challenges and benefits, is based upon a simple and steadfast faith in God."

—DR. MONICA LEE is Visiting Professor at Newcastle Business School, UK. A leading international expert in the field of Human Resources, she has published over 100 books and articles.

It was the best of times and the worst of times." Although Charles Dickens wrote in *a Tale of Two Cities* of another time in history, the Great Depression and World War II could be described in these words by B. Coyne in her first novel. Through excellent research, interviews, and stories handed down through generations, B. Coyne has given us another viewpoint in seeing the struggle or ordinary people—ordinary people doing un-ordinary things to survive. And people who are proud to call themselves "Americans." Yet in spite of difficult times, Coyne shows us the love of family and how neighbors helped each other to live and find work.

Is the time ripe for another Laura Ingalls Wilder to appear on the scene? Someone who can take us back to a gentler time in America? Someone who can produce a series like the *Little House* books? Coyne may be that writer! Readers will be strengthened by reading this pictorial account of this historical era.

—CAROLYN TOMLIN is co-author of *The Secret Holocaust Diaries: The Untold Story of Nonna Bannister* and co-founder of the Boot Camp for Christian Writers.

Praise for
Treading Water on Ripple Creek Farm

B. Coyne is a hypnotist whose artistic trances are born in common things that spring from the waters of *Ripple Creek*. In some ways *Ripple Creek* reminds the reader of Tinker Creek, that charming, shaded rill from which Annie Dillard lived in simple splendor that bought her a Pulitzer. But beware all of you who read this work. There will be water moccasins and choking brambles, hidden here. But the struggles are worthy battles. The pen always wins in these pages.

The reader is set free from the ennui of all drudgery in here. Boredom is never welcome at *Ripple Creek*. So settle in. There are many pages to be turned, and you will feel betrayed when B. Coyne's final words fall out on paper and the sentences that bound you at last release you. The book you may finish and shelve, but the trance will hold you forever.

—CALVIN MILLER, Birmingham, AL., is a professor, pastor, poet, artist, novelist and evangelist, and has authored more than 40 books and numerous articles on religion and preaching.

If you ever long for a slower, simpler way of life among God-fearing folks who love and truly care for their families and local community, then take a trip back to the time of the Great Depression and World War II. TREADING WATER ON RIPPLE CREEK FARM—LILY is a delightful story of pain, sorrow, joy and victory, revealed in the lives and loves of an economically deprived southern rural family. B. Coyne gives the reader a glimpse of the past among people who manifested three foundational pillars—love for family, God and country—that enabled America to survive nearly a decade and a half of economic depression and world war.

—LYLE W. DORSETT, Birmingham, AL, has authored twenty books of biography and history, is a professor of evangelism.

Although the cast of characters of *Ripple Creek* are fictional and the places and incidents are products of the author's imagination, Dr. B Coyne writes in such a personally reflective manner that the readers are bound to see themselves in characters and to hear themselves as the recordings of the characters life experiences are played for their hearing. This literary treatise serves as a profound mirror for identity – it carries within its bosom the seed of potential to bridge the gap between lamentation and laughter, hope and despair, faith and futility.

—ROBERT SMITH, JR., Cincinnati, OH, is a professor of divinity, as well as a pastor-preacher and author for over 45 years. He speaks in Bible Colleges, Universities and Seminaries in the United States and abroad.

This is a delightful tale of a single family's love, courage and resourcefulness as they work together to keep their farm and community intact. Its fascinating description of life on a southern American farm of the early 20th century transports the reader into a world where survival was not guaranteed and always hard work, but where the joy of honest labor and the bonds of love made life rich with meaning.

—FRANK THIELMAN, Birmingham, AL, is a professor and noted New Testament scholar, concentrating primarily in the Pauline epistles. He has written many books and articles.

Treading Water
on Ripple Creek Farm

~ Lily

TREADING WATER

on Ripple Creek Farm

~ LILY

Beulah S. Coyne

BORDERSTONE PRESS

2011

Author's Note: I have tried to present life as it was in the Great Depression/World War II Era in southern rural America. However, this book is entirely a work of fiction. Names, characters, places, and incidents are either products of the author's imagination or are used fictitiously. Any resemblance to actual persons, living or dead, events or locales is entirely coincidental.

First Edition

Treading Water on Ripple Creek Farm - Lily

Beulah S. Coyne

BorderStone Press, LLC., PO Box 1383, Mountain Home, AR 72654
Dallas, TX - Memphis, TN
www.borderstonepress.com

Text © 2011 by Beulah S. Coyne. (additional copyright information may be obtained by contacting BorderStone Press, LLC).

Editor: Roger D. Duke
Copy editor: Rachel M. Mooney
Supervising editor: Brian R. Mooney

All rights reserved. With the exception of short excerpts for critical reviews, no part of this publication may be reproduced, stored in a retrieval system, or transmitted in any form by any means, electronic, mechanical, photocopy, recording, or otherwise, without prior permission of the publisher, except as provided by USA copyright law.

Reasonable efforts have been made to determine copyright holders of excerpted materials and to secure permissions as needed. If any copyrighted materials have been inadvertently used in this work without proper credit being given in one form or another, please notify Thesis Imprints at BorderStone Press, LLC in writing so that future printings of this work may be corrected accordingly. Thank you.

Internet addresses (Web sites, blogs, etc.) and telephone numbers printed in this book are offered as a resource to you. These are not intended in any way to be or imply any endorsement on the part of the editor or BorderStone Press, LLC, nor do we vouch for the content of these sites and numbers for the life of this book.

BorderStone Press, LLC publishes this volume as a document of critical, theological, historical and/or literary significance and does not necessarily endorse or promote all the views or statements made herein.

ISBN: 978-1-936670-06-2

Library of Congress Control Number: 2011936214

ACKNOWLEDGEMENTS

A special thanks to my husband, *Edward J. Coyne, Sr.* whose faith in me never waivers.

Thanks to my *family, friends and neighbors* who assisted in my research.

Thanks to granddaughter and artist, *Molly Coyne*, for the artwork.

Thanks to my unfailing friend, *Devon Bagwell*, whose readings and suggestions made TREADING WATER...a better book.

Thanks to *my colleagues* who supported my efforts to complete a life-long dream of writing fiction, many of whom read and commented on the book.

Last, but not least, thanks to *BorderStone Press, LLC* for appreciating my work and publishing TREADING WATER ON RIPPLE CREEK FARM – LILY. A special thanks to *Roger Duke* (my editor) and to *Brian Mooney* for their professionalism and humility in seeing this project through.

DEDICATION

For my sister Shirley

1934 - 1976

Cast of *Ripple Creek* Characters

IMMEDIATE FAMILY MEMBERS	RELATIONSHIP
Anna Howell	2nd eldest child
Ross Wesley Howell	Papa
Jan Wingate Howell	Mama
Lilly Howell	Narrator and eldest child
Mathew Paul Howell	5th child and 3rd son
Tom Howell	3rd child and eldest son
David Howell	4th child and 2nd son
Katie	Family mule
Pearl	Family mule
Bertie	Family mule
Bessie	Family cow
Lad	Family dog
Skip	Family dog

FAMILY RELATIVES	RELATIONSHIP
Bob, Eddie, Rick & Russell Howell	Papa's brothers
Cynthia, Jill, Megan, Sarah, & Teresa Howell	Papa's sisters
Dan	Grandpa Howell's prize horse
Grandma Howell	Papa's mother
Grandpa Claude Howell	Papa's father
Pattie Ann Howell	Wife of Rick Howell
Nadine Howell	Wife of Eddie Howell
Roberta Agnes Wingate	Mama's mother
Thomas William Wingate	Mama's father
Great Grandfather Wingate	Mama's grandfather
Great Grandmother "Little Flower" Wingate	Mama's grandmother
John Wingate	Mama's brother
Ralph Wingate	Mama's brother
Stephen Wingate	Mama's brother

Friends & Neighbors	Relationship
Rena Hogan	Mr. Jeremiah's granddaughter
Hal Bennett	Neighbor
Amy Cole	Neighbor's daughter
Bradley Cole	Neighbor
Irene Cole	Neighbor's wife
Jack Cole	Neighbor's oldest son
Adam Cole	Neighbor's youngest son
Lucy Bowman	Midwife
Mark Bowman	Son of Sam & Lucy Bowman
Sam Bowman	Husband of Lucy/Walsh's worker
Colton Harris	Friend from neighboring town
Dr. Hayes	Family doctor
Mrs. Hayes	Family doctor's wife and assistant
Dr. Barnes	Country veterinarian
Mr. Jeremiah	Neighbor
Hilly & May Jeremiah	Mr. Jeremiah's daughters
Bob & Sherry Parkman	Neighbors
Pastor Luke Lawrence	Church pastor
Mr. Parnell	Truck Peddler
Mrs. Parnell	Teacher/wife of family peddler
Ron Vickers	Friend of Megan in nearby town
John & Martha Walsh	Neighbors
Gloria Walsh	Mr. & Mrs. Walsh's daughter
Matt Walsh	Mr. & Mrs. Walsh's youngest son
Nathan Walsh	Mr. & Mrs. Walsh's oldest son
Sal Black	Uncle Rick's friend in Nashville

Contents

PART I - Our Family

1 - Mama Cried 1
2 - Papa 21
3 - Mama's Indian Heritage 43
4 - Our First House 73
5 - Ripple Creek Farm 95
6 - Killing Time 117
7 - Mama's Friends 129
8 - Lad and Skip 145

PART II - Our Community

9 - Depression and War 159
10 - Our School 173

PART III - Holidays Come to Ripple Creek

11 - Thanksgiving with Papa's Family 189
12 - Finding the Perfect Christmas Tree 20
13 - Christmas Surprises 213
14 - Christmas Dinner 23
15 - The Surprise 245

PART IV - New Year, New Hopes

16 - Mathew Paul Howell 255
17 - Wash Day / Flying Jenny 273
18 - Spring Time 287
19 - Mr. Jeremiah 303
20 - The Swimming Hole 315
21 - Let Him Live 327

PART I – OUR FAMILY

CHAPTER 1

Mama Cried

ACCORDING TO MAMA, I came into this world kicking and screaming. When the doctor slapped me on the buttocks, he informed Mama that she had a rambunctious baby girl. I was born in October 1934. Life was a lot different back then than it is today. I don't remember much about my infant and toddler years but I know that I, Lily Howell, was the first born child of Ross and Jan Howell, small rural southern farmers. Papa had hoped for a boy, but loved me all the same. Farmers generally wanted a boy to be their first born— a son would be able to work the fields alongside them, to inherit the land, and to bring forth many children to continue the family lineage and carry on the family tradition. When I was two, my sister Anna was born. Papa finally had his boys when Tom, my brother, was born a year after Anna with my second brother, David, coming two years later.

2 Treading Water on Ripple Creek Farm

Even though I am in the twilight of my life, memories from growing up on the farm as a young child are still as clear as the water that flowed from Ripple Creek. One particular incident still burns bright in my mind like it was yesterday. As a child, I only saw my mother cry once—November of 1943 when our mule, Katie, ate some poisonous bramble.

In 1943, good working mules were a farmer's lifeline. Farms with large acreage were worked by four, and sometimes six, mules. Farms with less land had at least one mule. We were blessed because Papa had two mules, Katie and Pearl. He used mules to plow the fields for planting, spreading manure and other fertilizers, sowing new crops and then turning the old crops under for soil enrichment. Papa worked with the mules in the fields every day except Sunday. Sunday was the seventh day and a day of rest saved for church and giving thanks to God for his many blessings. Southern farmers in our neck of the woods were God fearing, God believing, non-denominational Christians. Our family was like everyone else—trying to survive the hardships of farm life, doing the best you could for your family and being thankful for what God had given you.

On this particular morning in November, Papa woke early and hitched Katie and Pearl to the double plow which was the biggest plow in the barn. He planned to plow the cotton stalks under in the lower forty section of the farm and needed both mules and the double plow to finish the job in a few weeks. The land would then rest until spring planting. Papa routinely turned the old crop under after the fall harvest to make the soil rich for the next crop and to save money by reducing the need for store-bought fertilizer. Sometimes, however, he would have a winter crop of alfalfa hay to supplement the feed for the farm animals. If the money earning crop was good quality and plentiful, he would turn the soil under and let the soil rest until spring. If the crops were not as good, it was necessary to plant a second crop to help ease the money burden. This November he was turning the soil under to rest.

It was noon. Mama sent me to fetch Papa from the field for dinner. Anna and I were out of school for two days. Our teacher, Mrs. Parnell, had a teacher workshop to attend in town. I was glad to help Mama by getting Papa from the fields.

This time of the year was particularly beautiful in the rural south. Brilliant colors dotted the hills and woodlands as far as the eye could see—bright yellow, burnt orange, deep burgundy, vivid amber with deep chestnut brown and rich chocolate foliage began covering the hardwood trees as they got ready to shed their leaves in anticipation of winter months ahead. It was easy to get lost in the colors and dream about spending time lying on the ground counting various gifts from God while watching a speck of an airplane leaving a white trail of smoke across the sky. We often found ourselves waving "hello" to the plane thinking people inside could see us on the ground below. My daydream was shattered when Mama called to me as I walked slowly down the path, kicking the dirt as I went. "Lily, hurry up! Your Papa's food's getting cold, so get a move on!" Her shouts jolted me back to reality and I broke into a full trot making my way down the trail to the field.

Meals were a major part of farm life. Farm labor was hard work and farmers needed hearty food to keep up their energy and strength. During spring and fall harvest seasons, farm families ate three meals a day—breakfast at 5:00 am; dinner at 12:00 noon and supper at 5:00 pm. In winter months and during mid-summer, two meals were sufficient with milk and bread served in the early evening if you were hungry.

I called to Papa as I neared the end of the field. "Papa, Mama has dinner ready!"

He waved to let me know he heard me while he softly guided the mules. "Come on girls! That's the way, go a little left Katie. Come on Pearl. We'll rest when we get to the end of this row." Papa spoke soothingly to the mules as they obeyed his commands.

Papa had a special working relationship with Pearl and Katie. He respected them and they appreciated the extra treats that he gave them after a hard working day. Sometimes, it was just a larger portion of feed. But when tomatoes were in season, both mules loved a juicy ripe tomato from Papa's hand.

Papa and the mules made the turn at the end of the row, throwing up dark rich soil and leaving a small trench in the wake of the plow. Papa pulled the reigns and the mules stopped as soon as he said, "Whoa." He carefully unhooked the mules from the large plow and led them to the shade of the nearby trees. Papa tied Katie and Pearl to a low branch of a large hickory tree near the end of the field.

I ran over to him and gave the mules a gentle rub on the neck. Papa reached down and with one big swoop hoisted me up on his shoulders. I sat astride his neck with my feet and legs dangling on his chest.

"Comfortable?" He asked as I giggled.

"Un huh," I replied between giggles.

"Hold on tight," He said as he flipped his old work hat on the freshly plowed ground and began the walk home with me on his shoulders. He whistled as we walked down the lane.

I loved riding my Papa's shoulders—he was so big and strong. I loved to feel his dark hair under my hands as my legs swished back and forth with each step he took. I loved the smell of my father—the combination of sweat, sun, and soil, made me feel protected by his strength.

I was Papa's first born and even though I was a girl, he made me feel like I was his favorite. I am sure my younger siblings, Anna, Tom, and David, all felt they were Papa's favorite too when he carried them on his shoulders this way. Mama and Papa had a new baby every eighteen months to two years—just like clockwork. With each new sibling, I feared that my parents would love the new baby more and me less so I tried very hard to obey their rules. I studied hard, read my Bible, and participated in church when possible. I did my chores and helped the other children without complaining.

After a quick dinner, Papa headed back to the field. I wanted to tag along, but he explained that he still had plowing to do and I would slow him down.

"No Lily, stay here and help Mama," he said. "I will be back before supper and Mama needs your and Anna's help more than I need it."

My face fell, but I understood. I tried to hide my hurt at the rejection. Without being told, I climbed onto the stool at the sink and began washing the dinner dishes. Anna began drying and putting the dishes away. Anna began humming a hymn and I joined her singing the words as we passed dishes back and forth,

*"Amazing Grace, how sweet the sound,
That saved a wretch like me..."*

Singing helped to make chores pass quicker. After the dishes were done, we were off to play soldiers with Tom and David in our room.

After about an hour, I excused myself from the soldier game and went to the kitchen to see if Mama needed help preparing supper. She was stirring a pot on the stove when I came through the door.

"Everybody, okay?" she asked without turning around. Something smelled very good. She finished stirring the pot and turned to face me. She moved to the sink area and got two cups. Mama poured coffee for the two of us. I automatically got the milk jug from the cooling box just inside the kitchen door and added some to both cups. Mama occasionally let me have coffee when it was just us girls, but she insisted that I add about half milk. Since Mama milked our cows daily, we used fresh sweet milk throughout the day, stored unused milk in the underground cellar beneath the house in cold pans of water to keep it from spoiling, and churned soured milk once a week to make buttermilk and render the butter.

"I just got tired of playing the game. Anna is reading and the boys are fine without me," I replied as I pulled out my chair from the table and sat down. "Besides, I thought you might need some help with supper."

"I can always use the help," she replied, smiled, passed my cup to me, and took a long slow sip of her own coffee. As she closed her eyes and tilted her head slightly back, it was plain to see that she enjoyed the taste of fresh coffee and the moment of resting with me.

I watched Mama and then did the same with my coffee. When I opened my eyes she smiled at me.

"It's good, isn't it?" she said as her eyes twinkled slightly. I wondered what Mama was really thinking.

"Very good, thank you," I replied just as Papa burst through the backdoor. He looked tired and irritated.

"What's wrong, Ross?" Mama asked with concern showing on her face. He had planned to plow until dark and here it was only mid-afternoon.

"That stupid ole mule," Papa began. "Katie broke the lead and ate some bramble bushes. Bramble can get stuck in the throat and cause breathing problems. She was eating away when I got back from dinner. Now she is having difficulty breathing so I cannot continue to plow. I just unhitched the mules and left her in the pasture near the barn."

"Will she be alright?" Mama asked soothingly as she stood up and pulled out Papa's chair from the head of the table. I sat very still, hoping that he would not see me and that I could stay. He plopped down in the chair dropping his hat on the floor beside it.

"I just don't know, Jan. Mules have died from getting choked on bramble." He sounded so defeated as he ran his fingers through his hair that draped down near his ears.

With his head in his hands, he was silent for a moment.

"Had you better fetch Doc Barnes?" Mama asked as she patted him on the shoulder. Mama pulled the coffee pot from the stove, poured a steaming cup and placed it in front of Papa. She waited for his reply as she replaced the coffee pot. He lifted his head, took a long swig of the coffee and said,

"We have no money, Jan. I can't ask Doc Barnes to come out again. We paid him in milk and eggs when the sow gave birth to the litter of pigs."

"But Ross, everyone pays Doc Barnes in goods when money is tight. He doesn't mind," Mama replied as she sat back down. I continued to try to make myself small and invisible by sitting still and barely breathing. I wanted to hear this conversation between my parents.

"I just can't ask him to come. Maybe she'll get better. I fed her and Pearl. She ate. Maybe she didn't eat enough to kill her. We can only pray that God will intervene and lets Katie live." Papa sighed with his head still in his hands on the table. "I really need that ole mule."

He took a long sip of the clear black liquid before putting his head in his hands again. I tried not to breathe, thinking he might hear and send me away.

Doc Barnes, the only veterinarian for miles around, treated everyone's animals. He often took farm goods in payment for services rendered. He was a good man and had made a difference in the quality of life for the farmers in the Dry Valley community. Doc had saved a lot of sick animals that would not have survived without him. He had saved Mr. Bennett's prize mare when her colt was turned the wrong way and she had a breech birth. The Walsh's famous stud bull had gotten tangled in a barb-wire fence and Doc Barnes had stitched up the wounds making him good as new. The stories go on and on about Doc's good deeds.

Papa went to check on Katie a couple of times that evening before going to bed.

I was going to ask Mama if I should help the children with their prayers and overheard Papa talking to Mama after the first time he checked on Katie. He came back, sat down putting his head in his hands. He was weary. Mama dropped her sewing and knelt beside Papa. She clasped his hands and head in her hands. Papa said, "This can't be happening, Jan! It just can't be happening!" He shook his head back and forth lifting it a little off his hands and from hers.

"Ross, it will be alright," she consoled him while patting him gently on his shoulder.

He continued, "I don't know what we will do if Katie dies. I was just beginning to have a glimmer of hope for us and now this. Jan, if Katie dies, we could lose the farm!

Bank notes are due in a few weeks. Taxes are due now. We had a good crop but barely have enough money to cover debts. With only one mule, I don't know how we can continue to work the farm." He paused again to get control of his shaky voice. He pulled out his hanky and blew his nose. I strained my ears to hear, listening from outside the door, my heart aching with each word from Papa.

"God always provides—even if we don't understand at the time," Mama reassured him. She stood and Papa stood with her. They embraced for a moment and Papa spoke again.

"If I cannot get the lay-by work done before winter, the additional fertilizer will cost more than we can borrow. By laying-by the crops now, it enriches the soil so that I need less fertilizer and is actually better for the land. God knows how I need Katie."

"Go to bed and ask for God's mercy. You are so tired, get some rest and perhaps Katie will be fine in the morning," Mama suggested as she kissed him on the cheek.

"Jan, you are my rock," Papa said gently. "I think I will check on Katie once more then turn in. Will you be long?"

This was my cue, I backed a few steps down the hall and walked back up to the door, scuffing my feet and opening it as though I had just walked up. Papa was putting his hat back on his head.

"I won't be too late," Mama replied to Papa, then turning to me, Papa said,

"Goodnight, Lily" as he passed me on his way out the door.

Since we did not have electricity, it was sunup to sundown for the Howell family. Often late at night in the fall and winter before I fell asleep, I would see Papa and sometimes Mama sitting near the fire reading quietly under the big oil lamp. Papa spent the time reading his Bible and writing things down. He read Zane Gray western novels that his brothers passed along. He also read how-to books about science and carpentry and electricity. He loved to read. Occasionally a neighbor would share a newspaper and Papa would read and re-read it several times before putting it in the outhouse for toilet paper.

Mama sewed quilts and blankets when she had time, especially in the evenings. She stitched fabulous quilts to keep us warm and won a blue ribbon for the most beautiful quilt at the County Fair in 1942.

Late in the evenings Mama repaired shirts for Papa, darned holes in socks and sewed by the dim light of the oil lamp. Papa would throw another log on the fire to keep the farmhouse toasty warm. The kitchen and living room were the only heated rooms so once the fire died out, the house got cold.

Mama said she would come in and see us before she went to bed. That evening she came to tuck Anna and me in for the night. The boys were already asleep. At night she helped us with our prayers before we fell asleep. This night we said a special prayer for Katie. I remember how blessed I felt to have such a wonderful Mama and Papa, a younger sister and little brothers. I should have been praying for God to save Katie but instead thought to myself, *please God I don't want more sisters and brothers*. I didn't realize how selfish my thoughts were, I just liked our family the way it was. Although I did not fully understand the burden Papa would have to shoulder if Katie should die, after Mama prayed with us that night, I fell asleep thinking Katie would get well.

The next morning the air felt chilly but not as cold as the day before. The frost pattern on the windows looked like the first snow of winter. Jack Frost had been busy during the night while we slept warm in our beds.

The sun peeped brightly over the barn. Jack Frost's work would melt away fast. It was the second teacher workday so Anna and I were free from school again. All of us children awakened just before 6:00 am. Mama hurried with breakfast. We had steaming hot biscuits with melted butter, homemade blackberry jam, piping hot oatmeal and large slices of bacon with soft scrambled eggs. We ate all we could as breakfast was the most important meal of the day for farmers.

Papa was out early. Today he had hitched Pearl to the one mule plow and continued in the lower forty turning the cotton stalks under to enrich the soil. Mid-morning found us children under Mama's feet, pushing, teasing, and pestering each other. Mama said she had a headache and sent us outside to play.

Anna and I headed for the barn. We wanted to find old Katie to see if she was okay. We also needed to gather the eggs and feed the chickens so we did everything at the same time to save a second trip. Hearing a noise, we looked up and saw Tom with David as his shadow, running as fast as they could for the opposite end of the barn.

"What should we do now?" Anna asked. "Do you want me to shoo them back to the house?"

"No," I replied. "It will be okay, but you need to help me watch them. I don't want Mama's wrath coming down on us. You know how she is when she has a headache." We knew well that when Mama had one of her headaches, she lost her patience with us and spent a lot of time in her room.

Sometimes, that meant another baby was on the way. Anna nodded in agreement so we waited for Tom and David to reappear at the north side of the barn.

"We want to help you look for Katie!" Tom called as they entered the barn together.

"Okay" I replied. "But you must do as we say. Okay?" I gave their heads an affectionate pat with my hand as they walked beside Anna and me.

I continued, "First Anna and I have to feed the chickens and gather the eggs. While we do our chores, you may look for Katie, but don't go too far and don't get into trouble." I warned.

"Now stay close to the barn and don't go into the woods, do you hear me?" I cautioned. They shook their heads in agreement.

"Okay," they finally called over their shoulders as they raced for the pasture area.

I opened the barn door and peered out. Katie was nowhere to be seen. I called her name but no response. Anna called her name and got the same echo of silence. The silence in the barn seemed to overtake the universe. There was not a bird in sight, just complete silence as the sun continued shining high in the cloudless sky. Anna and I walked to the feed room.

We each got a bucket of feed for the chickens. This was a necessary chore that either of us could do with our eyes shut.

"Do you think Katie is okay?" Anna questioned as she filled her bucket half full from the yellow corn bag. First, I took feed from the laying hen's special feedbag and then the yellow corn bag, mixing the two feeds together with my hands.

Anna's big green eyes were wide with wonderment as her thick blonde hair lay in tiny ringlets on her shoulder. She was a beautiful seven-year-old with fair skin and not a freckle in sight. Her looks came from the Howell side of the family. I, on the other hand, looked a lot like Mama's side of the family and her Indian ancestors. I had olive skin, long straight black hair that was shoulder length but usually held back in a ponytail. My eyes were large, round, dark brown, and set deep within my arched brow. My high cheekbones made people take a second glance, but I did not think I was pretty. I thought my sister, Anna, was beautiful. Anna and I looked so different that strangers would not recognize us as sisters. We were close in age with a little less than two years difference. We told each other our secrets, our dreams, everything in our young girl's heart.

We took the chicken feed out the south end of the barn and around to the chicken coop area. We began sprinkling the feed on the ground and calling the chickens to come to eat.

"Cluck, cluck, cluck, cluck," is chicken talk for the food's here.

I stepped around and opened the brooding hen doors one at a time and allowed the hens to descend to the ground. I quickly returned to the feed room, took the pail of water stored there, and filled the chickens' water dish with fresh water. Then, we scattered small amounts of the feed into their coops. I enjoyed raising chickens. It was easy work, but required daily attention. We gathered eggs daily and watched baby chicks appear as fluffs of bright yellow down snuggled under their mother's protective wings. The baby chicks were so cute and cuddlesome but grew up to be plain chickens. Grown chickens were not ugly, but they were not cute or pretty either. They also were not very smart. They didn't seem to mind that we raided their nests and removed all the eggs but one. Hens only laid one egg a day, so if you found twelve eggs in the nest that day, eleven hens had visited the same nest.

Anna and I sometimes played a game on the laying hens. We would remove all the eggs in one nest to see how long before they realized it was okay to return to that nest. They would usually come back the second day, but they would lay an egg each day if you left one egg. We were careful not to play this game too often as Mama would have been upset with us had she known. It was one of our little secrets. This day we gathered eighteen eggs. I took an empty bucket from the feed room and placed the eggs inside for safe keeping until we got ready to return to the house.

Looking around, Tom and David were still outside. The morning air was calm. It was dead quiet without the noise of chirping birds. Only a single hawk glided high overhead as he sought prey on the ground below. Some days when time permitted, I liked to lie on the ground and watch the hawks glide. It looked effortless—they could stay up a long time without flapping their wings. I found this fascinating. Forgetting about the hawk, I suggested, "Let's check the pasture. I heard Papa say he had left Katie outside in the fresh air."

Anna and I walked out into the clear crisp mid-morning air. As we stepped from the barn, the north wind blew a chill that cut through our clothes and to the bone. Even the beautiful sunshine could not warm us. We pulled our jackets close around our necks and headed for the north side of the barn.

Then I saw her. Katie was lying on her side under a tall oak tree where she loved to scratch her back by rubbing against the tree. David was sitting on Katie's back close to her buttocks. Tom was also sitting on her but nearer to her head. They were riding her! Katie didn't seem to mind. Fear gripped me as I saw at once that something was wrong. Katie was a gentle old mule with whom all of us had grown up. She never minded us touching her and would take a carrot or a tomato from a small hand that extended it without a bite. We heard stories of some mules biting their owners and disliking children. But not our Katie! She was like family. We loved her.

"Anna," I whispered. "Go get Mama."

"Why? They are just riding her." Anna asked looking puzzled. "What about the headache?"

"Please, just do as I say and quickly," I said trying to calm my voice and fears at the same time. We had all ridden Katie this way before, but this time, something was different. Her eyes were opened and she was lying very still.

Anna ran for the house without arguing. In a couple of minutes, but what seemed an eternity, I heard the slam of the door and saw Mama as she bolted through the kitchen doorway into the cold air. She wore only a light sweater over her blouse. Mama ran as fast as I had ever seen her with Anna close behind. She came through the gate, crossed the open pasture, rounded the barn, crossed the front of it and was standing beside us in a few seconds.

She didn't say a word, but reached up and removed David first, standing him on the ground, then Tom. As she stood Tom on the ground beside David, she said,

"Go on to the house now all of you."

"Yes Mama," Anna and I said together and turned to walk away.

"Are you mad at us?" questioned Tom as he and David stood beside Katie not moving. Anna and I stopped and stood quietly listening.

"No," Mama replied. "I am not mad at you. It's freezing cold out here and you will catch your death." At that moment, before anything else could be said, Mama picked David up, took Tom by the hand and motioned with her head for Anna and me to follow. I picked up the bucket of eggs from just inside the barn as we started to the house.

David, with the enthusiasm that only a four year old can have, asked, "Mama, is Katie sleeping?"

As Mama walked in silence, David continued, "She let us ride her but her eyes are open. Do all mules sleep with their eyes open, Mama?"

When Mama didn't reply to David's question, he stopped talking. We walked the remaining distance in silence. When we reached the kitchen door, Mama quickly pulled a lightweight jacket from the coat hook located just inside the door. She pulled the jacket over her arms and around her shoulders and said,

"Lily, I have to go see your father. I'm leaving you in charge! Please take everyone inside and play a game. I will be back shortly." With that, Mama turned around and with her head down, started walking down the pathway toward the fields.

About forty-five minutes later, while the children played house and paper dolls, I went to the kitchen to get a drink of water. Peeking out the kitchen window, I saw Mama kneeling on the ground beside old Katie. Her body was gently swaying back and forth and I could see she was shaking with sobs.

She knelt on the cold ground beside a dead Katie for what seemed like an hour. I was scared. What could I do? Should I go comfort Mama? For the first time in my nine years of life, I saw my Mama cry.

After a while, she got up, wiped her eyes with her hanky, blew her nose and slowly walked toward the house. She was totally unaware of the biting cold wind that whipped the sides of her jacket to and fro or of my child face at the kitchen window peering out.

I returned to the den and joined my siblings in their game before Mama came into the house. The others were concentrating on the game and didn't notice Mama's red swollen eyes and bright red nose. I pretended not to notice either. I didn't want to embarrass Mama by letting her know I saw her cry.

CHAPTER 2

Papa

PAPA'S PARENTS, the Claude Howell family, had lived in the area for more than 23 years. They were both born and raised in nearby counties. The Howell home sat in the middle of a 100 acre farm, 50 acres of tillable fields and 50 acres of hilly timberlands. Everyone in the neighborhood knew the Howells. Papa's parents bought the farm and moved to Jackson County before he was born.

Papa was born one beautiful spring day. Flowers were blooming, birds were chirping, and chipmunks and squirrels were racing on April 29, 1910. The spring crops of cotton, corn, sweet corn, potatoes, and hay were growing in the fields. The plants in the vegetable garden were covered with vast amounts of blooms while bees worked frantically securing nectar for their hives to make honey. All the signs were there for a good crop year. The mid-wife slowly came from the bedroom smiling down at the bundle in her arms. She handed the baby to Grandpa and through tears of joy,

Grandpa proudly presented Ross Wesley Howell, his firstborn son, to Papa's two older sisters, Jill and Teresa. A firstborn son, a special gift indeed to carry on the Howell family name for another generation, meant he and Grandma could relax now.

Later Grandpa and Grandma Howell had three more daughters, Megan, Sarah, and Cynthia and four more sons, Eddie, Russell, Bob, and Rick. But Papa, as their firstborn son, had his special place in life. Families needed a lot of children back then to work the farm. Children were a gift from God, and parents were pleased when God gave them a healthy baby, but were overjoyed with the birth of the first son.

Papa's sisters were thrilled with the birth of their handsome little brother. They loved him and spoiled him from the first day. This affection continued until the time he married and even afterwards—his sisters showered our family with love.

From birth, Ross Howell wanted for nothing. His sisters went out of their way to get whatever he needed or wanted. Most young men who had older sisters to spoil them grew up selfish, lazy, inconsiderate—just plain brats, but not Papa. He was a striking young boy and grew to become a handsome, outgoing, unselfish, polite young man and a good person who was liked by everyone. And above all, he was a hard worker and honest.

After his sixteenth birthday, Ross Howell started earning money doing chores for neighbors. His farm chores included the normal jobs for operating a farm—plowing, planting, laying-by the crops, repairing fences, clearing trees from new fields that were being converted to farm land, and repairs to machinery and buildings. He also helped grandpa design and build a new barn which became the envy of the neighbors. Word got around about his work and his talent as a self-taught carpenter. When his chores at home were finished, Papa worked a few hours a week for neighbor farmers. Finding work was easy for Papa. His reputation for being a strong, polite, hard-worker soon became the talk of the neighborhood.

"He's such a good, polite boy and can repair or build anything!" they said.

Soon Papa had more work than he could do. Except for week-ends, Papa worked nonstop-first, to complete his chores at home, and then for the neighboring farmers. In planting and harvest time, he would get up early and work a couple of hours before going to school and rush home after school to complete his chores. His reputation expanded to nearby counties. When farmers had special building projects such as new barns, fence lines, storage buildings and homes, they requested Papa to be a part of the team. Soon he spent Saturdays working on special projects. Papa really enjoyed the building and creating part of farming.

Papa continued to go to school and work part-time for two years until he turned eighteen. He then dropped out of school at the end of eleventh grade and began working full time, not only at farm chores, but more often at building projects for other farmers.

Except for buying clothes occasionally, Papa saved his money. He wanted to get married and raise a family like his father and grandfather before him. This was the American way in the 1920-30s. Most boys went to school, developed a skill, and either moved to a big city to work in a factory or worked on the farm until they could earn enough money to buy a farm of their own. Often they followed in their parents footsteps and became farmers. They married young and raised large families to help work the fields. Times were hard, but a good reputation, a strong back, and hard work could make a young man successful. Papa was becoming successful.

But, it was not enough. Papa wanted more. He wanted to have a farm of his very own, and to raise a family there. Then he met Jan Alma Wingate. She was eighteen when he first saw her at a church social in another county. He had been working to help a farmer, Mr. Bradley Cole, build a livestock barn. The team of four men had worked all day and Mrs. Cole had fed everyone a nice supper including pork, griddle cakes, string beans, fried potatoes, candied carrots, turnips with greens, and berry cobbler for dessert. The other three men went home to their families after supper. As the sun began to set, Papa lingered behind with a cup of black coffee, chatting with Mr. Cole. They discussed the progress of the project and the last things that needed to be done to complete it. Both Papa and Mr. Cole thought one more Saturday would finish raising the barn. Knowing Papa had a long ten mile ride home on his mule, the farmer asked if he wanted to spend the night.

"Ross," Mr. Cole said, "it's a long ride home, so why don't you go to the church social with us and spend the night? You can wash up in the sick room of the birthing barn where water is available."

Papa listened while sipping his coffee. The Coles used the "sick room" whenever they had a sick animal in their herd, or when a young cow had difficulty while giving birth to her first calf. Occasionally, they used it for other things. They stored clean blankets and clean towels in a self-contained cabinet in the room. The birthing room, with available water provided from a pump-well located inside the building, was nicer than a lot of farmers' homes, including the Howell home.

"You can take some of the blankets and either stay on the sick room floor or sleep in the hayloft," Mr. Cole continued talking. "Me," Mr. Cole chuckled, "I prefer sleeping with the sweet smell of new hay, but you can do which ever you like."

Papa was thinking about the invitation, but waiting patiently while Mr. Cole talked. That was one of Papa's strong points; he was a good listener.

Mr. Cole said, "If you leave at first light tomorrow morning, you can still make it home in time to do your chores before Sunday church service. Besides, Amy baked a cake for the cake walk tonight and she will be delighted if you participate."

Papa considered the invitation. It became more appetizing by the moment and he did like to talk with Mr. Cole's daughter, Amy. He was a little tired, but the thought of the church social and the possibility of seeing old friends and making some new ones energized him.

Finally, Papa sat his empty coffee cup down, looked Mr. Cole straight in the eyes and said, "Mr. Cole that is the best offer I have had in a long time." He said graciously, "I would be delighted to attend the church social and spend the night in your hayloft."

When working on Saturdays, Papa always brought a fresh shirt, his comb and straight razor tucked inside his mule saddlebags just in case he had an opportunity to visit with friends after work. He took pride in his appearance and did not like to visit unless he was fresh-shaved and presentable.

Mr. Cole's daughter, Amy, knew and liked Papa. Papa had a lot of friends who were girls. He also had his fair share of girlfriends. Papa was considered to be a "good catch" in those days. He was not too tall at 5' 11", but his lean muscular body, fair skin, blue eyes, and black hair that was cut short on the sides and in the back, but long and slicked back on the top, made him look striking when he was cleaned up. Papa had an outgoing personality and never met a stranger. He could talk with anyone in such an easy manner that he put people, especially the young ladies, at ease.

Tonight the church social was a Valentine Social with a cake walk to raise money for the church. This meant that after preaching, the young ladies would present a cake they baked to be auctioned off to the highest bidder. Young gentlemen in the audience would bid on the cake and the opportunity to spend time with the young female baker, even though they did not know which young lady baked which cake. The cake went to the highest bidder and the baker spent an hour of her time with the successful bidder. They would enjoy the cake at a quiet spot within the church. Often the girls' parents and family would be invited by the winner to enjoy a slice of the cake with them. It was a good way to raise money for church needs including supplies such as hymnal books and Bibles. Sometimes the money was used to pay the preacher when crops were poor. Most preachers were church pastors part-time, but also worked small farms and expected no payment for their services. They did it purely for the love of God and their community.

Papa rode with the Coles to the social that evening. Mr. Cole drove the family wagon while Papa sat on the top bench with Mr. Cole's seven-year-old son, Jake, seated between the two men. Mrs. Cole, their daughter Amy, and their youngest son, Adam, sat in the back of the wagon wrapped in woolen blankets to keep the cold night wind at bay. Everyone chatted while the farmer's two best mules pulled the wagon along the mile of dirt road to the church. Saturday night events at the church were a place for young people to get together in a Christian atmosphere, to enjoy time with each other, and to give thanks and praise to God. The local churches were the center of social events in the community.

It was a short sermon that evening as the pastor sensed the anticipation of the young men waiting for the cake auction to begin. First, the pastor would introduce the bakers and then the cakes were described and shown. After the cake was auctioned, the baker came forward herself to claim the cake and present it to the winning bidder. Then the couple would retreat to a quiet spot within the church to eat the cake, usually on a church bench. Cake was a special treat. Sugar and white flour, the main ingredients needed to make a cake, were in short supply.

The bakers quickly lined up in front of the church pulpit as the pastor called their names one at a time. There were twelve participants tonight, including Papa's younger sister, Megan, and Jan Alma Wingate—my Mama. Mama knew Megan before the social this evening and enjoyed talking with her the few times they had met at church. Mama also knew of Papa, but by reputation only. She had not had the opportunity to meet Papa, but knew who he was when she saw him in the church audience. Mama never tired of telling me the story of how she and Papa first met.

Mama said she was number eight in the line of twelve young women. Megan, Papa's sister, was number nine. Mr. Cole's daughter was number six. As they lined up in front of the pulpit, Mama could feel Papa's eyes transfixed on her, boring deep into her heart and mind. She had sewn a new dress for herself and had on her best shoes and a long scarf stitched from the dress material draped over one shoulder. Her thick, long, shiny black hair hung down her back striking her at the waist. Although she was usually confident in her appearance, this night she felt nervous.

Mama had baked the cake this afternoon from ingredients that she had squirreled away over several weeks. She had no idea that she would get to go to the social, but had heard about it days ago from John, her younger brother. News of church socials traveled fast among the young people living in the country. Sometimes friends would stop by to see if the Wingates (Mama and John) wanted to ride with them.

Mama did not have time to stop her chores long enough to bake a cake, so while completing other chores she overbaked it. Even the hot buttermilk icing she poured over the cake did not conceal the dark brown outer crust. It was not burnt, but was a deep brown color—the color of Mama's eyes.

Megan invited Mama and John to ride to the social with her and her two older sisters, Jill and Teresa. They stopped by early so Mama and John had time to dress for church. The Howell girls did not know their brother, Ross, would be attending the social. His sisters were surprised to see him when he entered the church with the Cole family.

The trip to the Valentine Social was a long wagon ride. The church was located in the adjoining county. It was well known throughout the county that Grandpa Wingate didn't believe in the social side of church, and that he would not let John and Mama use the Wingate wagon to go to a social. But Mama's brother, John, although two years younger than her, was a striking, tall young man and eager to find ways to attend the social functions at various churches. He did not mind Mama tagging along with him. It opened doors and paved the way for him to speak with more girls. Mama was delighted when Megan's wagon stopped at their house. John ended up driving the team of mules pulling the Howell wagon while the females rode in the back of the wagon. Megan, Jill, and Mama chatted away, trying often to pull Teresa into the discussions. Teresa was the aloof Howell sister and seen as a loner in the eyes of the community. She stayed to herself and preferred to spend her time at home with her parents and the younger Howell siblings.

Time passed by slowly as the young women waited patiently for the pastor to describe each cake as it was presented. The twelve cakes consisted of many flavors including a black walnut cake, a molasses cake, and Mama's hot buttermilk cake. Even the plain cakes were a sweet delightful treat to those who were invited to have a piece. Mama's feet began to hurt from standing for a long period of time in her stacked high heels. She felt like she was going to faint, but Papa's eyes never left her face.

The auction began and the pastor auctioned the cakes by random number beginning with the cake closest to him and running through all twelve cakes. Papa was the highest bidder on cake number six baked by Amy Cole. Megan's cake number nine was purchased by a friend of John's, Ron Vickers; while a young man named Colton Harris, from a church in another county purchased Mama's cake. Colton quickly asked John to join them as Mama received the cake from the pastor. Colton took the cake from Mama and she thanked him in a polite voice. Mama, Colton, and John walked to the back of the church. Within twenty minutes all cakes had been auctioned off and purchased by hungry young men just waiting to enjoy the sweet dessert.

Ron Vickers lived in a nearby town. Ron invited Megan's sisters to enjoy the cake with them as they came and sat on a bench near Mama, John, and Colton. As other church members joined the various groups to enjoy a slice of cake, it was obvious that Ron was smitten by Megan's beauty. They sat making small talk and laughing occasionally in the back left corner of the church.

Papa received Amy Cole's cake as she smiled at him. They had selected the left back pew across from Mama and Colton. Bradley Cole and Teresa joined them to eat the cake.

Soon Pastor and the other congregational members were all enjoying the taste of delicious cake. Papa, on two occasions, secretly glanced over to see Mama and Colton talking with John and some other church members who had joined them. He was much too polite and too skilled to let it be noticed by anyone other than Mama whose eyes met his.

The social part of the service lasted about an hour before Pastor dismissed the crowd for the evening. He announced that $12.10 had been raised from the sale of the cakes. Amy Cole's cake had brought the most money, selling for $1.10. Mama silently noticed Papa had been the big spender that night. Pastor thanked everyone for participating and dismissed with a prayer for a safe journey home.

Mama, Colton, and John were the first ones through the door of the church. They walked over to the Howell wagon and politely waited for Megan, Jill, and Teresa to say their goodbyes. Mama noticed that the Cole family and Papa had joined Megan's group in the back of the church as everyone prepared to leave. But it would have been impolite for Mama to excuse herself and join them. Colton had been a lovely partner for the evening and she and John had enjoyed spending time with him and others from the church. Colton said good night first as he had a distance to ride and it was getting late. "The cake was delicious and the browned crust enhanced the flavor," he assured Mama, placing his hand on her shoulder as she blushed.

Some members of the congregation stopped by to say goodnight to Mama's group, but the Cole family wagon was parked at the far end of the building. Papa excused himself and went to bring the wagon around while the family waited near the church door. Megan and her sisters finished their goodbyes and Ron Vickers walked them over to the wagon where Mama and John waited. The girls boarded into the back of the wagon, with Papa's oldest sister, Jill, volunteering to hold the lantern for John. She pulled a heavy driver's coat from under the seat and slipped it on. The coat would keep the night chill away. John lit the lantern and thanked her, gladly accepting her invitation to assist him. The girls settled in the back and pulled the woolen blankets close to their chest. The night air was cold as the wagon began the long trip home. Megan and Mama chatted about Ron Vickers, Colton Harris, and the other people from the congregation they had met. Teresa, Papa's shy sister, sat quietly and fell asleep quickly leaving Megan and Mama deep in conversation. It had been a lovely evening.

Mama listened as Megan spoke of the various young people she knew in the church. The mules pulled the wagon at a fast walk, snorting a few times along the road. The moon overhead was full giving great light to the road below. It was so bright that John told Jill she could blow out the lantern. She did and settled in on the seat beside John. They sang a few old church hymns to liven up their spirits and keep the sleepiness away. Nine o'clock in the evening was long past a farmer's bedtime. Teresa continued to sleep under the woolen blankets. Mama and Megan dozed for a while and then Megan began the chatter again. She called up to John,

"I think Ron is really nice. I would like to see him again sometime."

"Good," John called down to her. "I think he enjoyed himself. I don't know when I will see him again, but I will let him know."

Mama listened to this conversation. Megan turned to Mama and said,

"Do you know my brother, Ross?"

"I have not formally met your brother, but I have seen him from a distance," Mama answered.

"That was him with the Cole family tonight. He is working for Mr. Cole. We did not know he would be at the social." Mama watched Megan in the moonlight trying to sense where this conversation might go. Mama was interested in knowing more about Ross, but asking questions about a friend's brother could be troublesome at times. She waited for Megan to continue.

"He came over to our group tonight after the dismissal. I did not see you and John or I would have introduced you," Megan continued slowly.

"I'm sorry," Mama replied. "Colton, John and I walked outside after the dismissal prayer to avoid the stampede at the door and Colton had a long ride home. I wish you had called to me."

"Oh well, you can meet him another time. He bought Amy Cole's cake. Her family seems nice." Megan was on a roll. "I know Ross likes working for her father. They are rather wealthy farmers, you know."

"I don't know the Cole family at all," Mama answered. "I saw Amy only one other time before tonight at another church social. She is beautiful," Mama said in almost a whisper.

"Yes, she is," replied Megan. "But a lot of men are intimidated by her father. You know the type—wealthy, trying to find the right groom for his daughter."

"Really!" Mama sat up. This had gotten her attention. "Just seeing him from across the room, he doesn't appear that way," she said almost to herself.

"Oh Mr. Cole is very nice and big in the church—deacon and all." Megan had baited Mama's appetite now. Mama waited to hear more about the Cole family. She waited patiently as Megan continued.

"Rumor has it Mr. Cole has his eyes set on my brother to be his son-in-law." Her smile could be seen even in the moonlight.

"What about Ross?" Mama's heart pounded in her chest as she asked. "Is he interested in marrying Amy Cole?"

"Ross is very smart when it comes to people. He is too polite to hurt Mr. Cole's feelings, but he is also sensible enough not to marry for anything but love."

Megan continued, "Wealth would be nice to have, but a marriage can never survive without a special kind of love which bonds and holds a couple together in the hardships of this life. You need so much more than money. Your mate must be willing to work hard alongside of you to be successful. And, there is the entire church thing combined with sense of family. Ross wants a big family. I am not sure Amy Cole has that same kind of dream. Ross is a hard worker. The Coles have many workers. Ross would never accept anything he did not earn. He has too much pride for that. Papa and Mama taught us that once you lose your pride/dignity, you are a goner." She sighed, "I don't think my brother is ready for marriage, just yet."

There was no stopping Megan now. She continued talking. Mama listened intently.

"Besides, he asked me who you were tonight. Mr. Cole walked up before I could answer. Ross is a popular guy and can have any girl he chooses." Megan reached out and patted Mama's blanket. Mama hoped that she could not see the flush on her face at the thought of Papa asking about her. Mama flashed Megan a smile that said without words she might be interested in meeting her brother.

After that exchange, the wagon ride home was pleasant but uneventful. Everyone quieted to their own thoughts as the mules continued along the road. Rabbits scampered from the roadway to avoid being hit. One raccoon was climbing a tree to check out an old bird nest as the wagon rolled by. A mother deer and her small fawn were grazing near the road beside a lone creek bed. The moonlight captured a perfect scene of a grassy knoll with tall grass, trees and woods behind a perfect opening with the babble of the creek rounding out the scene. The mother deer gently lifted her head and moved closer to the fawn in case there was danger. Mama smiled as she turned her head to watch the pair as they fed for the night. *A perfect place to raise a family*, Mama whispered as peace and a calmness settled over her while the wagon continued a rhythmic pace.

Everyone said goodbyes when the Howell girls dropped John and Mama off at the end of the road near their house. Jill slid over into the driver's seat taking the reins from John. "Thanks for driving, John. It was a lovely time with you both," Jill said softly as she called to the mules to pull the wagon again. It would take them another half hour or so in the wagon to make it home. Jill was a skilled wagon driver and felt totally comfortable driving at night with just her sisters. No one would bother the Howell girls. Their father was known throughout the valley and was a man to be reckoned with when it came to his family.

Mama took the shoes off her tired feet. She wasn't used to heels and preferred no shoes. She walked barefoot carrying them in her hands as she hurried to catch John. She was several feet behind John when she felt a painful prick on the bottom of her foot and felt something smooth move under it. She froze.

"John," she cried out softly.

John stopped and whirled around. "What is it?" he asked, a bit irritated.

"I just got bitten by a snake, I think." She began to cry softly but was thankful for the full moon, praying silently that they could find the snake. If the snake was venomous, she could die if they waited too long. The poison would have to be drained from her foot.

"Don't panic." John picked up a forked stick that was lying near the lane and a larger broken branch to use as a weapon.

"I'll find whatever it was," he assured her as he spread out close to the edge of the lane while the moon gave perfect light. He walked a few feet from Jan while she held her foot and moved to a grassy mound and sat down. He moved the stick back and forth along the ground and then something moved beneath the stick. He touched the snake, which coiled up in a circle immediately.

"Gotcha!" John yelled.

Parents taught their children at an early age, how to survive in the wild which included how to swim, how to shoot a gun and a bow and arrow, and how to safely catch a snake. There were many snakes around. Non-venomous snakes were good for the farm and you lived in peace with them. They included king snakes, coachwhip snakes, rat snakes, chicken snakes, garden snakes, the scarlet king snakes, the red milk snakes, and the worm snakes. Venomous snakes were diamondback rattlesnakes, timber rattlers, pigmy rattlers, water moccasins, copperheads, coral snakes, and various viper snakes. Snakes could be recognized by the color of their skin, the skin pattern on their belly and the shape of their heads. Snakes with two venomous hollow fangs located near the front of their mouths had a triangular shaped head with vertical shaped eyes and a circular pattern on their belly, while non-venomous snakes normally have a set of small teeth, oval or elongated heads, round eyes, and a disjointed double pattern on their belly. John knew that if he could catch the snake or whatever had bitten his sister, he would know what to do next. He could determine what kind of danger Mama was in and save her life, if possible.

He could see that it was a long snake by the light from the moon. He pressed the fork of the stick firmly behind the snakes head as it wiggled and squirmed from the round coil to try and get free. The light from the moon shined bright above as John stooped and caught the snake's neck just behind the head and held it up in the air. The snake immediate swung its body up and coiled around John's right arm. John allowed it to do so. He was in no danger because he held the head firmly in his grasp. The snake actually relaxed as he applied pressure to the neck and settled on his arm.

"It is poisonous?" Jan asked as her heart raced.

John stepped from under the tree shadows into the full light of the moon, held the snake up and checked its belly pattern and its head. He took his time in the examination.

"John, hurry up!" Jan cried. "Is it poisonous?"

"Nah," John replied. "He is either a black racer or a king snake—I can't see good enough to tell you which, but his bite will only make the muscle sore—not kill you." John was playing with her and the snake now.

"Do you want me to take it to the house so I can examine it further?" he asked.

"Not if you are sure," Mama said as she rose from the place where she sat on the grass.

"I'm sure," John replied as he unwound the snake from his arm and walking to the edge of the lane returned it to the wooded, grassy area. It quickly slithered off into the night.

"We'll put a tobacco poultice on it to help keep the sting and soreness down," John assured her as he took her arm to help her walk down the lane to their front door. The moon guided their way as it silently moved across the sky spreading great beams of light while tree leaves cast long shadows along the ground. The brightness of the moon glowing and stars twinkling helped light the path. A lone owl hooted in the distance while creatures of the night moved about and crickets chirped along the wood line.

Mama and John had enjoyed the evening before the snake bite and were thankful. They had met some new people and had renewed some acquaintances. However, morning would arrive much too soon and daily chores would greet them as another day began. John quickly made a poultice from his father's chewing tobacco, wet it and placed it under a clean cloth on Mama's foot where small teeth marks showed a little

Papa 41

blood on her white skin. Mama got a white sock from the laundry basket that was located just inside the door where the shoes were stored and pulled it over the poultice draped foot.

"Thanks, brother!" Mama said as she gave John a quick kiss on the cheek. "I was rather terrified for a moment."

"Me too," John replied. "Don't know what I would do without my sister around to pick on." He gave Mama a small punch to the shoulder. They each went to their rooms to get some sleep. The liveliness of the night remained outside and the quietness of the house greeted them.

Mama thought about what Megan had said about Papa as she lay in bed that night. He wanted a large family, he would not accept anything he had not earned, he wanted success, and most exciting of all—he had asked who she was. What did it all mean? She said a quick prayer thanking God for the evening, for the blessing of the snake being non-venomous, for John being there, and for guidance to sort out the meaning of everything before closing her eyes. Sleep came soon.

At the Cole home in the next county, Papa said goodnight and goodbyes to the Coles when they arrived back at the farm. He would be leaving at first light before the family awoke. He unhitched the team, fed them, and put the wagon and mule bridles away for the night. He then went to the sick room, retrieved two large woolen blankets and crawled into the firm hayloft to settle in for the night. A big tabby colored tomcat came and stretched out his body with his nose touching his paws first and then Papa's hand as if to say hello. Papa stretched out, pulled the blankets near, patted the cat on the head, and it lay down beside him on the hay. It was warm and comfortable. Mr. Cole was right. There was nothing that could compete with the smell of fresh hay to relax you. The night had been enjoyable and the Coles were nice people. He had been delighted to be able to contribute $1.10 to the church fund and Amy's cake was delicious.

As he drifted into sleep, a mental picture of the olive skinned girl with high cheek bones, big brown eyes that pulled you in like eyes of a female deer, and the long shiny black hair draped down her back kept returning to his thoughts. He must find out more about her. He would talk with his sisters tomorrow, especially Megan who seemed to know her. Papa thought he knew all the eligible women in this and the surrounding counties. Why had he never met Jan Wingate? Where had she been hiding?

CHAPTER 3

Mama's Indian Heritage

THE NEXT DAY after the social Papa woke up at first light, saddled Pearl, his prize mule, and began the journey home. He rode faster than normal, stopping only once at a small creek so they both could drink water. The coolness of the water would help them both cool off quickly. While Pearl took long drinks from the stream, Papa took off his work hat and washed his face in the cool water. Then he took a long drink of water himself using his hands for a cup. Papa dropped Pearl's bridle lines, told her to stay, and walked a few steps into the woods to pee. Pearl was obedient so he took a few extra minutes to notice the beauty of this little spot in the road.

The creek flowed and widened to create a small pool of water a few yards off the roadway, although somewhat shallow, much like a small lake. Natural boulders of rock formed the edges of the pool and a tiny waterfall trickled from the center rocks. Nature is beautiful, he thought as his eyes took in the beauty of this grassy glade. Squirrels and chipmunks scampered around on the grass close to the rocks. They were finding food they had stored for the winter months and sought the nuts and dried berries they had stashed earlier. It was a sobering thought when you took time to think of the magnificent world and to read and know that God had created it in just six days. The seventh day God rested. Ross had grown up reading the Bible and going to church. His parents had provided a sound basis for his faith in God, but some of his friends did not have that solid background. However, they respected each other's beliefs and moved on.

 He walked back, adjusted Pearl's saddle as he swung his right leg up and over. She had finished drinking and was waiting to get on the road again. He gave her a soft pat on the neck and said, "Come on girl, let's go home." As Pearl galloped away, Papa made a mental note that this would be a good spot for a picnic. It wasn't too far from home, had lots of shade and a variety of small animals to keep a conversation and laughter going. There was even a firm bed of beautiful grass and moss near the boulders forming the top of the waterfall. It would be a great place to pass time on a Sunday afternoon with a spot for Pearl to graze while he and a young lady ate dinner or took a nap on a quilt. He must remember this place.

Papa's mind was still occupied with thoughts of the night before. He had slept fitfully with dreams of Jan Wingate. He wanted to find out more about her. He had not dreamed about a girl before, and it disturbed him. He wanted to see her, to talk with her, to find out everything about her.

When Papa reached home, breakfast was being served in the kitchen. He slid into his chair at the table, arriving just in time for Grandpa Howell's blessing. After everyone greeted Ross, Grandpa Howell gave thanks for the family, for health, and for the food, asking that it be used for the nourishment of our body through Christ our Lord. When the prayer was finished and everyone began eating, Grandpa Howell asked Papa about his work week and the progress on Mr. Cole's barn. He and Papa talked barn building throughout breakfast while others at the table had their own conversations going.

While Teresa ate her breakfast in silence, Megan and Jill talked about the church social and informed Grandma Howell that Ross was the big spender and about Amy Cole's cake. Grandma asked several questions about Amy Cole and for her daughters' opinions of her. They thought she was a beautiful young woman, very smart at school, who was looking for the right young man to get married. They both giggled when Grandma wanted to know if they thought Ross was sweet on her. When Grandma Howell looked at Teresa, she just shrugged her shoulders.

"Lots of men are sweet on her," said Jill. "But I'm not sure if anyone will meet all of Mr. Cole's requirements for a son-in-law."

"He's going to be very particular who wins the hand of his daughter," Megan chimed in.

"We have some mighty good stock to choose from around here," Grandma said smiling.

"Well you can bet he'll be doing the choosing and not Amy," Jill returned to the conversation.

"Now girls, don't be too hard on Mr. Cole," she cautioned. "He has a right to want the best for his daughter and they both should be choosy. Marriage is not for the weak at heart and there had better be a lot of strong muscles and deep down God given love to go along with it. It takes more than book smarts and beauty to make a good farmer's wife," she said firmly as the breakfast was finishing up. "Now let's get this table cleared so we can make it to church on time." They slid back their chairs and gathered dirty dishes placing them in a large dishpan for washing.

Grandma was delighted that the girls had a good time and that the social had made some money for the church. She explained that the pastors took a lot upon themselves to be there for the neighbors, counseling, and sometimes even lending supplies and food to parishioners during times like these.

Once everyone had finished and the dishes were cleared, Papa excused himself and found Megan washing dishes in the small pantry off the kitchen. It was just the two of them. Today was Megan's turn to cook and clean the kitchen. Papa asked her about Jan Wingate as Megan passed a drying towel to him. She washed and he dried while Megan told Papa everything she knew about Jan. She was the oldest child and only girl in her family. She had three younger brothers, the baby being her favorite. John, the young man with them last night, was her oldest brother. Megan told Papa Jan had a sheltered, but hard, life with very strict parents. She worked the fields in addition to doing all the household chores. Her mother was sickly and Jan was not allowed to go out or do anything outside of church functions. Sometimes she was not allowed to go to church.

Papa asked if she had a boyfriend. With this question, Megan laughed so hard that it irritated Papa. Megan sensed his irritation and calmed down saying, "Mr. Wingate would kill anyone who thought of courting his daughter. She doesn't even have friends and certainly not any eligible male friends. They cannot live without Jan doing the work for them. It's almost like she is a servant. So, no, she does not have a boyfriend." She laughed again and this time Papa stormed from the room flinging the towel at Megan as he left.

"I'm sorry," Megan called but Papa was already through the back door which banged as he left. She continued washing dishes shaking her head. She loved her brother and was sorry she had angered him. She would apologize after the work was done. Megan washed the remaining plates, cups, bowls, silverware, pots, and pans. She dried the ones Papa failed to finish when he got angry.

Papa took Pearl's lead and walked her to the barn, removed her saddle, bit, and bridle. He would curry her down with a long brush while he fed her. Pearl had cooled off while he ate breakfast. He went to the feed bag and got a generous portion of feed. He placed the bucket on the stall hanger and she began eating. Pearl had earned the extra portion of feed. It had been a hard ride home. Papa could feel her body relax beneath his touch as he glided the brush along her head, spine, back, and sides. Her ears wiggled letting Papa know she was enjoying the rub down. He spoke softly to the mule as he continued to work on her coat and he talked to Pearl while he groomed her. She was an amazing creature, worked hard and added a sense of calmness to his sometimes complicated life. She was one female that seemed to understand and always listened—unlike his sisters who made fun of him when they got the chance. He made up his mind, he would not ask Megan any more questions about Jan Wingate. He might ask Jill if the subject came up later, but if not, he would find the answers for himself. He continued to gently push the brush along Pearl's sides and back.

Pearl was a good mule and young enough to give many more years of service. Right now, she was his prize. Everyone wanted to buy her. Pearl was a crossbreed between a fine quarter horse and burro, so she was larger than your average

Mama's Indian Heritage 49

mule and had a beautiful head on her large frame. Papa had traded for her with the farmer who raised her.

The farmer had a young stallion quarter horse he kept in the pasture with his donkeys. This stallion did not get along with the farmer's other young colts. The other horses were pastured by themselves. The handsome quarter horse had become enchanted with the beautiful little female donkey. Where you saw the stallion, you saw the donkey. They ate together, went to the drinking hole together, ran the pasture fence together, and rolled on their backs together. The stallion snorted and the donkey brayed. The donkey calmed the stallion and the farmer was pleased. Soon, Pearl was born and had the best of both parents. Her stallion qualities from her father gave her the large frame and beautiful muscular body. Her donkey qualities from her mother gave her a sweet disposition and a small, beautiful head with the most incredible eyes for a mule. She was also very smart, whereas some mules are not. Pearl's mother and father were blessed animals because the mule is usually too big for the mother's small body to give birth to such a large baby. Most often the donkey dies. But in Pearl's case, mother and baby both survived. Pearl was not as large as a horse, but larger than a donkey. Papa had taken her as payment for some work he had done on fence lines for her owner. Papa's wages for two weeks paid for young Pearl. They made a good pair, Pearl and Papa. They understood and respected each other, man and mule. Papa trained the young mule to have good working skills and to mind him like she was human. He treated her like one. He took pride in Pearl and she never disappointed him. Once the currying job was finished and Papa's temper had cooled down, he went to his room to change his clothes before going with the family to church.

Megan spoke with Papa again later that day after church. She apologized for laughing at him and offered to help him meet Jan. Papa put his arm around her, tousled her hair, gave her a small peck of a kiss on top of the head, and said he couldn't stay mad very long but he did not like her teasing him about girls he showed an interest in. After all, it was healthy to look and usually did not come to anything. Once he got to know them, he knew they were not the one. Megan agreed to introduce Papa to Jan at church the following Wednesday evening after prayer service.

On Monday morning Megan told Grandma Howell about her plan. It was easy to get permission to visit Jan. Grandma Howell suggested that she take some fresh baked bread to the Wingates for tea. Megan knocked on the Wingate door around 11:00 am. It was a little later than she had planned and would not allow much time for her to visit with Jan, but she could discuss the idea with Jan quickly. Mr. Wingate greeted Megan at the door and she presented Mrs. Wingate with the fresh bread. Jan's mother called to her that she had a visitor and Jan peeked around the door. Smiling, Jan gave Megan a hug to greet her and the two girls went in the kitchen to talk. Megan told Jan that Papa wanted to formally meet her at church on Wednesday. Jan quickly put the kettle on and water for tea was boiling in no time. She took a mixture of elderberry leaves and rose hips and made a delicious smelling herbal tea. She poured coffee for her parents from the already hot pot on the stove and poured tea for the two of them. Jan and Megan placed the fresh bread with soft butter and jam on a tray and together they brought it in the parlor where Jan's parents were. Mr. Wingate put his Bible aside, and Mrs. Wingate placed her mending basket with bits and pieces of cloth in it on the floor beside her.

"This is lovely, Megan," Mrs. Wingate said in a nice, sweet voice. "Won't the two of you join us?" Mr. Wingate took his coffee and added, "By all means, please do. You can tell me how your family is coping with hard times."

"Thank you," Megan smiled. "I can only stay for a moment," she continued. She sat for a few minutes and answered Mr. Wingate's questions about her father and her two brothers. She was polite but guarded about the personal stuff. She had been schooled by her folks just like Mama and Papa schooled us—if it's family business, you don't discuss it outside the family. After a few minutes had passed, Megan asked,

"I was wondering if Jan and John could join Jill and me and attend prayer service Wednesday night? It should not be a long service so they would be home early, it being a week night and all." Mr. Wingate gave Mrs. Wingate an agreeable glance and she spoke for them,

"Well, can't be any harm in it. Going to church is a Christian virtue so I suppose it will be alright." Jan's mother then glanced at her while Mr. Wingate took another bite of the fresh bread followed by a long swallow of coffee, and said, "You will need to finish all your chores before you go."

Jan replied, "I have only a couple of chores left today. I can do some chores that I normally do on Wednesday so I can finish in time. Thank you, Mama; thank you, Papa." She and Megan clasped hands and excused themselves to return to the kitchen for tea and bread. Once inside the kitchen door they hugged each other like five year olds who had just received a new pony. The tea was perfectly brewed, so each girl put in a spoon of honey to give it a sweet taste and buttered a slice of the fresh bread, chattering about the plan and how they would pull it off.

Wednesdays were Mama's easiest day to finish work in time to go to church. She lined the chores up that way, because she enjoyed the worship services and visiting with neighbors who attended regularly. Grandpa Wingate never balked at his daughter's attending church. He had strong faith in God and read his Bible and prayed daily. His faith had strengthened since his wife's health had been failing over the last few years. Strong faith in God and confidence in his word, according to Grandpa Wingate, is what kept families strong and together.

Mama did not tell Megan, but her heart did a big flip and she felt faint just thinking about it. Could it possibly be true?

Ross Howell wanted to meet her? Ross Howell—who could have any girl he chose! The week passed ever so slowly until Wednesday arrived. Mama completed her chores early in the afternoon on this day.

Mama and John were ready when the wagon came and the group arrived at church early. Papa was already there sitting outside on Pearl under a big oak tree. He looked handsome in a crisp white shirt with brown sackcloth slacks. When they arrived, he slid down from the saddle and walked over to greet them. He flashed his biggest smile and Mama froze. When Megan introduced them, Mama managed to say, "It's nice to meet you." She had gone shy all of a sudden. Papa, too, had lost his ability to chat so they stood there looking at each other. John, however, came to the rescue. He reminded Ross that he had seen him around and had actually spoken with him briefly one Saturday outside the county store in town. John was with a mutual friend, Ron. Papa vaguely remembered the incident, but John was younger and did not hang out with the same guys as Papa. The five of them sat together during the service that night. Papa tied Pearl to the back of the wagon and drove the wagon to the Wingate farm. Papa and Mama sat up top, but not too close, so they could visit while John sat in the back with Megan and Jill. John was a good story teller and kept the sisters in stitches with funny stories that happened when he was younger. Papa and Mama talked about things each of them liked to do and what their aspirations were.

Papa wanted to have his own place and raise beef cattle and horses and to raise cotton and corn and have a vegetable patch in the spring and fall that would include greens, tomatoes, squash, lettuce, cucumbers, radishes, beans of all kinds, and melons. He even wanted to have some fruit trees scattered around the property. He wanted cows, horses, pigs, and maybe even a lamb or two, perhaps some chickens so his family would not go hungry in winter months when things would not grow. It seemed like an impossible dream with the economy down, the country marred in a deep depression, friends and family getting hammered left and right. But one can dream—he continued, "Jan, don't ever give up on dreaming and imaging your life in a better time and place. What *are* your dreams, girl? Do you sit around and dream like I do?" He smiled as he asked.

She turned and looked him square in the face as he kept his eyes mostly on the dark roadway, but she could still feel his blue eyes boring holes into her as she responded,

"Of course I have dreams. Maybe not as elaborate as yours, but this is my dream for my life. I want a little place of my own too. Perhaps one that is not so big that my partner and I cannot work it with the help of our offspring. I love children and I want to have several—I don't care if they are boys or girls. I just pray to God that they are healthy in mind and spirit and have strong backs and a stubborn streak that will help them through life's many crises. I want my children to have open hearts that will love their neighbors and family and will help the poor and less fortunate when times are abundant and will support the church and God through all times. And that they will be filled with faith, forgiveness, and foresight beyond comprehension but a gentleness and voice for the least of these." Ross had remained silent for several minutes just listening to her talk.

"I'm sorry, I got carried away," she apologized. "As you can see, I have dreams."

"Please tell me more," he said as the rhythm of the horses walking gently along the road added quietness and tenderness to the evening. John, Megan, and Jill were enjoying themselves laughing and talking about various things they had in common.

She touched his shirt sleeve and asked, "Are you sure you want to know more of my thoughts. My brothers are always laughing at me, saying I have my head in the clouds again."

"Without dreams, or goals is what I call them, you never will strive to do anything different or better. It's very easy to get stuck into a rut and never crawl out." He sounded so serious but his smile lit up the sky with the moonlight glowing through the tree tops, putting her totally at ease. "Please tell me more. I enjoy hearing your perspective on life and the future." He looked ahead now at the road waiting for her to continue her thoughts.

"I want a house, not fancy but plain and livable, large enough to raise the children I give birth to. And perhaps have a spare room for my parents or friends to come and visit for special occasions. A small rose garden with climbing roses and wild roses, an herbal garden, and flower bushes that I've gathered from the forest with green grass like a carpet located near a babbling brook so my family and nature can live in harmony together—us and the land. Perhaps have a couple of log chairs outside under a big oak tree. The boys and girls can climb up the tree and scrape knees and elbows as they grow and learn from each experience. Sitting in those old log chairs, parents can watch them grow from babies into boys and girls and then young men and women. I dream of a good sturdy barn and strong fences that keep our animals inside, making them want to work hard and respect their owners." Jan was on a roll now. Ross giggled a little at her last remark and said, "What animal, outside of Pearl, respects its owner? And Pearl is one in a million. So, I agree with your brothers and think you are in the clouds a bit with that one." Papa reached over and patted her briefly on the arm.

"I was just making sure you were listening," Mama laughed. For the next few minutes, the conversation moved from dreams to the weather and the coolness of the night time air and to upcoming days ahead as the Wingate farm house came into view. It had been an interesting evening. They said goodbye to Ross, Megan, and Jill at the end of the lane as they had the night of the church social, and Ross began the drive home with both sisters now seated next to him.

Mama and Papa saw each other at church and social events over the next few months. Ross managed to stop by the Wingate farm a couple of time to see John and had met Mr. and Mrs. Wingate without raising any alarms that he was interested in Mama. Mama recalled over and over again for us girls one of her favorite stories about Papa's visits during that time.

Papa and John became friends and Papa found excuse upon excuse to stop by the Wingate farm to shoot the breeze with Mr. Wingate and the young Wingate boys, especially John, or so they claimed. Papa's real reason for coming to the farm was to catch a glimpse of Mama and he hungered for those brief times when they could talk together at the fence line while Mama either hung the washing or took the clothes from the line. Papa would help Mama while John stood around to cover the obvious reason for Papa's visit. One afternoon in early summer, Papa stopped by in the early evening to see John. Mr. Wingate, Papa, and John talked for a long time about the Depression and the plight of the farmers. Papa has not been able to spend any time with Jan who was busy doing chores and only came in once to serve them coffee. As supper time rolled around, Jan's father asked Papa if he would like to stay for supper. Papa jumped at the chance as he knew they ate family style, all the family together. During the meal, John managed to get Papa seated next to Mama, who prepared the food and placed it all on the table before seating herself. During the Wingate blessing,

Papa took a bold step, while all heads were bowed, reached over and put his hand on Mama's just for a moment. Then while passing the various dishes of food back and forth their hands touched more than once. The meal was pleasant and the men and Mrs. Wingate moved into the parlor for coffee afterwards while Jan was left to clean up. Papa and John offered to help Jan, but Mr. Wingate made it known that Jan was very capable of cleaning up. He wanted to continue the conversation they were having before supper. Mr. Wingate was interested in the projects Papa was working on for the area farmers and the progress of each. It was obvious that Mr. Wingate enjoyed conversing with Papa and that he had taken a liking to him.

Mama finished the clean up and moved into the parlor with everyone else with her basket of sewing. She seated herself on a large cushion on the floor across from Papa and near the fire. The discussion continued and Papa stole glimpses of Mama from the corner of his eyes, but was careful so her parents would not catch on.

The sun set in the west and it got dark outside. The Wingate farm sat back at the end of the lane and the farmhouse was enclosed in a rustic but workable wooden fence. The fence poles were cut from trees on their land. The poles were etched with grooves that fit inside each other somewhat like logs used to build homes. It was a natural and cheap way of fencing, but worked fine although it took a long time to fence a section of property. Once the fence was in place, it lasted for many years. The natural lane ended with a plank gate made from strips of smooth lumber nailed onto logs for support and was located not far from the farmhouse. Most of the time, the gate remained open. Today it had been closed when Papa arrived on Pearl, so he closed the gate behind himself after entering.

By the time Papa left the Wingate place that evening the sky was dark and it was beginning to rain. Papa mounted Pearl, said goodnight to everyone, and rode away from the farmhouse. His mind wandered, going over the events of today. He was a bit agitated that he had not been able to spend more time with Jan but was thinking about what a good cook she was and completely forgot the closed gate.

Pearl was in a slow trot when she hit the fence gate with such a force that it brought her to her knees and threw Papa over the gate into the road in front of them. Papa moaned under his breath, then rushed to Pearl to see if she was hurt badly. She had gone down on both knees and now limped slightly as she turned round.

"Whoa, girl," Papa soothed and he caught the reigns as lightening lit-up the sky. Rain came down hard on his brow and he tasted blood in his mouth. Wiping the blood from his head on his shirt sleeve, he discovered that Pearl had lost a shoe and picked it up from the ground as he ran his hand down each of Pearl's legs to make sure that was all that had happened. The gate was broken in the middle with two of the planks splintered, and it had come off the homemade hinge holding it in place. The lightening continued while Papa inspected the damage. He had a hammer in his saddle bag. As a carpenter, he also had some long nails that would temporarily allow him to jimmy the gate so that it would hold through the night. The night was pitch black with the exception of the lightning flashes that allowed him to do a minor repair. He continued to talk to Pearl, trying to keep her calm. Pearl did not like lightening and each flash unnerved her. She pressed her nose into Papa's back more than once as he hammered nails into the broken gate. At last, he lifted the repaired gate onto the homemade hinge and it caught. He then walked Pearl through the opening and placed the gate rope across the mount, hooking the gate in place.

 Pearl was walking with a slight limp, so Papa and Pearl began the long walk home through the lightening and the rain. A few hours later, Papa had Pearl safe in her stall, unsaddled and rubbed her down, placed a blanket across her back to keep her warm and once again inspected each foot and leg. Pearl had a small cut above the knee of the leg from which she had lost the horseshoe, so Papa treated it with some turpentine. The turpentine spirits burned Papa knew as he used them on himself when he got a cut to stop infection from setting in. Pearl was a good patient and didn't flinch. Papa gave her a small handful of corn and then poured another portion into her feed bucket.

Papa then went inside the house where Megan was still awake and heard him come in.

"Bout time you got home," she teased without looking up as she sat sewing near the fire with the lamp burning close by. Once she saw Ross all wet and bloody, she put her sewing basket aside.

"Ross, what happened?" Megan asked concern showing in her face. She followed him to the kitchen where she got a fresh pan of water and a clean cloth. He sat in the chair near the table. Megan began to wash the cut above his eye as he went through the events of Pearl slamming into the gate and the long walk home.

"You should have gotten John to help you repair the gate," Megan said, putting a special beeswax salve on the cut followed by a clean bandage.

"I was too embarrassed," Papa said sheepishly. "I was the one that closed the gate and then forgot about it. I could have killed Pearl!"

"Is Pearl alright?" Megan asked again.

"She will be a little sore and I have to re-shoe her, but she only got a small cut above her knee. She's a strong one," Papa said shaking his head.

"When the family gets up in the morning, will you tell Papa where I am? I plan to go at the crack of dawn and repair the gate properly. I don't want Mr. Wingate to be upset with my foolishness." He stood up from the table as Megan removed the pan and soiled cloths.

"How is it going with Jan?" Megan quizzed. "You seem to be spending more time there than here lately with your chores and work." His sister had been eyeing this romance from afar closer than he thought.

"I don't know," he said. "I spend very little time with her. Most of it is spent with John and Mr. and Mrs. Wingate. Jan is constantly working. She does all the chores and cooks, cleans, and sews most of their clothes, cares for her little brothers in addition to milking the cows and working the fields." He spoke in a low voice, almost a murmur.

"So, do you like her, Ross?" Megan picked, but in a loving way.

"I've never met another girl like her!" Papa replied as he made his way to the back door. "I'm going to sleep in the barn with Pearl, just to keep an eye on her," he said, opening the door. "I'll take one of the horses in the morning and may be back before breakfast." Then, he disappeared into the rainy night.

The rain had stopped sometime after Papa went to bed in the hayloft above Pearl's stall. The air smelled clean and fresh and a little cooler than most summer mornings. The rain was nature's way of scrubbing everything. Papa was up at sunrise and saddled Dancer, his father's prize horse, making sure to load supplies he needed to repair the Wingate gate. He took two boards to replace the splintered ones, tying them across the back of the saddle. Papa also took a small

Mama's Indian Heritage 63

handsaw which was sticking out of the saddle bag, being too long to fit securely inside.

Dancer was eager to have a good run so the ride to the Wingate farm was quick. Papa dismounted Dancer at the gate and tied him to a nearby tree limb. In the daylight, the gate wasn't busted as bad as Papa first thought. He could have it repaired in a little while. He unloaded the supplies and went to work, removing the splintered boards that he had nailed back in place last night. Then he measured the length for the new ones, sawed them to the correct length and hammered them in place. Once that was done, he tackled the hinge holding the gate in place. It had not been destroyed in the accident, but he could make it stronger by adding a new clamp on the fence portion, which he did. The entire repair job was over in less than two hours.

Now came the hard part. He had to face Mr. Wingate and explain what happened before he saw the gate. No better time to do it than now. Papa gathered up the pieces of broken lumber from the accident, tied them onto his saddle, returned the tools to the saddlebag and mounted Dancer. He rode the few hundred feet to the farmhouse. Mr. Wingate was coming from a trip to the outhouse and tipped his hat in greeting to Ross.

"Ross, you're out mighty early," Mr. Wingate broke the silence. "Is anything wrong? What happened to your head and where's Pearl?"

"That's three questions in one," replied Papa as he stuck out his hand and Mr. Wingate took it in a firm shake. "Everything's fine, now." Ross started.

"It was pretty late when I left last night, pitch dark outside and raining cats and dogs." He continued, "I forgot that I closed your fence gate when I came in late yesterday afternoon. Pearl forgot it too and she ran right through the gate last night." He put it out there, straight forward and to the point. "It splintered your gate, knocked Pearl to her knees, and she tossed me over the fence."

Mr. Wingate looked surprised and somewhat amused by this tale coming from Ross Howell. "I'm sorry, Ross," he laughed. "But that would have been a sight to see!" He slapped his pants leg. "Sure glad Pearl and you are alright—the gate can be repaired."

"I just finished repairing it, Sir," Papa said not too sure he was enjoying this conversation. "But, I wanted to let you know why it looks a little fresh in some areas."

"Come in and have a cup of coffee with us." Mr. Wingate patted him on the back. "John left a little while ago to check the lower field. Sometimes it can wash out in a rain like we got last night. But Jan, the little ones, and her mother are waiting for me to come to breakfast. Are you hungry? Jan cooks a good breakfast so you are in for a treat." He took Papa by the arm and they went inside.

Papa and Mama's relationship grew and one afternoon Papa asked Mama to meet him at the small creek with the tiny waterfall where boulders framed the pond along the road. Jan knew just where to find him and turned her small horse to approach the green carpet of the grass near the waterfall and boulders.

John had ridden part-way with Jan but stopped by a friend's on the way over so Jan could see Ross and not be disturbed. It was middle of the day and in the wide open area so what harm could come from them having a conversation together and an afternoon with nature?

Ross surprised her with a picnic dinner and a mandolin. He knew Mama could play guitar from talking with his sisters who had both heard her play and sing, but was not sure of this instrument. He took it as payment for some work he did on a fence line for a friend. It made a perfect engagement gift for Mama. Mama didn't read music but played by ear and cords. Papa was pleased when she gave him a shy kiss on the cheek, tuned the instrument, and played real music on it for him the first time she tried.

Mama had a nice raspy voice. She could sing a ballad with the best of them and could belt out a hymn with the ladies in our small church. At first she was caught off guard and said she did not accept gifts from men. Papa, turned her around and replied, "Well then, you will have to marry me to get the mandolin. It can be an engagement present since I don't have a ring."

That afternoon John wasn't ready to go home after dinner so Ross agreed to ride along with Jan most of the way home.

When they stopped at the lane to say good-bye, he leaned over from Pearl and surprised her with a quick peck of a kiss on the lips. It was so quick. She looked up, startled, thinking she was in real trouble if Grandpa Wingate saw that exchange. He would not let her see Papa anymore. But no one was around to see the brief first kiss between them.

They were married in a small private ceremony several months after the night of the cake walk at church. Ross Howell was twenty-three and Mama, Jan Alma Wingate, was nineteen. John, Megan, Jill, Teresa, and a couple of Papa's other siblings made up the wedding party. Grandpa and Grandma Wingate did not go to the wedding. They were upset about Mama marrying. Mama was not upset that they were absent because she loved her parents and in many ways understood the burden she was leaving to them. Mama always said it was not Papa. Everyone liked and respected him. But it was because her mother could not do the chores and take care of the men of the house. Her health was poor. For years, Mama had been doing the lion's share of all the duties, including working in the fields and taking care of the younger children.

At first, Mama and Papa lived with Mama's parents, Thomas William Wingate and Roberta Agnes Wingate. Since they had no money, it was common for newlyweds to live with the bride's parents. After the wedding, Papa moved into Mama's room. Mama was the oldest child and the only daughter. Her duties as the oldest child and only girl included helping her mother with household chores. She cooked the meals, cleaned the house, washed the dishes, and washed and ironed the clothes and bed linens. Mrs. Wingate was an excellent seamstress and taught her the fine art of sewing. Mama was a talented seamstress and could make men's, women's or children's clothes from memory after seeing a picture or seeing someone wear an item. She learned to sew trousers for her brothers, Papa, and Grandpa Wingate that looked store-bought.

In addition to her household work, Mama worked in the fields. Even after the fieldwork was done, Mama milked the cows and helped with other daily farm chores. After Papa and Mama got married, she continued doing the chores. By doing so, she earned room and board for herself and Papa. When I was born, Mama stopped going to the fields to work, but continued her other chores while taking care of me. Mama seemed to never get tired back then. Some of her work ethic came from her Indian heritage. She told me many stories about her Indian family and customs that grandma Wingate had shared with her.

My Great-Grandpa Wingate had fought in the Union Army and my Great-Grandma Wingate's mother was a Cherokee Indian. They had met in 1864 following the Battle of May's Gulf during the Civil War. My great-grandpa's army regiment helped win that battle but great-grandpa had been wounded. Great-Grandmother "Little Flower," a beautiful Cherokee Indian girl, lived nearby with her family. She found great-grandpa lying on the ground unconscious, bloody from his wounds and starving. Over the next several weeks, she fed him, treated the injuries and nursed him back to health. They hid him from Confederate soldiers until the war was over. After the war ended in 1865, Great-Grandpa Wingate moved to the south, married Little Flower, who saved his life and began farming a small area of land near the Gulf in the southern part of the state. He never went north again. He loved southern people and their lifestyle. He wanted to be a part of the southern culture and raise his children in the South.

Mama's long black hair, big brown eyes, and beautiful smooth olive skin came from her Indian heritage. She cherished her grandmother's stories of Little Flower and continued to practice some Cherokee traditions. For example, Mama never cut her hair after I was born. She would trim just the ends sometimes leaving it long and flowing, a sign of fertility. She wore it up most of the time in braids or twisted into a large bun on top of her head or at the nape of her neck.

Mama used a lot of natural herbs and spices in her cooking and made potions from herbs to treat many of our illnesses when we were sick. Our food included edible green plants from our woods, poke-salad, mushrooms, wild onions, berries, persimmons, and crabapples. She carefully selected the plants she used. Her knowledge of these plants and medicine came from her Indian ancestors' wealth of information about survival and living with nature.

Mama taught us to remove the resin from the sweet-gum tree and chew it to clean our teeth and sweeten our breath. She took long pieces of the sweet-gum tree and flattened the tips spreading them outward, making toothbrushes. She kept extra brushes on hand and had an abundance of them so there were no excuses for bad breath or dirty teeth.

Mama had three brothers—John, Ralph, and Stephen (Steve for short). John was the eldest son. Although John did a lot of social things with Mama through church, they fought sometimes. John never appreciated how hard Mama worked. He teased her relentlessly and dirtied up the house so her work was on-going. Ralph, the middle brother, was the peacemaker. He got along with everyone. Sometimes Ralph helped Mama when she carried firewood or washed the clothes. Mama and Ralph understood and helped each other. Mama appreciated and loved Ralph. They talked together, each sharing plans, dreams, beliefs, and faith. He was her rock, solace, and friend and she was the same to him.

Steve, the youngest, was Mama's favorite. To Mama, Steve was much like her own child. Grandma Wingate was sickly after Steve's birth so Mama had major responsibility for taking care of him. As a baby, he was constantly under foot, playing in the kitchen while she cooked, and in the other parts of the house while she did other chores. He was the apple of her eye and remained so even after she and Papa married and I was born.

Mama was blessed as a mother. Babies arrived regularly. Anna was born a few months shy of two years after me with Tom following eighteen months later and then David. Young mothers worked hard taking care of their children, doing all the chores of running the home, and providing meals for their family. Mama worked exceptionally hard with two preschool children. Papa was gone during the day working at jobs and saving money to buy their own farm. Although she was excited about moving to their own place, she was sad about leaving her little brother, Steve, behind.

Mama longed for female companionship sometimes, just a female friend, someone to share life's joys and sorrows. Mama always prayed to Jesus for guidance, but thought it would be nice to have a close friend she could talk to about woman things. Not that she was unhappy, but she did get frustrated sometimes just like Papa. Even though Papa was her best friend, some things she did not want to worry her husband about. Farm wives had no one outside of their husbands to talk about personal things. Family things stayed within the family. The family pride never allowed you to share secrets and hardships with anyone outside the family. Wives were expected to be strong and hold the family together regardless of the daily crises farm-life held.

Mama was friends with the other farm wives, but children, running the household, and farm work did not allow time for visiting with any of the women. Mama knew, as did the other women in the neighborhood, that when something happened, neighbor women would drop whatever they were doing and come to help. Dry Valley was a close community, but social visits were reserved for church on Sundays, harvests, births, deaths, and tragedies that required assistance and understanding and sometimes just an extra set of hands to help with chores brought on by the event. Occasionally, a visit with a close neighbor was possible during the winter months after field work was laid by.

Mama read the Bible to pull her through many days. One of her favorite chapters in the Bible was Proverbs 31. She picked up the Bible that day and read, *"She gets up before dawn to prepare breakfast for her household and plan the day's work for her servant girls."* (Prov.31:15). Mama closed the book and her eyes and said out loud, "If only I could have servant girls just for a day."

Everyone in our small community went to the same church. We had service on Sunday morning and again on Wednesday night for part of the year. During the spring, summer, and fall harvest months, Wednesday night services were cancelled as the farmers were in the field by sunup and at home after sundown. By the time evening chores were finished and supper eaten, it was bed-time.

After a harvest service, the families at church would join together under the trees outside and have Sunday dinner on the grounds. Wives and daughters, and sometimes grandmothers, prepared food and assisted each other in setting up a feast spread on long homemade tables in the shade of the trees. Families brought their favorite dishes— homemade biscuits and cornbread fresh from the oven, fresh beans, steaming gingered carrots, piping hot mashed potatoes with smooth brown gravy, and turnip or collard greens from a late garden. For dessert, cinnamon smelling apple pie, decadent chocolate cake, and sometimes coconut cake with mounds of icing piled as high as a mountain lined the table. After Pastor Lawrence blessed the food and thanked God for a glorious harvest, the feast began.

I loved those times, when we children ate our fill and then excused ourselves to go play. We often played kick-the-can, crack the whip, or dodge-the-ball as a group or the girls might play hopscotch while the boys played marbles. None of these games required store-bought equipment except marbles and boys with marbles shared with those who did not have them. Someone usually brought an old tin can for kick-the-can. The church had a large rubber ball for dodge-the-ball. Other favorite games were softball and touch football. With the children out playing, the adults were free to discuss grown-up matters. Mama encouraged us children "to speak when spoken to and to be seen, not heard."

CHAPTER 4

Our First House

A LITTLE OVER a year after they were married, Mama and Papa moved to a small farmhouse they rented from a nearby large farmer, Mr. Hal Bennett. Papa bartered with him to work for the rent by checking his fence lines monthly and making repairs as needed to keep Bennett livestock corralled.

The small log house had two rooms with a fireplace and chimney at the end of the larger bedroom-living area. Although there was not a well to supply water, the house was built on a hill above a small creek that flowed into Mr. Bennett's livestock pond. The house itself was built behind the knoll and had a high crawl space underneath the house itself. Papa would use this space for storage and shelter for Lad, an older dog his parents gave them as a protector for Mama and me when Papa was working.

Lad was a Border collie, livestock and snake dog. Living near water in a house that had been vacant for a while could be a hazard for young children. The vacant house could become a perfect habitat for water snakes. Since the house was located on the knoll, it could also be a den for wood rattlers and ground snakes, which chose to make their dens in the rocky, grassy area of the hills. Papa and Mama were both knowledgeable about snakes and could readily tell the difference between a good snake and a bad snake. Good snakes were helpful to keep venomous snakes at bay. Good snakes also kept rats and field mice from taking over. Mama was delighted to have Lad and was not surprised that he killed three snakes the first week with them.

The Wingates gave Papa and Mama the bed from her room and a small chest to put clothes in, which outfitted the fireplace room. Mama sewed a new mattress ticking and she and Papa stuffed it firmly with fresh hay. She sewed ticking for new pillows and they stuffed those with a combination of wild goose feathers and cotton from which she removed the seeds.

The kitchen had a shelf built along the wall near the stove for storing pots and pans. Mr. Bennett gave Mama a small table with two benches attached to use in the kitchen. The house also had a wood burning stove with a small oven and two cooking eyes on top, one for the coffee pot and one for the skillet. The small outhouse toilet was located to the east of the house, between the hill and the creek bed.

In a few days, Mama had the place clean and had sewn curtains for one window in the fireplace room and a second window in the kitchen. There was also a small porch located off the kitchen with steps leading to a path to the creek below.

Papa came home at the end of the first week with a gift from another neighbor—enough logs and lumber to build a washstand for the kitchen. Papa measured, then cut, hammered, and made the perfect size stand, large enough to hold two wash bowls; one for Mama to wash dishes in and the other as a hand wash basin. He had enough logs and lumber left over to make a small crib for me to sleep in when Mama was busy cooking or cleaning. He gave Mama a hug and told her he would make a baby holder the first rainy day that he could not work outside.

Papa's routine of long hours continued as he worked as much as possible for farmers around the area. Odd jobs, using the building and logging skills he possessed, kept him in demand. Mama was left alone during the day to run the household and take care of me, except on Sundays. Papa and Mama went to church and reserved that day for family time.

Although the house was not perfect, it allowed them an opportunity to be on their own without the input of Mama's family in our lives. Although Mama and Papa were happy, sometimes the smallest misunderstanding or disagreement was a problem in a two family house. I was a growing baby but Mama and I returned to her parents three days a week to do household chores for them—their cooking, cleaning, and laundry. Grandma Wingate doted on me and Steve loved having a little niece to play with. This also allowed Mama to keep her eye on Steve to make sure he was fed and healthy. She took mending and sewing home with her. Her mother was getting stronger again, but Mama continued to help them not just because they needed her, but because Mama enjoyed spending time with her family.

About six weeks after moving into the small house, Mama seemed to be more tired in the evening and fell asleep some nights with her sewing basket in her lap. Papa would gently remove it and pick her up and place her on the bed beside me. Sometimes she did not wake up but would continue to sleep. After the third night in a row this had happened, Papa asked,

"Jan, are you overworking yourself? I have never seen you this tired. Perhaps it is too much for you to continue to take care of your parents, Lily, and me. You need more rest. I'm worried about you." He spoke with concern on his face as she woke when he placed her on the bed.

Mama yawned, listened and let Papa finish before she said,

"Ross, I'm okay. I am more tired these days than usual. But, it's not the extra work. I'm healthy as a horse. It's just that I'm pregnant."

"Well, I'll be." Papa hugged her tightly. "That's wonderful! How far along?"

"If I counted right, somewhere around five months. I wanted to be sure before I got your hopes up. I know you want a little boy, so this may be a boy that God has given us." Jan smiled as Papa got up from the bed and leaned over and gave her a watery kiss.

"Oh, Jan. We'll take whatever God wants us to have." He sounded so excited. "I better get that crib built soon since we will have two little ones to watch over."

"Come to bed now, so we can get in a good day's work tomorrow," Jan said then continued, "If it's okay with you, I'll tell my parents tomorrow when Lily and I are there. They will need to make plans to get someone else to help them once the baby comes. I don't want to surprise them and destroy the relationship we have with my family. We need to tell your parents too."

"Maybe Pearl and I'll stop by my Pa's tomorrow and give them the good news. Jan, my parents will be thrilled for us. Megan, Jill, and even Teresa will too," he said as he placed his shoes under the bed and crawled under the covers. They were both so tired they fell asleep right away.

The next few weeks passed quickly. Papa made the crib larger than a normal one, covering the bottom with wire because he did not have enough lumber to make it solid. Jan sewed a small mattress ticking and stuffed it with the feathers and cotton. She also sewed a special blanket and pieced together a small quilt to cover the children while they were napping. She thought out loud that both Lily and the baby would continue to sleep in bed with them for a while. With that thought, the baby kicked inside. She automatically brought her hand to her stomach and rubbed gently until the baby stopped moving. The crib could be moved from the bedroom to the kitchen area without fuss, making it ideal to keep the babies off the floor. Lily was crawling and walking so it would be harder to keep her confined unless she was sleeping.

At this point in the pregnancy, Mama was still working at her parents' home. One benefit was she was able to continue to wash our clothes when she washed her family's so there had not been a need to set up a wash area by the creek. It would only be a matter of time as the baby grew inside her that she could not continue the work.

Grandpa Wingate had a small iron washtub in his barn which was not used. After a couple of months, Jan asked her father if she could have it to use at home. He gave her a little hug and said he and John would bring it over and set it up for her, which they did the very next day. They dug out a grassy area near the creek large enough to set up the four sided iron prong to hold the black iron tub. The fire would be built underneath for boiling water to wash clothes. Mama knew plants to use to make beautiful colors for dying cloth and would use the pot for this too. She was delighted and invited them inside for a cup of coffee.

"Jan, I must bring your mother over," Papa Wingate said. "You've made this little house into a nice home." She took the coffee pot from the stove and poured three cups of coffee. Papa Wingate and John drank their coffee black, but Mama added half milk to hers.

"We're getting there," she sighed. "Ross is working every day, so it is slow going. We want to build a couple of chicken coups and a small shelter for Pearl—nothing elaborate, just something to keep Pearl, Ross's saddle and tools, and some hay and feed dry." She placed her hands on her back and pushed into them. Her back was hurting more today than usual.

"If Ross can come up with the logs or wood, John, Ralph, and I will come over and give him a few days work." Papa Wingate continued, "Not much going on just now in the fields so we could all pull together and have it done in a couple of days."

"Why, Papa, that's wonderful. I'll tell Ross."

"You're my daughter. We will be happy to help get the buildings up." Grandpa smiled as he patted his daughter's shoulder.

John had taken his coffee to the porch area and had been sitting on the steps when Lad wandered up with a large dead timber rattler in his mouth. He laid the snake at John's feet and wagged his tail seeking approval.

"Good dog," John said as he turned the snake over with his shoe and patting Lad's head. "Where did you get this beauty?" Lad lay down beside John on the porch. He continued petting Lad, scratching him behind his ears as the tail swayed back and forth and up and down hitting the floor, making a gentle thumping sound. John had a way with animals almost as good as Ross.

Mama and Grandpa Wingate came through the door just as John finished his coffee. He passed the empty cup to his sister. "Some dog you got here, that's a big timber rattler he just brought to me. It's dead but fresh," he said turning it over with his boot. "It will keep moving until the sun goes down. Have you seen many snakes round here, Jan?"

"Lad is constantly bringing them up. He has killed about six or seven in the few weeks since the Howells gave him to us," she replied as I pushed through the opened door and onto the porch. John instinctually picked me up into his arms and I patted his face.

"Don't want to frighten you Sis, but if Lily gets bit by one of these, it will kill her. This snake carries enough venom in one bite to kill a grown man or a mid-size calf. You must keep Lily out of the grass until the dog no longer brings catches to you. By then, he will have killed most of them or will have the snake population on the run."

"Not all of the snakes have been venomous," Mama offered.

"But you can't afford to take a chance. Any snake, good or bad, will bite if it feels threatened and little feet and hands don't always watch where they are going or what they pick up."

Grandpa Wingate joined in, "John has a point. We still have several weeks of warm weather before the snakes go into hibernation. Just be careful and take good care of this dog. He is worth his weight in gold."

"His name is Lad," Jan replied as she stroked Lad's coat.

Papa Wingate and John began to move toward the steps to leave but before going John passed me to Mama and took a large stick that was lying close by, removed the dead snake from the porch and tossed it into a wooded area; they mounted the horses they had tied to the tree when they arrived.

Mama shared the good news of the offer her family made to build the chicken coops and combination shed stall building for Pearl and Papa's tools. Papa thought his brothers would help also so he thought the work could be done in a day.

They also talked about John's conversation about the snakes and Lad's role in protecting them. Papa suggested that Mama bring Lad inside the house when we were there alone. He agreed they had to be careful especially with me since I was a very active toddler at this stage of life, exploring everything and running away from them every chance I got. Lad spent his first night in the house lying on an old quilt that Mama placed on the floor in the corner of the bedroom. He became my protector and stayed beside me at each step when I was outside. Even with Mama standing near me, Lad was at my heels or beside my hand.

The Howells and Wingates worked together later in the summer to build three chicken coops and a small combination building for Pearl and Papa's tools. The work was completed over a long, hard day of in-laws working together under Papa's supervision. Pearl's stall was designed so that Mama could also use it for a milking stall when we got a cow. We continued to use milk from the Wingate or Howell farms which Papa or Mama retrieved every two or three days. Mama kept the milk cold by tethering it in the deep water of the creek with a rope that she or Papa could pull up when needed. Lad continued to bring gifts of various dead snakes including venomous ones, but less frequently.

More weeks passed as Mama's belly got more round and she suffered back aches coupled with headaches. Papa surprised Mama with a brood hen and a flock of six baby chickens that he had taken as payment for a recent job. The next day he brought a rooster and a beautiful laying hen, which filled all three chicken coops—mama hen and babies in one coop, the rooster in a second coop, and the brood hen rounding out the third coop. Papa bought a small bag of crushed corn for feed and used an old white wash bucket to store the feed in by hanging the bucket on a peg high at the back of Pearl's stall.

A couple of weeks later, Papa and Pearl came home early one afternoon. Mama had not been feeling well and both of us were taking a nap on the bed with Lad asleep on his quilt in the corner. Papa roused Mama and I awoke immediately. He took her hand, picked me up in his arms and led the way through the door onto the back porch of the tiny house. Lad followed on our heels. There, standing below, with a single rope tied as a halter over her head, stood a beautiful jersey cow. Mama was overwhelmed and started to cry softly. Papa held on tight and led Mama, with me still in his arms, down the steps.

"Jan, meet Bessie," he laughed as tears of joy rolled down Mama's cheeks.

"Now, we will have our own milk so we don't have to wait when we are out." With me in his arms and squirming, he reached up with his spare hand and gently brushed Mama's tears from her cheeks.

"Where did you get her?" Mama asked half crying and half laughing.

"Mr. Bennett was going to sell her anyway, so I bought her."

Looking through teary eyes she touched Bessie's face and rubbed her hand gently down her side and across the length of her spine. Bessie turned her head showing big round brown eyes to her new owner. She quietly chewed her cud while automatically swishing her tail to keep the flies away.

"Bessie, you are one beautiful creature," Mama said.

"I have been looking for a cow to buy for a long time. With the new baby on its way and Lily getting older and drinking milk on her own, it was time for us to have our own cow." Papa continued, "Hal gave me a great deal. He is going to let me work it off. Bessie cost me $10."

Papa continued saying, "Bessie has already been milked today but will need milking tomorrow morning, so that gives me this afternoon to make a milking stool for you, my dear."

"What will you make it out of?" Jan asked.

"I still have a few pieces of logs and can cut a round top from a couple scraps of board, so I have what I need. If you will make us a cup of coffee, I'll get started on the stool."

With that he passed me to Mama and I slid down her side to the ground and started going up the back steps, my favorite place to play. Lad was right behind me and lay down at the top of the steps, so I couldn't pass to go back down. Each time I tried to go around Lad, he would put his full body in front of me and block the way. Mama came up soon, took my hand and led me into the kitchen. She closed the door behind her and started the coffee brewing.

Papa finished the stool and left it near Pearl's stall. He fed Pearl for the night, fed Bessie some of Pearl's food, and tied her with a medium length rope to the end of the building. She had some shelter from the weather as she was protected on the north side by the building itself and it was still reasonably warm weather. Papa would have time to make an addition to the building and create a stall for her at the end. He promised himself to do that before the first freeze. Mama would be able to let the rope out further during the day so that Bessie could graze on the tall grass growing on the hillside. Currently, Bessie could only lie down, stand up, eat, and drink water as her rope was too tight for anything more.

Next morning, Papa was gone early and Mama left Lad in charge of watching me sleep. She took our water bucket and a clean towel and went to milk Bessie. She found and admired the stool Papa had made and checked out the sturdiness of it, noticing the correct height for milking. Mama spoke softly to Bessie, rubbed her down the shoulders and then the back to soothe her and allow her to smell her body scent so that Bessie would become familiar with Mama's smell and not be afraid. Mama positioned the stool near Bessie's back legs and lowered her own protruding body onto the stool. She took her hands and splashed the water from the pail onto Bessie's udder to clean it. By spreading her own legs wide, Mama was able to set the bucket on the ground directly under the cow. Bessie relaxed and the milk flowed from her swollen udder with each gentle squeeze of the teat by Mama's fingers. Mama soon had Bessie's first gallon of milk. Mama stood erect and moved the milk pail from the cow's path. She then took a large portion of feed from Pearl's feedbag and hung the feed bucket on the nail Papa had placed in the side of the stall for that purpose.

Bessie did not wait for an invitation but munched away at the combination of molasses, oats, and crushed corn. Mama praised Bessie in her soft voice and thanked God for the beautiful day, Bessie, the chickens, Pearl, Lad, Papa, me, the baby she carried inside, and her life in general.

She then moved the milk pail outside the stall, hung it on a second nail and pulled gently on the rope beckoning Bessie to follow. Together they made their way to the creek bed below. Mama first allowed the cow to drink from the creek and then tied her firmly to a sturdy fence post so she would have access to ample grass, trees providing shade, and the creek water. Bessie would stay there until evening, and then Mama would milk her again. She would determine the amount of milk Bessie was capable of giving after a couple of days on the same routine and whether or not Bessie could provide enough milk for their growing family or if they needed to think about a second cow.

Lazy, hazy summer days turned to an early fall. Papa continued to work with farmers by clearing land to increase their farming potential. As a timber crewman he earned $1 a day but the hours were from sunup through sundown. Mama got bigger and more uncomfortable as the baby became more active. I required constant attention which left no time for Mama to sew and mend as she did before I began walking/running. Either Lad or Mama had to constantly be at my side. I explored every nook and cranny of the yard, the house, and the creek getting scrapes and cuts along the way. Everything began to take a toll on Mama as time for the baby to be born grew closer.

It was Wednesday and Papa had left at 4:00 am leaving me and Mama in bed. He told Mama he would be late today as they planned to burn the grass and stumps from the field in the late afternoon and he would need to stay until the fire was safely out. Mama, half asleep, told him not to worry that she did not plan much that day except sewing, so we would be fine. Papa left and Mama turned over next to me and fell back into a sound sleep. She woke mid-morning to find Lad agitated and up from his bed whining in a soft low whine. He was pacing round and round the crib which was close to his quilt near the corner of the room.

"What's wrong, boy?" Mama rubbed her eyes thinking he needed to go outside for his morning walk. Mama rolled her round body off the bed and holding her belly with her hands started toward the door to let Lad outside, but Lad did not come when she opened the door. He gave a loud yelp instead and continued to whine as he circled the crib. I stirred on the bed but remained asleep.

"Quiet, boy, you'll wake Lily," Mama said as she used the chamber pot near the bed that Papa had gotten from her mother several weeks back. Now she would not have to make the morning trip to the outhouse that had become more awkward for her as the baby grew. Lad looked over at her but continued to pace and whine, circling the crib.

Mama was still fuzzy with sleep and did not understand what was going on with Lad. He had become the perfect house dog and never made noise before. He had not been bothered by the crib before either. Mama was not sure what to do.

"Come over here, boy," Mama coached, but Lad still continued the circles as his whining got more fretful. Mama patted the bed, but Lad ignored her with his eyes fixed on the crib. Mama thought she saw the green quilt on top of the crib move a little, but then thought her eyes were deceiving her. The crib was empty so she must be imagining the movement. Then she saw a portion of something round, tan and brown about the size of a large tree limb with dark cross-bands circling it. She knew immediately that there was a very large snake in the crib.

"Oh, God, help us!" she muttered under her breath. She moved from the bed instantly to the fireplace and pulled the poker from its stand. Lad knew that Mama saw the snake and he began to make small dives for the crib, still whining and jumping in and back out quickly. Mama cautiously came near the dog and the crib, poker in hand. She took the end of the poker and flicked the small quilt from the crib onto the floor beyond. She could not see the head but could see a portion of the body as the snake quickly ran under the blanket covering the small blue ticking mattress lying over the wire bottom of the crib.

She was scared. The snake looked like a copperhead but she had not gotten a good look at it. She took the poker and tried to flick the blanket as she had the quilt, but it only came part way up. The snake immediately ran under the mattress to the wire frame below. Lad went wild. A second flick of the poker sent the blanket to the floor near the quilt. Lad started darting in and out with lightning movements each time his teeth snarling and his jaws clamping trying to get a bite of the snake between the wire and frame of the crib. Mama again tried to flick the mattress off the snake, but unlike the quilt or blanket, it was too heavy to move from the crib. Lad's whining became louder and I began to stir in the bed. Lad was on a mission to get the snake and started a routine of one bark followed by a dart to the underside of the crib. After a few seconds, I sat up in bed.

"Dog," I said and started to scoot off the bed. Mama's loud scream stopped me.

"Lily, stay on the bed!" she yelled. I crawled back onto the bed, startled at the tone of Mama's voice.

"Down. Dog," I called to Mama.

"No, stay on the bed!" Mama screamed at me again and I began to cry.

Mama was not a coward, but the pregnancy and the snake unraveled her and she began to release low frightening screams. Lad's hair on his neck bristled and his eyes stayed fixed firmly on the crib as he continued to bark, dart in, snap his jaws, and jump back.

A portion of the snake's tail fell through an opening between the wire and the side of the crib, the same opening the snake had used to crawl into it. Lad sprung and clamped his jaws on the snake's tail and gave a hard yank with the full force of his weight. Thud, thud! Mama tried to hit the snake with her poker. Lad pulled the snake out about a foot, released for a second and grabbed the body of the snake again. Thud! THUD! Mama brought the poker down again, but this time on the snake's back. With the whip of his head,

Lad yanked the snake out again. Thud, thud, THUD from Mama's poker. The dog pulled as hard as he could and the snake came out another foot. Mama was shocked by the size. He was a big one, well over four feet long. Lad, released and simultaneously grabbed the back of the body again with another yank. The snake fell onto the floor about six inches from the crib. As the scrambling injured snake flicked its head to strike, Mama hit it as hard as she could with the poker, striking its head. THUD! That blow gave Lad enough time to come in for the kill. He caught the snake near its head and shook it violently until he had broken its back in several places. He dropped the snake and Mama went in for overkill. She lowered the poker on the snake's head again and again until its head was smashed.

I was terrified, and screamed at the top of my lungs. I buried my face in the bed frame and screamed loud sobbing cries, "Mama, Mama!"

Mama crumpled onto the floor exhausted, overcome by fright, fatigue, and blackness as she felt warm liquid between her legs. "Lily," she murmured and passed out on the floor.

Lad, sensing something was wrong, rushed to Mama and licked her face but she did not move. I sat in the middle of the bed screaming at the top of my lungs, "Mama, Mama!" Lad jumped onto the bed beside me, lay down and began licking the tears from my face, consoling me like a parent would comfort a child. Mama never moved as the dark reddish-brown liquid formed a puddle beneath her.

About half an hour later, Uncle John knocked, then, called out, "Anybody home?" He opened the door to find me and Lad sitting beside Mama's body lying on the floor. Lad jumped up and barked when John came in.

John picked Mama up and placed her on the bed. He checked her pulse and washed her face with a wet cloth from the kitchen. He noticed the dead copperhead on the floor next to the crib. He then checked Mama for snake bites. I clung to his pants leg as he tried to wake Mama. Her pulse was weak and he could not wake her. He covered her with the bed sheet and quilt, and patted the bed for Lad to jump up, which he did. John then picked me up, commanded Lad to stay and with me in his arms he rode his horse to get the local midwife who lived and worked on Mr. Bennett's farm. John returned with Lucy Bowman. Mrs. Bennett kept and took care of me until Grandma Wingate came later that day to take me to her house.

Mama had gone into premature labor and lost a lot of blood by the time Lucy Bowman, the local midwife, arrived. The premature baby girl inside her was born several hours later. It was a very difficult delivery with Mama going in and out of shock. Anna Howell, a little under weight, finally pushed through and took her first breath screaming loud cries to let everyone know she had arrived. Most of the danger was over, but Mama was still semi-conscious and fading in and out of shock when Papa arrived home to be told he had another beautiful daughter. Mr. Bennett had sent a farmhand to the burn field to get Papa when his wife explained to Hal about John's visit and the snake incident.

The midwife brewed special tea (sassafras and yellow root) to help replenish the blood Mama lost and to aid in building strength. Mama slept for seven hours after giving birth to Anna. Papa sat in a chair beside her bed throughout the night. The midwife did not leave her side. Instead, she sat reading the Old Testament and praying for Mama's life. She began by reading aloud: (Ezekiel 16:6-7) *"Then I passed by you, and saw you kicking about in your blood, and as you lay there in your blood I said to you, 'Live!' I made you grow like a plant in the field. You grew up and developed."* The midwife prayed to God for his help to heal Mama. From that moment forward, she read silently and prayed silently. Every hour she examined Mama, first her pulse and then her abdomen and private parts. She changed soiled bandages, had Mama drink the liquid teas and water she put to her mouth and continued her ritual of reading the Bible and praying.

She made sure Anna was fed by giving her warm water laced with sugar through a nipple she made from soft gauze cloth stretched over a small hollow reed from wild cane growing in the creek. When she first put the homemade nipple in the baby's mouth, Anna screamed in frustration. But after a few tries of allowing her to suck her finger and then shifting to the reed, the infant latched on and began pulling in the sweet liquid. The sugar water would sustain the baby until Mama could feed her properly.

The midwife suggested to Papa that Mama have three full weeks of bed-rest before taking on the responsibility of a toddler and a premature newborn. She would check by daily the first week to make the teas for Mama, wash the bed linens, the baby's diapers and other laundry, and to examine the new baby. She explained to Papa that Mama was out of danger but still extremely weak.

With Mama being sick, Grandma Wingate found a new purpose in life and came each morning to stay with Mama, me, and Anna during the day while Papa continued to work. She cooked the meals, cleaned the house and took care of me and the baby while Mama rested that first week. She read the Bible to Mama in the afternoons while I took my naps. After cooking supper for Papa and Lad each evening, she took me home with her and we returned the next morning. Mama gradually renewed her strength and Anna gained a little weight as Mama's breast milk provided the nourishment she needed.

Lad continued to watch over us. Although Grandma Wingate did not normally allow dogs in the house, she never questioned Lad's presence in the corner of the room.

Mama and Papa became more cautious and more aware of cracks in floors and made sure they were properly filled in. They also appreciated having Lad around for protection.

CHAPTER 5

Ripple Creek Farm

THE FIRST SMALL house served as our home for several years after the snake incident and Anna's birth. From the beginning Papa and Mama had their hearts set on buying their own small working farm. Fortunately, Papa's reputation as a hard worker and skilled craftsman placed his services in high demand among the neighbors in the community and surrounding counties. In addition to helping Mama's parents at the Wingate farm, Papa worked hard over many years on projects for neighbors to build the cash down payment that he and Mama needed to make their dream come true.

Finally, a few years after their marriage, my parents (with the help of the bank) purchased a small farm. They now had a place of their own to farm and raise children. Everyone in the neighborhood was excited for the young couple and delighted to have them as neighbors.

The former owners, Bob and Sherry Parkman, sold the farm because Mr. Parkman's father was dying from an incurable disease. They decided to return home to Louisville, Kentucky to be with his family. The Parkman family had lived in our small neighborhood of Dry Valley for six years. They purchased the farm and planned to build a home as soon as they could afford it. When news spread of the coming depression and the older Mr. Parkman's illness, everyone speculated about who would buy the property. Mr. Parkman would inherit a large horse farm outside of Louisville when his father died. His mother would live with them. He under-priced the farm to sell and Papa jumped at the opportunity to buy it. Papa teased Mama that the barn was "good enough to live in." He liked saying that he got the property for a steal. However, no one except Papa, Mama, and the banker, Mr. Barnes, knew how much he paid for it. Such things were private.

The farm was unique with a spring fed creek running through the north side of the property. Even during drought months in late summer, when the water level was low, flowing water rippled along making the gurgling sounds of a babbling brook to put you in tune with nature and with God. Quiet time beside the creek, fishing or just spending a lazy few minutes, was good food for the soul. In the early years, Mama and Papa spent their free time either lying on a quilt or fishing for catfish or brim from the creek bank. It was heaven on earth according to Mama. We love the stories they both told of their time at the creek when they were young and carefree. My parents gave our farm the perfect name—Ripple Creek Farm.

Our every day drinking water came from a well my parents had dug near the outside kitchen door of our home. A twenty-inch open pipe placed over the hole sunk deep within the earth provided access to the water. A metal cover over the top of the pipe kept critters out and dirt and debris from falling in. A deep narrow wooden bucket tied to a rope and pulley was attached to a wooden roller with a handle. We used the handle and pulley to obtain water from the well for the house. The well was considered to be a shallow well—only 600 feet deep. The drillers hit rock at that stage and could drill no further. The well did not supply enough water for the family, washing clothes, plants, farm animals, or "killing time" in the fall.

The federal government electric cooperative targeted our rural area for electricity but it would be years before power lines were installed in our farm community. It was in the planning stage in 1943 with a projected date for electricity in Dry Valley of 1948.

We cooked and heated the house with wood and some coal. Oil lamps and candles made by Mama provided light after dark.

Our natural spring well was dug close to Ripple Creek and among the Oak trees near the back of the property. It was an open well, only about 300 feet deep and six feet across but it had abundant spring water. The well was covered by thick, heavy wooden pieces placed over the natural rock well shaft. The wooden well cover kept animals and children from falling in. Papa made a homemade danger sign by burning the words DANGER – DUG WELL onto a large board and nailing it to a large towering oak tree that lived behind the well. The old Oak provided shade and coolness from the scorching heat of summer and its massive branches provided shelter from the chilling winds, sleet,

and snow of winter. We used a large wooden bucket, tied onto a long rope slung over that same big Oak that held the danger sign, to draw water. We kept a metal dipper for drinking hanging on a nail driven into the same tree. The beautiful old Oak served as "Keeper of the Water Supplies."

The ground around the well was covered with beautiful blue green moss that felt like thick carpet under your bare feet in summer. Wild flowers grew along the mossy edge—tiny blue bells and wild moss roses blanketed the area from early spring until late fall. Even during winter months, the mossy green carpet flourished. It was a quiet place to come and sit beside the well. I enjoyed quiet time watching a little green frog sitting on the moss, flicking out his tiny tongue, catching flies and insects that were unaware that he was there and flew too close. When I got the chance, I would sneak off with a book and plop down on the mossy edge and daydream while soaking up the words on the page. I often heard Mama's voice jolt me to reality as I scrambled to get back to the house as quickly as possible. She called, "Lily! Lily! Where are you?"

Water from this well had a cool and refreshing taste like none other in the area. Our neighbors often brought large glass jugs and filled them with the spring water. They visited the well most often in the spring and summer months. In the winter it was too cold for them to endure the harsh winter climate to seek the refreshing spring water.

Ripple Creek Farm was scattered with thick rich timberland—tall clusters of trees including pine, cedar, various hardwoods including, oak, hickory, sycamore, sweetgum, some chestnut, black walnut, and elm. The wooded areas were rolling hills while the flat lands had rich black soil mixed with just the right amount of red clay and a little sand making it suitable for farming.

When Papa bought the farm, it had one large barn building already built with a dirt floor. The barn was old but had an open design with a pathway running through the middle to allow access from both ends. The dirt floor inside had been packed solid to allow clean up of animal manure, which was used as fertilizer in the fields. The top section of the building had been floored creating a large hayloft for hay gathered in the fall and stored as winter feed for the livestock. Four stalls with gates that latched took up most of the ground floor and were used to house the cattle and mules. Ladders were built along the walls to allow access from the ground to the upper floors. Only minimal repair was required to make the barn usable.

Two storage rooms with wooden floors were at the north end on the ground floor of the barn. One was used to store corn and feed for the farm animals including chickens, turkeys, pigs, and the mules. This room was called the feed room. The other room was used to store Mama's canned goods from the summer and fall harvest. This room was called the food storage room and had many shelves that reached from floor to ceiling. The hay on the upper floor provided insulation for the food storage room and kept the glass jars from breaking during freezing winter months. We lined the back of the food storage shelves with a thick layer of hay for additional protection. This room also had two large empty feed drums used for storing extra corn meal, flour, coffee, white sugar, and grits. Ropes with large metal pulleys were used to lift items from the floor onto large hooks suspended from the ceiling. Storing food suspended from the ceiling kept it free from wild animals or rodents that happened to wonder into the barn. Popcorn and peanuts were placed in large burlap bags that held 100 pounds of produce. Sugar cured hams, cured sides of beef, and deer plus hickory nuts, black walnuts, and wild chestnuts were also stored in these burlap bags and suspended on the large hooks. Other portions of meats were smoke-cured or salted down and placed in a saltbox located in a small underground room called a smokehouse cellar located closer to the house.

The smokehouse cellar consisted of a six by eight foot underground room dug into the hillside. It had a wooden door that opened and locked like the front door on the house. In addition, fresh meat, milk, and butter could be stored in the smokehouse without spoiling for as long as two days in the summer and for a week or longer in the winter. The coolness of the underground location kept food fresh longer.

The barn had a tin roof. When you got caught in the rain, it was nice to hear rain drops pounding against the tin overhead. Mama called it music from God. It was an ideal barn and would last a number of years. Papa took every opportunity to extend and reinforce the barn to make it bigger and better.

Adjacent to the barn was an open shed attached at the roofline. It was the storage shed for our wagon, plows, bridles, harnesses, and shoes for the mules. When Papa plowed the mules, he put a piece of metal called a "bit" across and inside their mouth to keep them from biting their tongue while pulling the plow. The "bit" did not hurt the mules while a tongue bite could be painful. Long leather lead lines were hitched to each side of the bit and tied together so Papa could hold the lines in his hands and guide the mule in the correct direction. To go left, Papa pulled on the left lead line and yelled, "Haw!" To guide the mule right, he pulled on the right line and yelled, "Gee!" Other things stored in the shed included both of Papa's plows—a single plow and a double plow—wrenches, hatchets, shovels, gloves, and other tools farmers needed and used.

    We raised chickens on Ripple Creek Farm. At the end of the barn shed and along the back south side of it were ten chicken coops built with doors to open and close. These special coops were for hens that laid eggs, sat on the nest, and raised the baby chicks. They were called "brood hens." Chickens that produced eggs for eating were referred to as "laying hens." Laying coops, also called opened coops, were built outside on posts with shelter over the tops and around the sides. Hens shared the open coops daily when laying eggs. When gathering the eggs, you might find brown and white eggs in the same coop as more than one hen sometimes laid their eggs in the same coop. However, when they became brooding hens, they no longer used the shared coops with the other hens. They instinctively began using the coops used by brood hens. Eggs were left inside the nest until the hen laid a nest full. Then the hen would begin sitting on the eggs to hatch them. Once this happened, we would close the door of the coop and open it once daily for the hen to come out for exercise, food and water. The brooding hen instinct took over and they knew exactly what to do and which coop belonged to them. We kept other hens away from the brooding hen's eggs. The incubation period for hatching the baby chicks was twenty-one days. It was fun to watch the process and we enjoyed the excitement of the yellow, fluffy down-covered baby chicks' arrival.

With Ripple Creek located in the woods and near water, chickens were vulnerable to becoming prey for wild animals. Coops sometimes protected the laying and brood hens, but could sometimes become death traps when a hungry predator came along.

Lad and Skip were good at keeping predators out, but there were many. Raccoons, ferrets, foxes, chicken snakes, and weasels were the worst. It was sometimes difficult to keep the chickens safe. Even the chickens nesting on the barn rafters and high in trees during summertime were susceptible to attacks. Raccoons, ferrets, foxes, and weasels had paws that worked like hands and were capable of opening the coop doors unless they were locked with a chain. Even locking the coops could result in death as the hen inside could die of fright during an attack.

An early fall evening found Lad and Skip agitated at the back door, barking and looking toward the barnyard. We had just sat down to supper so Papa yelled at the dogs, "Shut up." Neither dog obeyed his master. They barked, then whined and ran off the porch toward the barn, and then ran back, repeating the act again. Papa was praying over the food and as soon as he finished, Mama said, moving her chair back from the table, "Ross, something's wrong at the barn." She reached behind the door and picked up the shotgun from its holder.

"I just checked everything, Jan," Papa assured her making no move to get up. "The dogs are playing a game."

"Skip's young, but Lad only acts this way when danger is near," she replied as she stepped outside the door leaving Papa with us kids at the table. The dogs ran full speed under the fence to the barnyard and around the north end toward the chicken coops. It was almost dark, but still light enough that Mama didn't bother to light the lantern. She ran behind the dogs at full speed through the gate rounding the barn on their heels. Lad had a large weasel penned inside one of the chicken coops but it had already killed three of Mama's prize brood hens and their entire flock of baby chicks. The dead chicks were strewn over the ground of the chicken yard with feathers everywhere. Skip chased a second weasel into the woods at full speed.

"Lad," Mama yelled and the dog backed off enough that the weasel leapt to the ground below. Mama swung the gun to her shoulder and opened fire, leaving the weasel lying in a heap not more than a foot from the dog. Lad sniffed to make sure it was dead then headed for the woods in a full run following Skip's bark.

Papa rounded the barn in a full sprint. "What on earth is...?" He stopped in mid-sentence as, even in the dim light, he could see the carnage. He walked over to Mama and took the shotgun, put his arms around her and they stood there for a moment in the midst of the dead weasel and the squawking and fluttering of the other chickens inside their coops.

Mama pulled away close to tears and went to each remaining coop speaking gently to her chickens and her prize rooster quieting them down. Papa got a feed bucket from the barn and removed the dead chicks leaving just the feathers sprinkled over the ground. It would take months to rebuild the chicken stock to where it was before tonight's weasel raid. Next morning, Papa found the second weasel dead on the back porch, a present from the dogs.

Papa designed and built our house to the north of the barn. Timber to build the house came from trees located in the woody section of the land. Papa paid the sawmill crew to split the logs into lumber for the house. He sold a section of the timber and did a barter trade for the log splitting service. Papa paid for the tin to cover the roof and for the roofing nails. He had no suitable barter for either. The cost of the tin roof wiped out most of their savings and Papa found it necessary for him and Mama to tighten their belts and be frugal with expenses. For several months and even years, they bartered for most of the goods they needed for the farm, only paying money for emergencies.

You could see the open center aisle of the barn from the windows of the fireplace room and the kitchen areas of the house. It was a shotgun style track house—slim and long with a covered passageway running through the center of the house. This passageway, also called a breezeway, was designed so the family dogs would have shelter from the weather and a dry place to sleep at night. The breezeway allowed the wind to blow through which kept the house cooler in the summer. The fireplace room and kitchen areas were on the left side and the bedrooms on the right side of the house. This style house was popular throughout the South. The house was built with a wood frame three feet off the ground. Large rocks supported the frame and were placed at each of the four corners. Additional supporting rocks were placed in the middle of the house frame on both sides to ensure adequate support. We had no basement, but the area under the house was used for storage. Two rooms were located across the breezeway from the fireplace room and kitchen. The fireplace room had one door opening into the breezeway. The kitchen had two doors with one door opened into the covered breezeway; the second door located at the back of the room opened to steps leading to the ground. The breezeway ran east and west to allow the best protection from the elements while obtaining the coolest breezes in the summer and the warmest ones in winter.

The bedrooms were located across the breezeway. Mama and Papa's bedroom had a door opening onto the breezeway and, like the kitchen, a door at the back of it which led to steps descending to the ground. The other bedroom was larger with a curtain dividing the room into two sections. Anna and I slept in one bed in the front portion of the room and Tom and David in another bed located behind the curtain in the back section of the room. Only one door opened from the children's room onto the breezeway. A wall separated our room from a large closet called a pantry located between the bedrooms. A small doorway with a pull curtain across it separated the pantry from our bedroom. A solid wooden door opened into the pantry from the breezeway. The pantry was used to store foods that were in short supply and precious, like white flour, white sugar and coffee. A large wooden box kept dried beans, potatoes and onions ready for cooking. Soap products and cleaning supplies as well as linens for the beds and seasonal clothes were also stored in the pantry.

If weather permitted, Mama and Papa left the fireplace room/breezeway door open at night until they went to bed. Sometimes, while Anna and the boys slept, I would sneak into the pantry from our room and press my body flat against the floor. If I opened the door slightly and lay very still, I could hear their conversations undetected. I listened sometimes when I got worried about something I had overhead them say. I realized it was wrong to eavesdrop on my parent's conversations, but I found myself yielding to the temptation more often than not. I prayed about eavesdropping, but it only helped sometimes.

Tom and David's section of the bedroom was located at the back. Although we shared the bedroom with our brothers, their section was separated by a long muslin curtain hung on burlap twine string tied to long hooks pulled tight to the ceiling. The curtain was split in the middle to allow parting for entrance and exit from their section, so it was like two bedrooms. The curtain served as a sound buffer as the boys required more sleep.

We tried to be quiet in our room so we would not wake Tom and David. Anna and I did our homework in the kitchen. Burning the oil lamp in our bedroom might keep the boys awake. We were allowed one candle in our room for light except when doing homework. Since I was the oldest, it was my responsibility to light the candle and blow it out. Each bedroom had a window looking out over the meadow. You could look out and see how to dress each morning. Rain meant you should wear clothes conducive to staying dry. Sunshine meant cooler clothes, especially in summer. Leaves changing into a ray of colors and slowly falling ever so softly from trees brought fall temperatures. The weather would be cool in the morning and sometimes uncomfortably hot in the afternoons. As the fall weather turned to early winter, the window panes would have patterns of frost scattered across them and would feel cold to our touch. This meant it was close to heavy coat, mitten, and scarf time and sometimes two pairs of socks for our shoes. My favorite time was awakening in the winter to snowflakes gently coming down as if the lady in the moon swept her house out and the dirt settled on earth in small and sometimes large flakes. It was also like soap bubbles gently floating down from the sky to cover the earth with a gentle soft blanket to keep it warm. I loved the seasons, but fall and winter were my favorite. I loved having the window to know how to dress for the day, whether it was for school, farm chores, or going to church. Sometimes Tom and David forgot to look out and Mama sent them back to redress before going outside.

    The house had no electricity or indoor plumbing in 1943. Our toilet facility was a wooden outhouse sitting about fifty feet from the house. A large deep hole had been dug in the ground. Our small outhouse featured a smooth shelf with a large open hole on the right side of the center of the shelf and a smaller child size open hole to the left of center. The outhouse had a door that opened to the outside and a wooden floor to keep snakes and animals away. They still got in, just not as often. The floor was large enough to house newspaper and catalog pages for wiping paper. Lime was poured into the holes onto the waste matter monthly during summer and twice during the winter to help sanitize and keep down the stench. The farmhouses in our area were constructed the same way with the same toilet facilities. Some farmhouses and outhouses were bigger and some were smaller. Depending on the number of children, some families had a five-holer outhouse.

    It was usually too cold for tub baths in the large metal tub during winter months. However, one tub bath a week was required, even in winter. We took "spit-baths" as Mama called them the other days. Spit-baths meant you washed your face, hands, arms, legs, feet, and stinky private parts, in that order, with a clean wash cloth soaked in a pan of warm soapy water. Spit-baths were taken in the kitchen hand washbasin. The washbasin was a large round bowl with a very large ceramic pitcher for housing water until it was used. We washed our hands in this basin before cooking, eating, or anytime we handled food or came into the kitchen. Mama was a stickler for keeping hands free of germs. She made strong pine scented soap just for washing working hands.

Summer baths were easier. Sometimes we just went for a swim in Ripple Creek to remove the dirt. Most often outside tub baths were taken during the summer. If the weather was bad, we took tub baths behind the curtain in the boys' section of the bedroom. During the winter, all tub baths were taken in the bedroom. For these baths water was added to a large galvanized sheet metal tub. Water was heated in a large pan on the stove and added to the tub last. Girls bathed together in the tub filled with fresh clean warm water; then the boys bathed together. We were too young to know or care about modesty. Mama took her bath next and Papa brought up the rear in the bath line, all using the same water.

We ate our meals together as a family in the kitchen. At the eating table, we had assigned seats. Mine was in the middle on the left side of the big round kitchen table, so kind of the middle seat. Anna's was directly across on the right side. Tom sat to Anna's right and David to my left. That way we could help pass the food and then help Tom and David get their food anytime they needed help. Mama and Papa's chairs were closer to the center of the round table, across from each other and separating us kids. Mama's chair was close to the stove, so she could readily get up to get whatever may remain in pots once the meal was served. We always had family style meals. The food was placed on the table near the center and then passed after Papa prayed over the meal. Everyone was encouraged to eat as much as they wanted. We were required to taste everything. Mama said you never knew if you liked it or not without tasting first. Our parents had a rule—you had to eat breakfast before you were allowed to go to school. Mama and Papa didn't want us going to school hungry. She said it kept our minds concentrating on our studies and not on our growling stomachs.

We did not always have food to take to school, especially in winter months, except perhaps an apple or an orange after harvest or near Christmas. When we did carry our dinner it was usually a piece of bread, some meat or occasionally some cheese. Sometimes we had a large cookie called a teacake or a small piece of Mama's homemade cake. The extras really made a terrific dinner. The children in our school rarely brought dinners to school and Mrs. Parnell, our teacher, never stopped to eat dinner. School sessions only lasted about six and one-half hours. A hearty breakfast could keep us going for eight hours.

We ate our evening meal (supper) early at night. It was the way families who worked farms lived. We never got real hungry while at school and Mama usually had a glass of fresh milk and a piece of bread with lots of her sweet churned butter waiting for us after school. We ate the snack before beginning our chores. Anna and I loved school, so we always ate breakfast without being prompted.

    Mama's chore routine did not vary except for laundry days. Every day she milked the cows, cleaned the breakfast dishes, swept and mopped the wood floors, prepared dinner for Papa and put dry beans, either pinto, great northern white beans, or large butterbeans, on the stove to finish cooking after soaking them overnight. Sometimes she would take leftovers and make a huge country stew for supper. We all loved her country stew, especially in the winter months. The seasoned steaming liquid mixed with vegetables with a hint of flavor from a small piece of salt pork or a left over bone, simmered all day. Mixed with cornbread, it made a meal fit for a king, or so our Papa said. It was one of my favorite meals too.

    Our supper usually consisted of dried pintos, northern white beans or big yellow butter beans cooked with a choice piece of salt pork for flavor, corn bread, and fried potatoes. Anything else, such as meat or a dessert was a treat. Mama milked the cows each morning and night, providing us with fresh milk, buttermilk, and butter. It was delicious.

    We had four milk cows—two jerseys and two Holsteins. Mama would milk our cows in the morning when Mr. Parnell, our peddler, wanted to buy the milk and butter to sell from his truck. But she only milked at dusk when the cows had small calves. Usually we had two cows with calves at one time so Mama had the opportunity to sell the milk and butter to Mr. Parnell continuously while not depriving the cows of feeding their babies. Mr. Parnell had grown dependent on Mama's milk and butter for his route sales.

As the calves grew older and were being weaned from sucking, Mama would keep the calves in the barn in the morning and milk the cows twice a day. The calves were allowed to suck after the night milking. Mama saved one teat on the cow's udder for the calf. Mama did not let the calves go hungry. We had a special grain Mama made from finely ground oats and wheat. She mixed the two grains with honey and molasses for the young calves to eat as the weaning process took place. The mixture smelled good enough for humans to eat. The calves loved it. They would cry out for their mother during the first couple of days of weaning. They looked sad. The calves were kept in the barn while their mothers grazed during the day.

After milking in the evening, the calves were then let outside to exercise and take the full teat that Mama saved for them. Then the young calves were put back into the barn so as not to pester their mothers all night trying to suck her empty udder (milk sack). We began the weaning process by feeding each young calf a large bottle of fresh milk from their mother twice a day—one in the morning and a second one at night. The bottle feeding was a lot of fun. Sometimes Anna, Tom, David, and I would argue about who was to hold the bottle. Tom and David always got to feed the new calves while Anna and I fed the older ones. It was a lot of fun when your calf got finished because he/she wanted to suck your hand or finger. If you let it, it would walk around sucking your finger for several minutes after the milk was gone. Mama said they weren't still hungry, but just enjoyed the sucking noises it made. Silly babies, we thought.

Soon the young calves began eating Mama's special mixture and forgot about being weaned. Within a few weeks after they had eaten the grain mixture, they were ready for grass and were let out of their barn stalls daily with the other cattle. For a few weeks, Mama would continue to supplement their diet with a bit of the grain mixture and an occasional bottle of milk from their mother. If we went into the pasture to do something like feed the chickens, the baby calves would come running thinking we were going to feed them. They became our playmates and friends.

We grew different crops on the farm consisting mostly of the food we needed to live. We grew vegetables including carrots, sweet corn, onions, melons, beans, peas, lettuce, sweet peppers, hot peppers, turnip greens, rutabaga turnips, mustard greens, radishes, and tomatoes. At the end of harvest seasons in the summer and fall, Mama prepared and canned the harvest so we would have food for the winter. Seeds from crops were saved for planting the following year. We children planted and grew two rows of popcorn and two rows of peanuts, enough for munchies for our family through the winter months.

Boys and girls grew up quickly when raised on a farm. Farm children learned about life and death, sadness and joy at young tender ages. We also learned about God and the true meaning of Christmas. When boys were the younger children, older female children stepped in and assisted their fathers in duties normally performed by males, which was our situation. It was hard work and sometimes it seemed all for naught when crops failed for various reasons including storms and tornadoes, rainy seasons, drought seasons, dry rot in the corn fields, plagues of locusts, or boll-weevils and other insects.

Mother Nature did not always smile on farmers, but when she did it was a decent life. In my mind, the positive things about farming outweighed the things I did not like. Without a doubt, my least favorite thing and time of year was "killing time."

CHAPTER 6

Killing Time

ON THE FARM, fall brought cold weather and killing time. "Killing time" was *not* my favorite time of the year. Killing time each year came the first Monday following the first freeze. It was close to the same date each year but depended entirely on the weather. Temperatures needed to be cold, but not freezing. Killing required working outside and was easier when the temperature was just right. Our family routinely killed a young bull and a hog to provide meat to sustain the family during the winter months. Papa's family and our neighbors got together and killed every day for one week. During this period of time, everyone in our small Dry Valley community that needed animals slaughtered for their family meat worked together as a team—men, women and children.

School was closed during killing week. It was a necessary community event. Reading and arithmetic homework was given to make up for the school classes missed that week.

Many times the animal chosen for slaughter was one of the young steers that we had fed by bottle during the weaning process. Our favorite calf had followed us around the pasture for months thinking we were its mother. It was sad but necessary because the family had to eat. Animals were raised for feeding the family. Each time Papa saw us getting too close to a particular animal he cautioned us to hold on to our hearts as that may be the animal chosen at killing time. He never allowed visible tears in front of neighbors. It was our way of life and we should be strong and put forth a brave exterior. We knew our friends were going through the same thing we were by killing their animal friends.

We learned to get through the week and the process without flinching or crying in front of others. Sometimes at night, I heard my younger siblings crying on their pillows. When this happened, I went in to them to help comfort them. First it had been Anna, then a few years later Tom, and now David. Even though Tom and David were too young to participate in the actual slaughter, they still heard our neighbors and our parents discussing it and knew what was going on.

That night, hearing David's whimpering cry, I went in to comfort him, crawled into his bed and held him in my arms for a while. He sobbed because his prize bull and friend had been chosen. He had overheard Mama and Papa discussing which animal would be slaughtered. I softly reminded him that the animal had fallen into a hole a few weeks back and had damaged a back leg that did not heal properly which meant he was in pain and could never keep up with the other livestock. He could no longer run and play, only barely walk around the barn yard. David agreed that it was better that Papa chose him rather than a spunky, completely healthy young bull. Papa was good that way. If an animal got hurt or was handicapped, but was still edible, Papa would choose to sacrifice it over a healthy animal. But David was sad that his young animal friend would not be in the barnyard anymore to hobble over when he entered the pasture. David fell asleep in my arms but was actually glad the next day after everything was over that Papa had chosen the crippled bull.

After slaughter, the meat was either cured or salted down and stored for later use. The fat from the animals was rendered into lard for cooking and soap was made. One of the by-products of rendering the lard were "cracklings," small hard pieces of skin cooked down until very crisp. Beef and pork cracklings were stored in airtight containers and used as protein snacks and condiments during the winter. Mama would surprise us and chop up several cracklings for her cornbread. It added a slight salty flavor and a delightful crunch to ordinary corn bread. Mama used cracklings in other dishes to bring out a slight flavor of beef or pork. Sometimes, she sprinkled chopped pieces over green salads, used them in turnip greens while cooking, and as a flavor enhancer for potato salad.

Soap and candles were made as the last process after rendering fat from the animals. All parts of the animal were used. Skins were used to make various items needed on the farm such as tool holders, vests, rawhide string, and hunting accessories. The internal organs of the animals were cooked and sometimes used for dog food and the lining of the intestines were used to house blood sausage made from various portions of the body. Cattle feet were used to provide glycerin for the soap and the pig feet became a delicacy for eating after being cooked and stored in vinegar base brine. Nothing was wasted.

The neighborhood women worked as a team to make basic soap for washing clothes and cleaning. Mama was a leader in the group, guiding them through the processes. Basic laundry soap was made with lye from wood ashes and coal burned for fuel. Small amounts of the lye, some lanolin oil, and glycerin for hardening were added, but no fragrance. This soap was hard on the hands but cleaned stains instantly from clothes and dishes. Pots and pans shined like new when washed in this basic soap.

A heavy-duty all-purpose soap was the easiest and least expensive soap to make. The least desirable parts of the animals were used to make this soap. It had a greater percentage of lye and the men used it to remove oil and grease from their hands after working on farm plows and other tools. At the end of the day the women divided the basic soaps and the heavy-duty soaps. It was share and share alike, even if a family killed only one animal and another family killed three. Everyone had worked as a team and reaped benefits equally.

Mama had earned the reputation of "gifted soap maker." She gladly helped female neighbors with the process. She answered their questions when asked; however, she did not share all of her secrets with them. The week following killing time, Mama would make special soaps for our family. During this second week, she trimmed the fat and rendered lard from some of the better cuts of meat. Our soap was made from only the fattest part of the animals. She waited to make her special soap when she could work privately without scrutiny.

Mama's Indian ancestors were skilled soap makers. Her great-grandmother, Little Flower, taught her the Indian method and it was *special*. As a child, Mama became fascinated by the chemistry of finding a perfect balance when putting various ingredients together for special soaps. When she was ten years old, her great grandmother died, but Mama had been a good student and had committed the method to memory. She not only continued the family soap recipes, she concocted many of her own. She honed her skills in areas of adding fragrances from wild flowers and wild herbs that grew in abundance in meadows and near water. Mama knew which flowers and shrubs would retain the fragrance longest and how to keep it faint when she mixed the soap formula.

After moving to Ripple Creek, and being coached by her friend, Rena Hogan, our Negro neighbor, Mama had perfected her soap making skills even more by adding ingredients (flower extracts, lemon sage, and rose water) and spices. Miss Rena had come to live with her grandfather, Jeremiah, on a small piece of land located across the back of Papa's lower field. The house was old and had been there for many years, long before Papa and Mama purchased the farm. Jeremiah's family was the only Negro family living in our neighborhood or in the surrounding communities. They stayed privately to themselves and were fine neighbors. Papa enjoyed talking with Mr. Jeremiah on days that he worked in the lower field.

Mama had met Miss Rena when she visited our "spring dug well" a couple years before. She, like all the neighbors, came to draw spring water for their household. Neighbors from as far away as two counties came by wagon to take spring water from this special well, especially during spring and summer months. Many people claimed the water helped them feel better, particularly if they had joint pains or headaches. I remember distinctly the first time Miss Rena came to the well. I was seven years old, Anna was five, and Tom was the baby at twenty-six months of age. Mama was very pregnant at the time with David. We had experienced a dry spell without rain for over a month and our well near the house was running low on water. It was early June and a very hot day. Mama had moved the laundry to the spring well and she and I were busy washing clothes. Anna was on a quilt spread under a large oak shade tree watching her younger brother sleep. Anna was almost asleep herself when Miss Rena walked up with a large burlap covered jug balanced perfectly on her head. Miss Rena walked over to Mama and me and removed the jug in one graceful move that demanded our attention. Mama had her back to Miss Rena and was rubbing clothes across the rub-board. Mama jumped when Miss Rena spoke.

"Mrs. Howell, I'm Rena Hogan," she said sticking out her dark olive hand to Mama. Mama's hand was wet with soap suds but she quickly dried it on her apron and shook the outstretched hand. Miss Rena's skin was only slightly darker than Mama's, which was darkened after long periods working the fields in the summer sun.

"Pleased to meet you, Rena," Mama said as she turned to face the young woman fully now. Mama put her hands on her hips and leaned back into them as her back was really hurting.

"Grandpa Jeremiah said you let us take spring water from your well," Miss Rena said smiling. The smile showed the most beautiful white teeth I had ever seen. They were straight and sparkled.

"Yes, all the neighbors come to get water from the well. Some of them use it for medicinal purposes and others just choose to drink it. You are welcome to as much water as you need or want," Mama said as she moved to a nearby stump so she could sit down for a moment.

"Are you feeling okay?" Miss Rena asked. "You look kind of peaked to me," she said as Mama sat on the stump.

"I think I am just overly hot and tired," Mama said looking up at the young woman.

Miss Rena turned to look at me and asked, "What's your name, pretty girl?" Her smile put me totally at ease as I replied,

"I'm Lily."

"And how old are you, Lily," she said letting the Lily roll off her tongue in a crisp voice as she rolled up her sleeves, dipped her hands in the water and began to rub the clothes waiting to be washed.

"I'm nine," I replied noticing that Mama was leaning back with her eyes closed and was unaware that Miss Rena was doing her wash. Just then Anna stood up from the quilt where Tom slept and came and stood beside me.

"I'm Anna," she said as she smiled at Miss Rena.

"Well hello, Anna," Miss Rena smiled again showing her beautiful teeth.

"You are doing such a good job watching your baby brother," she complimented Anna as she continued rubbing the clothes and putting them in my rinse water without effort. Mama opened her eyes, stood up, and came over to Miss Rena.

"You should not be doing that," she smiled as she moved to take the rub-board back from Miss Rena.

"And why not," Miss Rena smiled but kept on washing the clothes.

"I think you need a rest." She turned to face Mama, dried her hands on her skirt caught Mama gently by the elbow and walked her over the quilt where Tom slept peacefully. A slight breeze under the tree made the space seem ten degrees cooler than the wash area. Mama did not object and seated herself on the quilt near a sleeping Tom.

"Now you just rest your eyes for a few minutes while Lily, Anna, and I finish these clothes and hang them out to dry. It won't take long."

With those words she turned and stood near the wash tub again, her hands quickly in the water and rubbing the remaining clothes on the rub-board. She chatted with Anna and me asking questions about school and the chores we did on the farm. Before too long the laundry was hanging on the clothesline that Papa had stretched between four trees. A nice breeze would dry them fast.

Mama had fallen asleep on the quilt beside Tom. Anna and I showed Miss Rena how to fill her jug from the well and I shared with her the legend of the spring that kept the well with an unending supply of spring water. The legend of the spring had been passed down from generation to generation. The spring was much deeper then and had a large ledge as its base where the water flowed from the mountain. It was a story of a young Indian maiden and a young warrior who wanted her for his bride. However, the tribes were feuding. Her father was Chief of the Cherokees and his father was Chief of the Muskogee, so their love was never to be. On the eve of the great council, the tribes voted to fight each other for property rights and the right to rule. The young warrior was killed in battle and being overcome with grief, the young maiden threw herself off the mountain ledge into the water and rocks below. Tears from her father's eyes flowed so vastly that the spring was blessed with plentiful water.

"That is a lovely legend, Lily," Miss Rena said. "Thank you for sharing it with me."

Miss Rena showed us how to take wild berries and paint our fingernails a light delicate pink color using the stain from the berries.

We had fun with her while the clothes dried and Mama took a nap. The wind and hot air dried the clothes quickly and Miss Rena helped me remove them from the line and fold them carefully so wrinkles would be minimal. She showed me how to use my hands to crease the boys and Papa's slacks so they would need less ironing. I thought she was the smartest lady I knew, except Mama, and she was so patient and gentle with Anna and me. We liked her. She suggested that we let Mama sleep until Tom woke up.

"Girls," she said with a smile, "Your mother is tired and since the laundry is done, there is no reason why she should not sleep a little longer."

We shook our heads in agreement as she hoisted the water jug up to the top of her head and balanced it. She put one hand on the jug to hold it secure and patted each of us on the top of the head with the other.

"Please tell your mother, thank you for the water and that I will stop to visit the next time I see her washing." She smiled and walked up the trail toward her Grandpa Jeremiah's house.

The old dug well provided the water supply that our well closer to the house could not. The water level never lowered regardless of how much water was used. It served as one of two washing spots on the farm. During rainy months when rain water was plentiful, we did laundry at a designated spot near the cattle pond in the south pasture below the barn. During the summer months and into the fall, Mama and I washed our clothes in large tubs near the dug well. White clothes were boiled in a big iron pot mounted on a make-shift hearth so wood for the fire could be placed underneath, then rinsed in clean water in a second tub. It was much easier to draw the well water from the dug well in the large bucket than to draw water from the pond or from our smaller well with a smaller bucket. Even though it was hot outside, the breeze that blew under the big oak tree made the area seem cooler than the temperature elsewhere.

If we had a lot of clothes to wash, Mama packed a picnic dinner and we started the washing around eleven in the morning. For smaller washes, we started at noon and she packed a light snack for us to enjoy in the coolness of the shade of the oak tree. Mama strived to make wash day a treat for us children.

CHAPTER 7

Mama's Friends

WHEN MAMA AND PAPA purchased Ripple Creek, three Negroes (Jeremiah Smith's family) lived on the back of the property. Mr. Jeremiah was an elderly man whose ancestors were slaves. During the times of slavery and many many years before, the owner of our property named Smith had slaves, when slave ownership was legal and practiced in the South. It was customary for slave families to assume their owner's name as their own during those early years. After the Civil War, Jeremiah's family was freed but chose to stay with their owner in Dry Valley. Mr. Jeremiah told Papa that his owner's family was the only family he had ever known. They loved and respected each other and took care of their own.

After freeing Jeremiah's family from slavery, the owner had written a stipulation as an addendum to his will and it had been passed down through generations that Jeremiah's family had the right to work and live on a small portion of the back forty property for the rest of their lives. If Jeremiah failed to produce a male heir to continue the family lineage, the right of occupancy would revert back to the owner at the time of his death.

    Jeremiah's family lived in a small three-room house on a five acre plot of land in the back forty acre section of Ripple Creek. He had married and was blessed with two daughters, Hilly and May. Sadly, his wife had died giving birth to May, the youngest daughter. Her death had devastated Jeremiah. He became a broken hearted man and lost his desire to work and live after the death of his wife. Hilly, his oldest daughter, had grown up, gotten married, and moved away. However, Jeremiah's youngest daughter, May, had suffered brain damage from the lack of oxygen during childbirth. The birth was an exhausting, long ordeal resulting in the death of his wife. Baby May was born breech with the umbilical cord wrapped around her neck cutting off the flow of oxygen to her brain. The brain damage was slight, but she was never normal. She was a shy child and neighbors considered her to be "slow" or mentally handicapped. She often sang songs at the moon outside in the open air in the dark, sometimes in the bitter cold. Her problem worsened when a full moon appeared. She had grown up with a stigma of mental illness. She did not attend school, but her grandfather showered her with love and affection and taught her how to grow things, to read a little, and to sign her name. She was a good gardener.

He devoted his life to her needs and sheltered her from unkind rumors and the outside world.

She was allowed to go outside only when Jeremiah or his granddaughter Rena, his daughter Hilly's child, was with her.

Everyone in Dry Valley had heard rumors about May's illness. One early evening, Anna and I had gone to our room to get ready for bed. Shadows were forming with the trees blowing slightly in the breeze outside our window. I closed our curtains but left the window raised a little to let in fresh night air. I thought I heard a noise and stopped dead still for a moment to listen. I heard it again. A distant crying sound came through the woods.

"Anna, did you hear that noise?" I asked in a low voice.

"What was it?" Anna questioned.

"I'm not sure. It sounded like a hurt animal," I replied.

"Let's see what it is," Anna suggested.

So we decided to investigate. Quietly, we raised the window until we had room to crawl out. We were careful not to make any noise as we sneaked through the front gate near the barn and through the pasture, past the dug well, through the back fence, then moved carefully through the trees and underbrush to get close enough to see where the noise was coming from. The tall shrub grass shielded us. Then we saw her! It was Miss May dressed in a long, white, flowing nightgown. We were afraid. Anna's body shivered as we hunkered down together out of sight. She moaned and mumbled words unfamiliar to us as she swayed to and fro.

Miss May moved in dance-like rhythms as she gathered several pieces of dry logs and stacked them together in a campfire. She then brought hot embers in a long metal pan from inside and began dumping them onto the wood. The hot coals scorched the dry rotted wood and created a giant bonfire as the flames caught and leaped high into the night sky. She spun around in a childlike dance as the flames leaped higher into the sky creating an eerie illumination. We watched undetected for a while.

I nudged Anna and pointed for us to retreat. With unspoken words, Anna and I made our way back through the woods until we could see the safety of our house. Outside and close to the barn, I whispered, "That was spooky!"

"If we don't hurry and sneak back inside, we are gonna get caught for sure!" Anna whined, as we rounded the corner of the house. Old Lad and Skip were sleeping soundly. Skip opened his eyes and raised his head, but lay back down when he saw the two of us. We removed our shoes and tiptoed quietly across the breezeway and into the quietness of our room. We could hear the gentle breathing of our two younger brothers coming from behind the curtain separating our rooms. They were both asleep. We slid beneath the bedcovers knowing that we had gotten away with an adventure.

After pulling the covers tight around her chin, Anna spoke first.

"Lily," she whispered, "I think people are right about Miss May being crazy! Do you think she's a witch?"

"Not a witch," I whispered, "I think she's ill."

"But what's wrong with her?" Anna quizzed.

"I don't know," I whispered as I pulled the covers close under my chin adding, "I think she needs our prayers and a lot of help from God."

"I'm scared of her," Anna continued as she shivered in the cool night air that blew across our room through the opened window.

"There's no need to be scared. She is never out alone." I tried to sound comforting. "We cannot talk to anyone about what we saw tonight, Anna." I spoke softly but firmly.

"Mama and Papa would give us a whipping for sure for sneaking out and we don't want to cause any problems for Miss May and Miss Rena," I continued just above a whisper.

"Okay," Anna replied.

"Promise me, Anna," I spoke again. "You won't tell anyone—cross your heart and hope to die."

"Okay, I promise." Anna sounded serious now. Both of us got quiet, each one trying to forget what we saw in the moonlit shadows beside Mr. Jeremiah's house. I lay awake for a long time while my mind replayed the scene of Miss May dancing in the moonlight over and over.

When I heard Anna's breathing pattern grow shallow into gentle snores, I knew she had fallen asleep. Then, I prayed to God in a soft whisper,

"Lord, thank you for another day. Thank you, too, for not letting us get caught for sneaking out. Forgive us too, God, for spying on Miss May and help us to understand what we saw tonight. Give us strength to keep it quiet. She and Miss Rena are nice people and we don't want to cause trouble for them. Bless my family, God—Mama, Papa, Tom, David, and Anna. Don't forget our extended family, God. You know who they are, so I won't take up any more of your time tonight, Lord. Help me to be stronger, Lord, and to not yield to temptation. Good night, Lord."

I closed my eyes as sleep settled in and my small body allowed sleep to take hold without fighting.

At first Mr. Jeremiah did not know Miss May was different. She looked like a normal, sweet, good baby. She progressed slower than her older sister but Mr. Jeremiah did not know enough about babies to realize something was wrong. She was late in crawling, and did not fuss a lot. She was completely silent in those younger years, a happy child that never cried. She finally began speaking a few words around age eight, but never built a large vocabulary. He devoted his life to taking care of May. People talked, but no one seemed to know the whole story of Mr. Jeremiah's heartbreaking life. We heard bits and pieces here and there from one neighbor and then another. Papa said it was all speculation and should not be repeated or taken seriously.

After buying Ripple Creek, Papa got more details from various neighbors he trusted. Jeremiah's life had been saddened even more. About five years earlier, he had suffered a stroke upon hearing the news that his eldest daughter, Hilly had died. Although she had not lived with her father for many years, she had visited every year or so.

Hilly had a beautiful daughter, named Rena Hogan. After her mother's death, Rena had returned to Dry Valley to live with and take care of her grandfather and her Aunt May. Both women were quiet and stayed pretty much to themselves. Mama and Rena became friends and spent hours talking on wash days when Rena visited our dug well for spring water. Miss Rena coached Mama in her soap making. She had given Mama some avocado oil and castor-oil (Mama said it came indirectly from Africa where the avocado tree and the castor plant grew abundantly). Miss Rena told Mama that her family had brought some of the plants with them when they came to America. The plants had grown well in the harsh, dry deserts of Arizona, because the soil was a lot like the soil of the harsh, dry savannah area of Africa where her family originated. The plants that her family brought with them had multiplied and were still in her family. She taught Mama to use small amounts of castor oil in her soaps to make them gentle on the skin. The secret to using the avocado oil and castor oil was in using the exact amount needed. If you used too much, the soap would not harden. If you used too little, the soap would be crumbly and become rancid quicker. Miss Rena worked out proportions for Mama.

Sometimes Mama was able to buy castor oil from our peddler, Mr. Parnell.

Miss Rena was educated. She explained to Mama that she had finished high school and had gone to university where she studied botany and learned a lot about plants for medical uses, candle, and soap making. That all ended when her Mama died. She had no means of supporting herself and when her grandfather and aunt needed her, she was happy to come live with them. She told Mama she wanted to go back someday and finish school—after all, she was thirty years old. She was two years older than my Mama and my Mama was married and had four children. Mama liked Miss Rena.

Over time, Mama learned that Miss Rena's family on her father's side had migrated to the Arizona desert after the Civil War and had married into the Navajo Indian tribes of Colorado. Some of them married members of the Pima Indian tribes of the Sonoran desert located south of Phoenix. Miss Rena and Mama were too busy with their daily chores to visit together much, but when Rena came to the spring, she and Mama enjoyed the time together. So as to not interfere with Mama's work and farm chores, Miss Rena timed her visits to the well to fall on Mama's wash days during the summer and fall. She helped Mama do the wash or sometimes if Mama was real tired, she insisted that Mama nap while she and I completed the wash. Anna and I both liked Miss Rena and Tom thought she was interesting to play with. She had a special way with children.

The two women developed a special bond. They understood one another's plight in the struggles of daily life. They were alike in many ways and had several things in common.

After visiting with Miss Rena and Miss May at the spring one day, Mama mentioned it to Papa after dinner. From my secret spot on the floor in the pantry that night, I heard Mama telling Papa about Rena's family and how they were desert farmers—they grew crops of the saguaro cactus fruit and mesquite bean pods. The flower buds from the cactus were used for medicine potions and fruit jams and jellies. Mama explained that Rena's grandfather on her father's side was a Pima brave and her grandmother a Negro. Mama allowed that was why Miss Rena had such pretty olive brown skin. She told Papa that Miss Rena would share some of her medicine knowledge with her so that she could treat more of our childhood illnesses.

Papa reminded Mama that her chores did not allow lots of time for idle chatter. Someone might start rumors about Mama and her two Negro friends. Mama was downhearted and then she got angry. She reminded Papa that the Bible says in St. Peter 5:6: *"Humble yourselves, therefore, under God's mighty hand, that he may lift you up in due time. Cast all your anxieties on him because he cares for you."*

Mama said she had heard the gossip rumors that Miss May was crazy, but would not let gossip determine how she treated the women. Although Mama was hurt by Papa's words, she wanted to obey him. However, these women had become her friends and Mama would continue to honor that friendship regardless of what the neighbors said. She compromised and told Papa she respected his concerns and would visit with Miss Rena only when she visited the spring for water. Papa said that he liked and respected old Jeremiah too. He was intelligent and interesting to talk with. Papa said that old man has seen things that neither of them had heard of, and had experienced heartaches that would kill a normal man.

"He's a strong one and I respect him," Papa finished. "So, I understand your feelings, Jan. Sometimes though we have to see the larger picture and how others perceive us. We have good neighbors including the Smiths, so we need to get along with everyone. Just be careful is all I am asking." Papa turned back to his reading.

They decided to ignore the rumors and continue their friendship with the Smith family, and to help them when needed as Christians. Mama repeated St. Matthew 7:1: *"Judge not, that ye be not judged."*

Our neighborhood women loved to receive a gift of Mama's beauty soap. Mama's method of making beauty soap took longer and was complicated. The slow cooking process required patience. The temperature of the ingredients had to be just right. Mama used more glycerin, lanolin, and special wild mint leaves in creating soap for men and wild lavender mixed with honey suckle and little rose petals from the garden for soap for women. It was gentle on the skin leaving it smooth and silky unlike soap used for laundry. Her secret was having just the right blend of castor oil, lanolin, and glycerin to soften the skin.

Outside in the open air, Mama cooked the fats down, added the special ingredients to make the soap and continued to cook the mixture until it was the perfect stage to harden. Part of her secret was in judging the hardening stage—hard, but not too hard. She used small glass dishes and butter molds to make pretty gift soaps. Some molds had animals or flowers on top. Mama used plain molds too. She swirled pieces of rose petals and other flowers throughout the bar before they cooled creating bars of beauty soap. Sometimes for fragrance, she added other things during the cooking process such as lemon sage, mint, or tiny flakes of lemon or orange peel. The entire area surrounding Ripple Creek smelled clean and pretty on the days Mama worked her magic with the herbs while making soap. The hardening process took from one to fourteen days, depending upon the type of soap she made.

She continued talking with Miss Rena about her soap making. Miss Rena came and observed the last batch Mama made. She made some suggestions to Mama to shorten the cooking process that would cut the required time for soap making by a third. It was just a matter of rearranging when to add the ingredients—simple, but effective. Mama was delighted with her friend's suggestions.

Miss Rena returned to the well the next day and Mama took her to the barn and showed her the rows of soap bars laying on the feed room floor for the drying process. She offered to return to help Mama wrap and label them. Mama told her she would let her know when they were ready to be packaged. Miss Rena left with her water balanced on her head once more smiling to us as she looked back and waved.

Mama thought to herself how lonely Rena must be—an educated woman stuck in the country with a sick old man who was her grandfather, and an aunt who was mentally ill, both fully depending on her to take care of them. Mama's heart ached for her friend Rena's plight and it showed as Mama prayed softly:

"Thank you God for my family, Ross, and my healthy children, and my friends. Lord, especially my friend Rena. Lord, please give her courage to lay her burdens at your feet. Guide her, please Lord that she may find happiness and overcome loneliness. Help render a blessing to you through our friendship. As Jesus said in Matthew 6:25: *'Take no thought for your life.' May we live in glorification of your name.* In Jesus' name I pray. Amen."

Mama seldom prayed out loud in the daytime except at mealtime and usually Papa did the praying. It was a special treat to hear her praying for her friendship with Miss Rena. Mama understood Rena's plight and the loneliness. Farm wives were expected to be strong and independent in all things. And in most things they were.

Especially, farm families were self-sufficient in most foods. Mama occasionally bought white flour, corn meal, white sugar and coffee when Mr. Parnell, our town peddler, made his weekly run on Saturday mornings. Our lane was about a half-mile away from the main road. Mr. Parnell rang the truck bell when he turned into the lane. You could hear the bell from a distance. We children ran to meet his truck. Mr. Parnell owned one of the few motorized vehicles in the area. Motor vehicles were the latest thing in cities across America in the early 1940s, but they were still few in the country. Only cities and a few larger towns had gasoline and oil available for powering vehicles and country roads were rough. Most dirt roads existed because wagons passed over the same area many times a day. Over the years this created a hard packed surface suitable for wagon travel, but not designed for motor vehicles. Mr. Parnell's truck was designed higher off the ground than cars and could travel the wagon roads.

His old brown peddler's truck was special and unusual. It had a door that folded to the outside and a small two step entryway. Once inside, there was a center aisle down the full length of the vehicle. Both sides of the aisle were loaded with things that were rationed or hard to find such as white flour, white sugar, brown sugar, coffee, vanilla flavoring, pudding, and pie fillings. He also sold cornmeal, rice, dried peas, and dried beans. He had some medications such as St. Joseph's children's aspirin, castor oil, lanolin, liniment, special salves, iodine, rubbing alcohol and other items needed to treat scrapes and scratches.

Mr. Parnell sold fabric products such as linen, cotton, hopsack and sometimes seersucker, and nylon satin together with thread, zippers, and buttons. As Mama sewed most of our clothes, she was delighted with the selection of fabrics that he had available on his truck. She used cheaper priced cotton and hopsack for the main portions of the garments, linens, and other household needs but sometimes purchased a tiny bit of the expensive linen or satin to use for trim on our dresses or jackets.

For children he had rows of jugs filled with sticks of peppermint, liquorices, orange strips, and hoar-hound candies that cost a penny for two. Mama made sure that Anna, Tom, David, and I, each, had a penny for candy. We chose and paid for our own sticks. Mama always strived to teach us about money and responsibility at an early age.

Our cows provided fresh sweet milk daily, not only for drinking and using at our home, but for other people who needed to buy milk and butter. Mama used milk, butter, and eggs from our cows and chickens to barter for household staples she needed such as flour, cornmeal, and granulated sugar. We raised chickens for both eggs to eat and sell and to provide chicken meat for our family. Sometimes when Mr. Parnell purchased our eggs or milk, Mama would splurge and buy some vanilla or coconut cream pie filling. She would then make a fabulous mouth watering pie for dessert.

Mr. Parnell often purchased some of Mama's sewing goods to sell on his truck. She sewed napkins, potholders for the kitchen, and dishtowels with embroidery on the front or corners of each for Mr. Parnell. His town customers would seek out Mama's designs for gifts and personal use.

Each year during the months following killing time, Mr. Parnell purchased Mama's prize soaps to sell on his truck. The amount of soap Mama sold depended on the number of animals we killed and the amount of soap she made that year. Mama always reserved enough soap to last our family thirteen months and a few extra bars of the special soaps to give as gifts to special neighbors, family, and friends. In the winter, she knitted socks, hats and mittens to sell. By doing this, she supplemented the farm income and we still had the supplies Mama needed to run our household even when we had no money. Mama was a good business woman and a hard worker. She and Mr. Parnell worked out a deal. She would provide three or four gallons of milk, three or four pounds of sweet cream butter, and four dozen eggs each week. In return, Mr. Parnell set up an account for Mama and each week added the price of the goods to her account. Mama purchased the supplies she needed from him. He subtracted the price of the supplies she purchased with the remainder staying in the account. Both were happy with this agreement.

Saturdays were special because of Mr. Parnell and his peddler truck. We liked to play outside on Saturday mornings and watch for his truck to come rolling up the lane. The moment we heard the clang of his bell, we ran to meet him near the yard. Mr. Parnell would stop, open his door, let us in, and give us a ride to the house. His was the only motor vehicle we had ever ridden in.

CHAPTER 8

Lad and Skip

FARM FAMILIES HAD DOGS. Some families chose to have only one dog, but usually there were two, three, and sometimes more. Dogs were used to help move cattle from one pasture to another or from the pasture to the barn in the evening at milking time. Hunting dogs were needed and trained by the farmer to hunt all kinds of animals for meat. Particular species of dogs were better for various hunting seasons. During quail season, dogs assisted with locating the birds and retrieving the farmer's kill. During rabbit season, dogs helped search for rabbits and again would bring the dead rabbit to the hunter. In squirrel season, dogs chased the squirrels through the trees sometimes frightening them enough that they jumped, making a kill easier for the farmer. If a hunter killed a squirrel in the tree and it fell to the ground, the dog was there waiting to bring it to his master. No kill was lost with a good dog. Deer season brought on new challenges for the dogs. They were not used as much for hunting deer since deer hunting required quietness.

Our family was small, but we had two great dogs, Lad and Skip. Lad was the older dog, a large border collie. Skip was younger, a large yellow and white collie who was gentle and smart. Each was unusual in his own way, almost human.

Lad was a gift from Papa's family when he and Mama rented their first house and I was a baby before Anna was born. He was known for his gentleness, loyalty and protection of the family. He was an exceptional snake dog and would not back down from the most venomous snakes. Lad loved children, played and protected us, but was getting older. So Papa got Skip as a puppy and a backup dog for Lad. The dogs became friends quickly and shared their responsibilities of taking care of us and protecting the family.

Skip helped Mama with the cattle and went hunting with Papa more than Lad. He loved to retrieve the quail that Papa killed for our dinner. Skip was an outside dog and quickly became my best friend. He quickly learned from Lad to watch over us children like we were his puppies. We fed Skip and Lad scraps from our dinner table. When times were really hard I would save a piece of potato or bread from my plate just for Skip or Lad. If we had a t-bone steak, I would leave some meat on the bone and break it in two so Skip and Lad could enjoy a bite of steak. We all loved the dogs and they returned our love every day. They were there when we played outside or went to the creek to catch bullfrogs. Both dogs were guardians, friends, and playmates for our family. Mama and Papa did not worry about us, not even when we played in the woods, as long as Lad or Skip was beside us. Skip, being the youngest, had proven many times that he was a loyal protector and could step in when Lad was not around.

Once on an extremely hot wash day, Lad was not feeling well so Mama let him continue sleeping on his quilt in the den. Anna, Tom, and I took the baskets of clothes down to the well and made the fire. Mama filled the big iron pot with water and after sorting the white clothes from the dark clothes, she put the soap and bleach into the water followed with the white clothes. It was really hot and the gentle breeze did not cool the air even in the shade.

It has been raining off and on for about a week and a small puddle of water had formed from the rain runoff. It wasn't deep, but had formed a few feet from the top of the well near the quilt Mama had spread on the mossy grass. Mama put the quilt on the soft grass so Tom and David could nap. Anna wasn't feeling well either that day, so Mama excused her from helping with the wash. Instead, Mama asked Anna to stay on the quilt with her two brothers. If they woke, Anna was to keep them occupied. Anna, Tom, and baby David lay on the quilt and all fell asleep. The wash-pot was located about fifteen feet away and we could see the sleeping children while doing our wash. Skip lay down on the moss near the top of the quilt.

Mama completed washing the white clothes and I rinsed and hung them on the line. As Mama began washing the colored clothes, Miss Rena walked up with her jug to get water. Mama stopped rubbing the clothes on the rub-board and walked over to the well. Miss Rena removed the jug from her head, smiled, gave Mama a hug, and then drew her water with the rope and bucket. She filled her jug as they exchanged hellos. After she filled her jug, Mama motioned for her to sit on a nearby log. Mama sat beside her, taking a break from the wash, while they visited.

As Mama and Miss Rena sat chatting on the log, I walked over to Mama's rub-board and began rubbing the rest of the clothes. I remember looking up once. Anna, Tom, and David were still asleep on the quilt. Skip was still lying on the ground near them. I turned my attention to the remaining clothes to be washed. The clothes were lying on the ground near the wash tub.

To wash a garment correctly, you checked each one for stains, before placing the item in the tub of water. Once the piece of clothing was wet, you rubbed the piece of clothing across the rub-board as hard as needed to remove dirt and stains from the item. You then checked carefully for stains or areas that needed additional rubbing. Sometimes it took several rubbings to remove a specific stain. The last step was to place them in the rinse tub filled with clean water. Once I had rubbed all the colored clothes, I then moved to the rinse tub to finish the process before hanging them to dry. Once they were rinsed I placed them in the large aluminum pan and moved to the clothesline to hang them up.

Mama was standing up now near the log with her back to the quilt. She was deep in conversation with Miss Rena and was not aware that I had moved to the clothes line. I worked fast and concentrated on getting the clothes on the line. I wanted to get the chore done so that I could visit with Miss Rena too. I forgot that it was always my responsibility (no matter what) to keep an eye on the younger children. At age three, Tom could be up and into the woods without a sound.

Not more than five minutes could have passed while I hung the clothes on the line and had my back to everyone. Skip barked, showed his teeth and growled. Tom was standing on the backside of the water hole made by the rain runoff. Skip had positioned himself between Tom and the waterhole. The dog was pushing on the boy with his rear and barking at something in the water. Mama and Miss Rena looked up. Anna woke up and baby David starting crying at the top of his lungs all at once.

Anna grabbed the baby and yelled, "Snake!"

With David in her arms, she rushed down near Mama and Miss Rena, who were looking around frantically to find something to kill the snake. Tom started to cry. Mama yelled for him to stand still. She could see that Skip was between Tom and a large dark colored snake with copper rings across its body coiled on the ground with its head darting in and out in a striking stance. Just then Miss Rena grabbed a large stick and moved toward Tom, Skip, and the snake. Tom really lost it then, he was screaming at the top of his lungs as the snake continued to strike at Skip. Miss Rena snatched Tom and somehow lifted the three year old into her arms, bounding out of the way.

Skip jumped this way and that way missing the snake's striking blows. Each time the snake's head went back into the coil after a strike, Skip went in for the attack. Skip was quick and knew the danger of a large poisonous snake. He managed to miss the strikes once, twice. On the third strike, Skip dove in for the kill. The snake struck again, this time striking Skip in the upper front leg, but the snake's bite was too late. Skip had the snake by the center of its back near the head. Skip yelped at the pain, but held on and shook the snake as hard as he could. The snake could not hold on. Skip kept shaking the snake violently breaking its back into several places. He shook it until it was dead.

"Lily," Mama yelled. "Run get your father and tell him to hurry and bring Pearl. Skip has been bitten by a cottonmouth."

I did not wait to be told twice. In shock, I ran as fast as I could through weeds and tall grass and through the stand of woods, taking the shortcut to the field where Papa was working. I yelled to him that Skip had been bitten by a cottonmouth and that Mama said for him to bring Pearl. He quickly unhitched Pearl from the plow, lifted me onto her bareback first and then swung onto Pearls' bareback himself. We returned to the dug well in a few minutes.

Skip was lying on the mossy grass with Mama consoling him. A foamy substance was beginning to form around his mouth. Miss Rena was holding David while Anna held Tom, who was still crying softly, on her lap. They were all seated on the log where the women had visited earlier.

Papa picked up the dead snake and put it in a pillow case from the laundry. He then took Skip and laid him across Pearl, then taking the pillowcase with the dead snake inside, he swung up behind Skip.

"We need prayers by all of you that Skip survives the ride to Doc Barnes," Papa said as he urged Pearl forward and they left in a gallop. Doc Barnes lived four miles from Ripple Creek. It was a long ride on a mule.

Once Mama got us all calmed down, she sat us all on the log and explained, "The snake was a poisonous cottonmouth."

Miss Rena then spoke, "It was most likely a mother snake that had come on land to lay her eggs. The run-off from the rain had created an ideal moist spot for her eggs. She saw Tom as a threat to her nest and eggs."

Mama then spoke again, "Skip came to Tom's rescue." She bent down and gave Tom a hug. She continued, "Tom, this is why you should stay away from snakes. You never know when you will frighten one. When they are frightened, they bite. It's hard to tell a poisonous snake from a good snake. Until you know your snakes, you should leave them alone."

"But, I didn't see her until Skip growled and barked." Tom started crying again.

Mama hugged him again before saying, "I know, sweetheart. It's okay." She soothed, "But when we are in the woods, we must *all* watch for snakes. They are God's creatures too and they are everywhere."

To lighten things up, Mama asked if we wanted to say a prayer to Jesus for Skip to get well. We all bowed our heads while sitting on the log, near the dug well and Mama prayed for Skip to have a full recovery.

Miss Rena suggested that Mama take Tom, Anna, and David and go to the house. She would help me finish the wash and bring it in. Mama thanked her and took Tom by the hand. Anna carried David in her arms, and they began the walk to the house.

Miss Rena and I dumped the dirty wash water and took the dry clothes from the line then folded the quilt and packed up the snack basket that we had brought with us, but that no one had time to enjoy. Rena then helped me carry everything up the hill to the house. Mama thanked her and invited her in for coffee. Miss Rena said she needed to get back to check on her grandfather. She appreciated the offer and would like to have coffee another day.

"Jan, I don't know how you do it, with so many little children. So many things can happen. You are a remarkable woman to keep it all together," she said as she stepped outside the door to leave.

"Some days, I don't," Mama smiled as she replied. She smoothed her hair and added, "I have God's help, Rena. I couldn't do it without Jesus."

"Take care of yourself and those babies. I hope Skip is okay," Rena said as she began walking away.

Mama watched as Rena walked down the path to the dug well area. She knew she would get the jug they had filled with water earlier before going home. Mama enjoyed her friendship with Rena. It was a blessing that they had time together at the well.

Mama helped me and Anna do Papa's chores. Tom watched baby David who played with a rag doll on a quilt Mama had put in the middle of the floor in the feed room. Since David could not crawl, Mama felt comfortable putting Tom in charge of keeping David happy and she had Lad for a backup. Anna and I worked together to feed and water the farm animals, while Mama milked the cows. Mama complimented us on our quick completion of the tasks as we walked to the house just as night began to fall. A whippoorwill bird sang out into the stillness of dusk. Mama and I each carried a bucket of milk that Mama had milked from the cows. We were tired. It had been a long day.

Once inside the kitchen, Mama said; "Lily, if you don't mind, strain the milk while I check on and change the baby. We are going to have milk and cornbread for supper tonight." Tom, who appeared in the kitchen from the den, started clapping his little hands—it was one of his favorite supper meals. "Anna, you get Tom and yourself washed up while Lily gets supper ready." Mama left us to check on David and Lad, his guardian.

Tom waited for Anna to get the water ready to wash him up. I strained the big buckets of milk into fresh jugs, then poured a large pitcher of the fresh milk and placed it in the center of our kitchen table. I took corn bread from the oven of the big stove. I then got a large dishpan and began crumbling the bread in the pan. When the bread was crumbled, I got bowls from the cabinet and spoons from the silverware drawer. Lastly I set the bowls and spoons beside each plate. Just as I completed setting the table, Anna finished with Tom and Mama came in. She had changed David, let him nurse, and he had fallen asleep. We were all tired as we sat at our places and Mama gave thanks for the food and asked God to take care of Skip and Papa. She prayed for a safe journey home for them tonight. Cornbread and milk never tasted so good.

After supper, Mama tucked Tom into bed and told him a bedtime story while Anna and I cleared away and washed the dishes from supper. Anna and I were given permission to stay up until Papa got home. We each decided to read our Bibles while we waited. Mama settled in with some mending that she needed to complete. Anna and I sat on the floor

Lad and Skip 155

beside Lad who was curled up on his quilt and already half asleep.

A little later, Papa came through the door with Skip in his arms. Skip had his eyes open looking weary and tired. Papa relayed details of how Doc Barnes saved Skip's life by opening the wound and draining the poison. He had an antidote for a Cottonmouth's venom and gave Skip a shot of it. The next twelve hours were critical. If Skip made it through the night, he would most likely be alright. Mama was to add the medicine to his food and force him to eat. Over the next few days Skip would lie around not interested in playing or anything. The antidote was usually successful, so in time Skip should be fine.

Doc Barnes told Papa we were blessed that the snake bit Skip, not Tom. A bite from a big cottonmouth, without an immediate antidote given, would mean death for a child.

Papa said we could let Skip sleep in the house tonight along side of Lad. He patted Skip affectionately on the head placing him on the floor near Lad, who gave Skip a face lick in welcome.

Papa asked Mama if there was any supper left. Mama got up from her mending, gave Skip and Lad pats on the head, before taking Papa's hand and heading for the kitchen. Anna and I scratched Skip behind his ears and rubbed his long coat of fur down the back the way he liked. The big eyes looked at us as he gave each of us a lick and put his head across his legs. We could see he was tired so we left him there on the floor with Lad as we went to the kitchen to say goodnight to Mama and Papa. It had been a long day and sleep was calling.

PART II - OUR COMMUNITY

CHAPTER 9

Depression and War

AMERICA WAS IN THE middle of World War II. Farmers, even small farmers like my family, shared the responsibility of growing wheat, rye, corn, potatoes, vegetables, cotton, soy beans, ducks, chickens, turkeys, pigs, goats, and livestock to keep America fed and to provide the raw material necessary to keep industry running. Times were hard and money was scarce. Farmers used portions of their crops as barter for necessities for the family, farm animals, and supplies.

The prior years had been hard on the Howell family as well as their neighbors. In 1941, America was still climbing that long bumpy road out of the Great Depression gripping the nation. The Japanese bombed Pearl Harbor on December 7, 1941. Although we did not want it, America was at war. The rationing of coffee, sugar, lard, flour, and meal were common.

Times were even harder in 1943 with little money and loads of work for farmers, but life was good. Farmers were proud to see their sons go into the military for service to their country. With heavy hearts but strong faith, they watched as the draft caught many local boys.

Wagon ruts became the base for farm country roads. The wagon wheels ran over the same dirt many, many times creating hard ruts. Rain pelted the ruts and made them wash, and wagons beat them down again until they eventually became the road. Some main roads had gravel, but most were dirt or clay packed down by the wheels of wagons passing over them. In our rural area, roads good enough to drive cars on were scarce. My family could not afford a car. Only two neighbors in our valley area had cars. The Walsh family to the north of us and the Bennett's to the south. I had never ridden in a car and wondered how it felt.

For church going we used the family wagon pulled by one mule. If Papa needed to go to town on business, he rode a mule. If he needed supplies, he took a wagon. Most of our friends and neighbors used wagons and mules to travel. Some had horses, but most were like us and had mules.

Farmers in rural America were responsible for growing food to feed the nation gripped by World War II. Papa had suffered the loss of one of his two work mules, Katie. Papa worked even harder trying to get the lay-by work done with just his one mule, Pearl. He left the house, hitched Pearl to the one-mule single plow and was in the field before 6:00

each morning. Papa worked six days a week during this time. He took Sundays off to attend church and give thanks to God for our family, our food, and our blessings. He was so tired that sometimes he took a long nap on Sunday afternoons. We children had to play outside when the weather permitted. We played quietly inside when it was raining or too cold so we would not wake Papa. He was so-o-o tired.

I often heard Mama and Papa whispering about how bad things were. We had no money. Papa worried that he would not get the decayed cotton stalks plowed under in the lower forty in time to enrich the soil for the spring planting. He always rotated his crops. In the spring, he would plant corn in the fields where cotton had been harvested from the past fall. In fields where corn had been planted the season before he planted cotton. He did the same thing in our garden areas. He would plant carrots where onions had been, beans where peas had been, popcorn were peanuts had been and peanuts where popcorn had been. He planted tomatoes where okra had been, beets where potatoes had been and cantaloupe where watermelon had been and on and on until all crops were not where they were the year before. He called this crop rotation. Papa said it made the earth healthier and the plants stronger to give better yields.

Without the decayed cotton stalks being turned under to enrich the soil, Papa would need to buy fertilizer for the corn crop. We could not afford to buy fertilizer. We barely had money for emergencies like seeing the doctor if someone got sick. Sometimes late at night, I heard Mama and Papa talking.

"Jan, I don't know how much longer I can hold out working such long hours. And Pearl is getting very tired. She is not a young mule, you know," I heard Papa say late one night.

"It seems to be getting colder at night. We have been lucky so far not to have a hard freeze," Mama commented. "Ross, what will we do if we get a hard freeze?" Mama asked.

I had gotten out of my bed and sneaked quietly inside the pantry, being very careful not to let them hear or see me. I stayed low near the floor pressing myself close to the wall hardly breathing. With the pantry door cracked slightly and the den door opened just a bit, I could barely see and hear them. Mama was working on her sewing and Papa was sitting in a squatting position on the hearth near the fire with his elbows resting on his knees holding his head in his hands.

"If we get a hard freeze, Jan, we are done for!" he raised his voice. "I don't even want to think about it. With just one mule, I can't work any harder and neither can Pearl. She has been very good, but she is tired—perhaps more tired than me." Papa shook his head back and forth. He then pushed his hands through his black wavy hair like he did sometimes when perspiration was on his brow.

When he plowed he wore an old straw hat to keep the sun off his face and out of his eyes. The hat caused the perspiration to collect on the brow and he would remove the hat and run his fingers through the hair shaking the perspiration away. But, tonight there was no perspiration to remove, just frustration.

"I just don't know," he continued, "I know the Bible says God will help us through all life trials and by faith we can handle anything. But I am beginning to think He is not listening to me right now."

With this, Mama put her sewing down and came and stood alongside of Papa. "Now Ross," she said. "You have always had such a strong faith. Please don't talk that way." She patted Papa's arm. "Why don't you go to bed and get some sleep. Four o'clock in the morning will be here before you can turn over. You are just tired."

"What about you, Jan? You are working too hard. It pains me to see you sewing every night in the dim light. Why don't you come to bed, too?" Papa encouraged.

"I'll be along shortly," Mama replied. "I just want to finish this new dress for Anna before I go to bed. The children are getting so big. It's hard to keep things hidden from them. Christmas is just around the corner. I still have a lot of sewing and knitting to do before it gets here. But don't you worry. Things are going to be okay," she reassured.

"God has never let us down yet. And I believe He will bless us this time too," she said as she picked up the sewing, sat down and began again. "I won't be long, I promise."

Papa got up from the hearth and went to their room. Mama continued sitting and sewing. She was humming "Amazing Grace" softly as she worked.

The house was getting colder as the fire died out. I stayed just a little while longer and then crept back to my bed, snuggling under the cold covers until only my nose and eyes were above them. I couldn't help but worry. I should help Papa more. Or perhaps some of the neighbors could help Papa with his work. I had to remember to ask Mama tomorrow.

Next morning, Mama was up very early and Papa had already gone to the field when we children got up at 5:00 am. I was the first in the kitchen. Mama had walked outside to feed Skip. I set my schoolbooks down on the cabinet and poured myself a glass of milk. Mama came through the kitchen door just as I pulled out my chair at the breakfast table.

"Good morning, Sunshine," she said. "Burr-r-r-r, it's much colder this morning! Did you sleep well? I gathered eggs and fed the chickens this morning so chores are done," she said as she worked at the stove.

"Very well, thank you," I replied as I tapped my foot.

I wanted to ask Mama about getting some neighbors to help Papa before the other children came in for breakfast this morning. Not knowing exactly how to begin the conversation, I blurted out, "Mama, do you think we can ask

Mr. Walsh to help Papa with the plowing or maybe Mr. Bennett?"

"Child, whatever brought that on?" Mama shot me a quizzical look while she dished up scrambled eggs, grits, and hot biscuits for me. As she placed the plate in front of me, I quickly looked down. I would be in trouble if Mama and Papa found out about my listening in the hallway last night. I did not want my guilt-ridden face to give me away. Mama had this way of seeing deep into your soul. It was like she had eyes in the back of her head and could anticipate what you were doing sometimes even before you did it. Anna and I had talked about this before. We reckoned it came with motherhood. It was an instinct or something, perhaps even a gift from God. Her ability to anticipate our thoughts and actions sometimes kept us from doing things we shouldn't.

My parents were firm believers in obeying rules such as speak when spoken to, do all your chores, help your siblings do theirs, be seen but not heard, always be polite and respectful not just to your elders but to everyone, clean up after yourself and make A's in school. Also, girls must act ladylike and boys should be all boy with none of that sissy stuff. Boys played with boy toys and girls with dolls. Boys were to follow in their father's footsteps and girls were to grow up, get married, and have babies. Boys were expected to do better in school than girls. Papa thought it was a waste of time for girls to be required to go to school when their Mamas could teach them everything they needed to know about being a wife and a mother. Deep in my heart, I wanted to prove Papa wrong about that.

"If Mr. Walsh and Mr. Bennett knew how hard Papa worked, I bet they would help," I said with my eyes still on my food and my head down as I took my first bite. The food tasted good. I got the courage to look up at Mama. She looked at me with a questioning glance.

"Lily," she began, "they both have large farms with many more acres than ours. They have lots more work than your Papa. They are not finished with their own work." As she turned back to the stove to stir the grits and cover the eggs to keep them soft for the others, she added, "But even if they were finished with their work, we could not ask for their help. That would be asking for charity. We could never do that. That would take away your Papa's dignity."

"But if they offered, could we accept their help?" I quickly asked while putting more butter on my hot biscuit. Biscuits hot from the oven overflowing with butter were my favorite part of breakfast. Mama did not reply to my question, but poured hot coffee into her half-filled cup to warm it. After taking a sip, she replied, "You should not be worried about grown up stuff. Everything will be alright. God has always come through for us and He will again. Your Papa is strong as an ox, and he will get the work finished on time." I wondered if Mama was trying to convince me or herself.

About that time, the kitchen door burst open and three hungry children ran into the kitchen, plopping down in their chairs. Mama dished up the breakfast as they chattered away. Anna asked me to help her with braiding her hair before we started the walk to school, two miles down the road. We left the kitchen after putting our dishes in the large metal dishpan filled with hot water and suds on the counter.

I had a plan, but decided to keep it to myself and not mention it to Anna. I wanted to see Pastor Lawrence when he came to school today. Pastor Lawrence had been pastor at our community church for ten years. He was well respected in the neighborhood, had three children of his own, and knew absolutely everyone for miles around. He was going be at school for recess this morning to hold a special service to bless fifteen new desks the farmers had built for our school.

Communities in the rural South did not always have a church, so our community was blessed to have a place to worship. The church was built by the farmers from timber cut from the Walsh family's farm. The community joined together to erect a chapel to give thanks and praise to God— not only in good times, but in bad times to seek help and guidance from neighbors and the Lord. Ours was a close knit community where everyone knew everyone.

The neighborhood women taught Sunday school. Texts came directly from the Bible as we had no printed Sunday books. Towns and particularly large cities in the South were different. They had Baptist, Methodist, Church of God, and Church of Christ churches; some cities even had Presbyterian, Pentecostal, and Lutheran churches. Some cities had an Anglican or a Catholic Church as well. Most Dry Valley residents rarely visited town and many of us never saw a city but we were happy in our small community church.

Anna looked kind of shocked when I made her swear to secrecy. I told her about my plan to ask Pastor Lawrence for some help to get the crops laid-by. "You are going to get the whipping of your life, Lily Howell, if Mama and Papa ever find out," Anna said shaking her head. "Is there something you and I can do to help?" she asked.

"You are too small," I said kicking a stone with my foot as we walked along the road.

"I'm almost as big as you," Anna replied looking quite hurt at my remark.

"I guess you are, but we are both too little." I kicked another rock as we walked along.

"Besides, I am going to ask Pastor Lawrence to keep my secret and not get me in trouble. If you tell, I'll never trust you again," I said looking at her beautiful blonde braids bouncing under her winter cap. "Now, we are going to be late, if we don't run."

Anna quickly leaped out to a head start as we ran the last quarter of a mile to the school door and pushed through it just before Mrs. Parnell rang the school bell.

We quickly found our desks. Mrs. Parnell called the roll. With our hands held over our hearts, we recited from memory the pledge of allegiance to our flag, which was mounted on the wall above the blackboard. Mrs. Parnell gave us older students some reading to do, while she taught reading to the first grade class. After reading, spelling was scheduled next for the second grade class, followed by history for the third grade and English for the fourth grade. The fifth and sixth grades had some classes together, such as math. But today recess had been changed from after third grade history to follow second grade spelling. Mrs. Parnell has asked me and another student to assist her in lining up the older students' desks around the wall to make a place for Pastor Lawrence to speak. He was due about five minutes before the lesson was completed. Mrs. Parnell then asked me to watch for him and offer him a drink of water while she finished spelling class. I was delighted to see him coming up the front path to the door. I whispered to her and slipped outside the door to greet Pastor Lawrence.

Pastor Lawrence said, "Hello," and asked me which subjects I liked best in school and I replied politely. He asked me about Papa and Mama, Anna, Tom, and David which gave me the opportunity I had been waiting for.

I explained to Pastor how worried I was about Papa and about Pearl. I told him that Katie had died. He was already aware of the circumstances. News travels like a brush fire in such a small community. Everyone knew.

I explained how hard Papa and Mama were working and how worried they were about the lay-by work. I questioned, "What will happen when the weather gets cold enough to freeze the ground? What will we do if something happens to our other mule, Pearl?"

Pastor put his hand on my shoulders. "Lily," he said, "You should not worry about things you cannot control." He gave me a big hug, agreed to keep our conversation a secret between us and told me not to worry. "God always provides," he said. "Let me see what I can do." Just then, Mrs. Parnell walked to the doorway and invited him to come inside.

I felt a great sense of relief just knowing that someone with a direct link to God was going to see what he could do. To be frank, I put the thoughts out of my mind for the rest of the day until on the way home when Anna asked, "Did you ask him?" She quizzed me while skipping and dancing backwards in front of me.

"Not exactly"—I stumbled across my words. "I just told him we were having a hard time and how hard Mama and Papa are working—that's all."

"You didn't ask for his help?" Anna sounded angry and surprised. "What was the point of telling him if you were not going to ask for his help?" Anna quipped looking very disappointed. She stopped dead still in the road waiting for an explanation from me.

"I didn't have to ask for help," I yelled over my shoulder as I broke into a run down the road home. Anna began running fast to catch up.

"What do you mean you didn't have to ask for help? I don't understand," she exclaimed slightly out of breath while running beside me.

"Pastor said for me not to worry about such things. He told me he would keep our secret and see what he could do." I smiled, "I didn't have to ask for help or charity as Mama calls it."

"Do you think he will help Papa with the work? Do you think he will?" she sounded totally astonished.

"I don't know. I sure hope so. Not another word about this, Anna. We will have to wait and see," I said as we entered the home lane.

Chapter 10

Our School

Mrs. Parnell taught first through sixth grade in our one large room school. She was married to our peddler, Mr. Parnell. They did not have children. However, she had twenty-six students spread between the grades who respected and loved her.

Our school was the only one in the community. It was called Dry Valley School. The building itself consisted of one big room that was divided by wooden sectional dividers mounted on pulleys, into three rooms—an area for grades one and two, another classroom area for grades three and four, and a final area for grades five and six. We had a small room to the right of the main room called a cloakroom. We used the cloakroom to store our dinners; we even had pegs for our coats and shelves for boots and shoes when they were wet or muddy. A large water pail and a large aluminum dipper were stored in the cloakroom and used for drinking water when we were thirsty. The water came from a small fresh water brook running through the back of the playground. We used some of the water to wash our hands in a small basin at dinnertime and at the end of recess.

Nothing much happened that day at school. Mrs. Parnell kept us in at recess where we played indoor games. The weather outside was too cold and she did not want students getting sick. It was fun to play inside sometimes. One of my favorite games was to pass a piece of chalk from the board from one student to the other. Everyone pretended to have the chalk then someone guessed where the chalk was in the line. If you did not guess correctly, you had to sit down until everyone was in his/her chair.

Another game was "pin-the-tail on the donkey." Someone drew a large donkey without a tail on a large piece of cardboard. Mrs. Parnell had a large black cardboard tail with a push pin in it. A volunteer student was blindfolded and spun around a few times and then he/she tried to pin the tail on the donkey. The rest of the class would encourage with shouts of "you're warm, cold, left, right, high, low." Everyone laughed a lot while playing this game.

As Anna and I came home from school, the weather was getting chillier. Although we had pulled our sweaters close up to our eyes we could see what was about to happen to us. Tom and David were waiting at the end of the lane hidden in the bushes. One of their favorite games was to hide, then jump out as we walked past them. To make them happy we always pretended they had scared us. They always hid in the same place and were easy to spot from a distance. Today we all finished the walk to the house together. The boys laughed and giggled, and we scolded them for giving us such a fright.

Anna and I put our books on the cabinet and said "hello" to Mama. We changed into clothes that could be worn while doing chores and quickly began our usual after school routine without waiting to be told. I filled the wood box with wood for the fire, and brought salt pork from the smoke house for the pot of beans that Mama would begin cooking tonight after dinner. Then, I made the beds in our rooms and picked up the toys that were on the floor in the boys' room.

After the inside chores were completed, we moved to do the outside ones. The boys fed the chickens and Anna gathered the eggs. While I fed the pigs, Anna began to churn milk to make buttermilk for supper.

We never wasted food and used all milk supplies. When fresh sweet milk soured, Mama placed it inside a wooden churn to clabber. After it sat for a couple of days and soured some more, we churned it. Our milk, fresh from the cows, contained lots of butterfat. The churning process allows the butterfat to rise to the top, leaving the remainder as buttermilk. Once all the butter had formed a nice ball at the top, Mama would remove it with a slotted spoon and put it in a bowl. She then washed the milk from the butter she collected by pouring clear water into the container and draining it all out again. She added a pinch of salt and smoothed it to form a long bar or a round ball. We then placed it in the cold storage cellar until it got chilled. Our butter was the best. Mama knew the right amount of salt to make it taste so good on biscuits or fritters.

Tom and David placed the silverware at the appropriate place beside our plates for supper. After washing up, Anna and I sat at the kitchen table and began our homework. Tom had replaced Anna at the churn to finish the buttermilk while David played with their wooden blocks in the corner of the kitchen. Mama came in from her bedroom where she had been sewing most of the day.

Papa came in late that evening. He was extremely tired. After a small prayer, he ate supper and went immediately to wash up and then to bed. He mentioned plowing progress was slow going. "But, tomorrow is another day," he said.

Mama sent us to bed as soon as dishes had been washed and homework finished. We said our prayers before going down the long hall to our rooms. We took sponge baths, put our pajamas on, brushed our teeth, and were ready for bed before a cat could purr. In the winter, we did not always take a tub bath. It was cold and too hard to heat the water for the big silver galvanized tub that was our bathtub. Baths were more fun in summer when the water was room temperature.

Mama said she was going to bed very soon. She felt tired this evening. She asked us to blow out our candle and stay quiet until we fell asleep. Anna was asleep as soon as her head hit the pillow. I lay awake watching the moon rise up over our window. The house was completely quiet. It was a clear, crisp night so maybe it would not rain. Papa could get more plowing done. I fell asleep asking God to please let Pastor Lawrence hurry up and help Papa with his work.

Next morning was uneventful. We got up, did chores, ate breakfast, and headed out the door for school. The weather was crisp with a cold breeze blowing out of the north. Anna and I pulled our scarves tightly under our chins and wrapped them closely over our mouths to keep out the bite of the wind as we walked to school. The leaves along the road were brilliant colors of deep shades of red, orange, and yellow. Very few green leaves remained on the hardwood trees. It was evident that fall was in the air with winter following on its heels. I loved this time of year. It was fun to experience nature at its best. The woods gave brilliant hues to dying leaves and they rustled in the wind as it blew from the sky in a gentle send-off. It would not be long before the first frost came followed by the first freeze and later sleet and snow. Winter was just around the corner.

The weather continued to be cold, but rain eluded Dry Valley as a full week passed. Pastor Lawrence had not come to help Papa. He held church as normal and was his usual self on Sunday. He even asked Papa how things were going as he winked at me. Papa was not one to complain, so he told him the plowing was going slowly, but he would get it done, God willing, before the first snowfall.

Anna asked me on the way home from school one day, "Are you sure Pastor is going to help us?"

"I don't know," I said feeling downhearted.

Tomorrow was the end of the second week in October. The weather was getting colder each day and still Papa was plowing every day. The hay needed to be cut and stacked before it snowed. I heard Mama praying a lot at night. She and Papa had lots of low conversations.

I had been too frightened to sneak out in the hallway again to listen. If they caught me, Papa would whip me for sure and I did not want to get a whipping from Papa. Mama's whippings were strong enough that you learned a lesson and did not make that mistake again, but Papa's whippings were humiliating and they hurt so much. You knew why you were being whipped by Papa. I had only received one whipping from him. It was for lying about a dime I took from the kitchen window and spent with Mr. Parnell for extra candy. I shared the candy with my siblings, but when asked where the money came from I told Mama and Papa I found it in the roadway. One whipping was enough for me. I did not want to ever receive another one. After the whipping, Papa explained that he would have given me the dime, but the whipping was for lying. I must *always* tell the truth, no matter what.

Days passed slowly by as Anna and I waited for some sign of the help we asked for. Mrs. Parnell sent a sealed paper home to Mama and Papa on Monday of the next week. The note said there would be a meeting at the church at 5:00 pm the next afternoon. Papa told Mama that he could not stop plowing early to attend a meeting in the middle of the week. He said it was foolish of Pastor Lawrence to think people could just stop their work to come when he beckoned. My heart sank as I realized that we would not find out what was up.

Next morning at school, Nathan Walsh, our neighbors' son came over to me and asked why we were not at church. He was the eldest of three Walsh children. The Walsh's farm was named "The Broken Horseshoe" and bordered our farm on the north side of the lower forty where Papa was still plowing. They had 100 acres in fields, and almost that much in pastureland. Their farm was more than twice the size of my Papa's sixty acre farm. They raised horses mostly, but also cattle, chickens, pigs, corn, cotton, and soybeans—the same as almost everyone in Jackson County. Gloria, his younger sister, was Anna's age and her friend. His younger brother, Matt, was Tom's age and spent time playing with Tom after church.

"Papa couldn't stop plowing that early. Why wasn't the meeting held after church on Sunday?" I asked.

"That's okay. You didn't miss anything," he said as he covered his eyes to keep the sun out. Then he grinned at me in that shy way boys sometimes do. Nathan was in the fourth grade and everyone said he had a crush on me. He was always nice and offered to carry my books one day as we all walked home together. But I was a fifth grader and could not be hanging around with a boy, especially one younger than me. Mama and Papa had rules about that. You carried your own books and only talked to boys about general things, never about personal things.

None of the other kids at school mentioned the church meeting. The day flew by and classes were finished before we turned around twice. Mrs. Parnell let us off easy that evening—no homework. I was so happy I wanted to hug her. I needed to figure out some way to help Papa with his work. On the way home that night, it began to drizzle rain as Anna and I ran to keep from getting wet. There was just one big black cloud in the sky, but it was big enough to bring on the rain. As we ran into the house, Mama stood inside the door waiting with a dry towel.

"Is it getting colder, girls?" she asked with that worried look on her face.

"I don't think so," I replied drying off my books and then my face. "It's just the wetness of the raindrops that makes us feel cold. I think it's a little warmer than yesterday."

Mama looked somewhat relieved.

"Is Papa home yet?" I asked looking around. Anna continued drying herself off with the towel.

"I just saw him taking Pearl into the barn with the plow still hitched on," Mama replied, as Tom, David, and Skip came through the back door at once. They all were wet.

"Get Skip out of here," Mama scolded as Skip began to shake himself.

"Ah, Mama, he's cold!" Tom cried. "Can't we dry him first?"

"Oh, I guess it won't hurt, just this once." She was softening up as she handed both boys a dry towel. "Here's one for Skip—he can use Lily's. But get him dried and onto the back porch before your father gets here."

"Alright, Mama, we'll hurry!" Tom replied and began drying Skip with his own towel.

"It's a bad time for the rain," Mama said to no one in particular. "The ground needs a good soaking, but we still have a lot of work to be done before it freezes." She was almost talking to herself. As she came around the table, she asked me, "Lily, did you find out about the meeting at the church last night?"

"Not exactly," I said. "Nathan Walsh said not much happened and that we didn't miss anything." I put my books on the counter, ready to change into my chore clothes, and gulped the glass of milk Mama had waiting for us, before heading for our room. "No-one else even mentioned it." I called over my shoulder as I entered our bedroom and closed the door. Anna was already dressed and ready to feed the chickens. She walked past me and into the kitchen. Mama told her to feed the chickens quickly, gather the eggs and come right back. The other chores would wait. She didn't want her to get too cold.

Mama told me to set the supper table, bring in some wood for the fire, and she and Papa would feed the pigs when she went to do the milking later. She had supper almost ready, and we would eat as soon as Papa washed up.

Papa came through the door just in time to hear the part about washing up. He walked directly to the washstand and poured fresh water into the bowl as he spoke, "I don't think this will last too long. It's just a drizzle. Not enough to soak the ground, but too much to stay outside and catch a cold."

Mama had the food ready by the time I got the dishes and flatware set in place. Anna was back with eggs in the basket. Mama pulled cornbread from the oven, steaming hot to go with the country stew that sat in the center of the table. Anna got the milk from the storage box. I took it from her and poured glasses for everyone. Papa blessed the food and we ate the best food for a cold drizzling winter day.

Mama, Papa, and I finished the outside chores just before nightfall. Anna washed the supper dishes and watched Tom and David. She got them washed up and into their pajamas. She was seated at the kitchen table working math problems when we returned. She only had four problems. Anna was really good in math so she had those solved quickly. Mama asked me about my homework. I told her Mrs. Parnell had let us off the hook. She thought that was good since I had helped with more chores than usual. "Now, kids, get to bed early because I still have some sewing to do," Mama said sliding another log onto the fire. "It's easier when you aren't under foot." She gave us all a kiss before we headed in for bed. I told her that I would help Tom, David, and Anna with their prayers so she could begin her work. "Thanks, Sweetie," she said as she seated herself in the old rocker where she always sat to darn socks and sew by hand.

I slept fretfully that night, waking many times. I could hear the wind howling through the trees outside and wondered just how much the temperature had dropped. I woke once out from under the covers and my feet and hands felt cold. I silently said a prayer for Pastor Lawrence to please come tomorrow to help Papa. Sleep came slowly, but I finally drifted off.

It seemed like I had just gone to bed when I awoke early the next morning hearing voices outside my window. I dressed quickly, putting socks and shoes on while somehow making it to the kitchen.

I recognized Mr. Walsh's voice, but another strange voice I did not know said, "Ross, you should have asked for some help."

Then I heard Mr. Walsh say, "I finished my lay-by work last week so my mules have rested for a week now."

The other man was our neighbor to the south, Mr. Hal Bennett. He said he had finished plowing too. Each of them would lend Papa a mule to plow beside Pearl. That way, Papa could plow Pearl and Mr. Walsh's mule one day. Then plow Pearl and Mr. Bennett's mule the next day. The day after, Papa could team the Walsh mule with the Bennett mule. He could cover twice the ground and Pearl would get to rest every third day. All the mules would be more productive without getting overly tired. Papa could use his big plow so he could finish the plowing in the lower forty within a few days. Then he could continue to use both mules to get in the haystacks, corn, and anything else he needed. He had use of the mules for two weeks.

Papa didn't know what to say, but Mr. Walsh and Mr. Bennett reassured him that neighbors were suppose to step up and help when one suffered misfortune. Losing Katie was the worst thing that could happen to Papa. They were emphatic about their offer.

"Ross, we all fall on hard times occasionally. It's all around the county," Mr. Bennett said. "If the government doesn't do something to help us farmers, some of us might lose our land. During wartime, we can't afford to be choosy in what we do. We must stick together and help one another." Papa shook hands and thanked them for their generosity.

After the hand shaking and slaps on the back, the mules were led to the barn. One was housed in Katie's stall and the other at the end of the barn hallway near the door that opened to the north. Papa pulled the metal latch on Katie's stall door to secure it. Then he slid a timber bar (2 x 4) across the barn hallway to create another makeshift stall at the end of the barn for the other mule. Papa had gotten the idea from another farmer who had makeshift stalls in both ends of his barn for quarantining sick cattle. Both mules were given a portion of feed and a bucket of water so they would feel more comfortable in the strange barn.

Papa already had hooks for buckets of feed and water on the north door because occasionally he had kept a new mother cow there when she had a preemie calf or a particularly hard birth. The men left their mules in Papa's care and Anna and I raced for school, managing to barely make it as Mrs. Parnell rang the school bell.

At recess that morning, Nathan Walsh came over and tapped me on the shoulder. I did not see him walk up as I talked with another classmate.

"Did everything go okay this morning?" he asked in a whisper.

"Yes. Your Papa and Mr. Bennett brought some mules for Papa to use to finish the lay-by work. Thank you," Lily replied, smiling.

"I wanted to tell you yesterday," he said. "But Pa said I couldn't. I had to keep it quiet or I would be in deep trouble with him. I'm sorry, Lily."

"That's okay, Nathan. I understand completely. We do what our parents tell us to do and I respect that," Lily said as she touched his arm. "I'm just so thankful they came and Papa has help from two good mules to get the work done."

"Are we still friends?" Nathan questioned.

"Of course we are," I replied tilting my head up to see his eyes. "I really appreciate the generosity your family is showing us Howells, and the Bennett family's generosity too.

We may not be able to repay you anytime soon, but God will surely bless you all for it."

As their conversation ended Mrs. Parnell rang the school bell and everyone went inside to get ready for the next class.

That night, I heard Mama and Papa talking about what good solid neighbors we have and how they could never repay the community generosity in coming to our rescue. "You know, Jan," Papa said, "God was listening all the time, when I thought he had forsaken us."

I slept better that night than I had in weeks. My prayers included a big thank you for Pastor Lawrence, our neighbors, and God for his blessings.

Part III – Holidays Come to Ripple Creek

CHAPTER 11

Thanksgiving with Papa's Family

THE FIRST WEEK in November flew by once Papa had three mules to finish the plowing. As the weather continued to get colder each night, the frost got a little heavier and winter arrived. The morning walks to school became swifter, especially the foggy mornings filled with misty rain. We skipped along and sometimes ran to stay warm. Anna and I pulled our scarves closer to our necks, wore mittens on our hands, long socks under our jumpers, and sweaters over our white blouses. Our coats were old, but heavy enough to keep us warm. Some days the wind blew so icily that we looked like the rosy-cheeked girls in the Ivory Soap posters from the Five and Dime store in town.

Children in our neighborhood walked to school. Occasionally someone's father went into town for supplies and we children all climbed into the wagon and rode to school. It did not matter whose father it was, we all accepted a ride when offered. Parents looked out for each other's children, so you always wanted to be on your best behavior.

November weeks rolled by quickly and Thanksgiving was upon us. Papa had almost all the lay-by work done. With only a few stacks of hay remaining in the field, he returned the borrowed mules and continued, when weather permitted, to do the remaining work with Pearl. After working Pearl long hours, he gave her an extra bucket of corn at night to keep her strong. Papa said Pearl was earning her keep this winter.

During Thanksgiving week we had school Monday through Wednesday. Mrs. Parnell worked us hard those three days but did not give us homework to do over the Thanksgiving holidays. Most of her students were farm kids with lots of chores. Thanksgiving was time for family and she respected that.

On Thanksgiving Day, we went to Papa's parents, Grandpa and Grandma Howell's farm. Papa's entire family came for Thanksgiving and sometimes for Christmas. Papa was the eldest son of ten living children. He had two older sisters and three younger ones. All four of his brothers were younger than Papa. The aunts and uncles were all married and everyone but Papa's youngest brother had children.

Papa's youngest brother, Rick and his wife, Patty Ann, were our favorites. She loved children but for some reason they did not have any. She showered us with love and sometimes presents. They lived in the city and Uncle Rick was in the Army. I had overheard Mama and Papa talking one night about why Uncle Rick joined the military before being drafted.

From their conversation and my eavesdropping the story I pieced together was that Uncle Rick was a little wild, especially when he could sneak a nip of liquor to drink. He liked to have fun with his friends. One night, while visiting a friend, Sal Black, who was getting married the next day in Nashville, Uncle Rick joined some other friends of Sal's at a local hangout in a town just outside the city. This was where guys got together to play poker, shoot dice, and sometimes take a nip of white lightning from the local bootlegger. This was Sal's special night and even though Rick did not know any of the other guys, he went along with the plan to celebrate his friend's upcoming marriage.

Once the friendly poker game got started there was no turning back. They started out playing penny poker, but as the bottle was passed around the stakes got higher. Uncle Rick was not normally a drinking man and only took a nip for medicine when he had a cold or for an extra special occasion. Grandma Howell did not allow the stuff in her home and did not allow her boys to drink liquor. Later in the evening a couple of other boys from Sal's old neighborhood joined the game. Rick was not an expert card player but was convinced after a few hands that one of the strangers was cheating. Rick called him on it. Without warning, the stranger leaped to his feet, turning the poker table over, and came at Uncle Rick. As the stranger made a lunge with a knife visible in his hand, Uncle Rick reacted quickly to get in the first blow to protect himself from being cut.

Rick's punch landed right on target, square on the man's chin, knocking him backwards toward the overturned table. As the attacker stumbled, his legs got tangled up in the table and down he went. The man emitted a loud grunt-like moan and went still on the floor, face down without another sound or movement. As Uncle Rick and his friends looked down at the man, a stream of red blood slowly trickled from underneath the still form creating a puddle on the floor beside the body. Rick knelt down and gently turned the stranger over. Evidently, when the man became entangled with the legs of the table, it spun him around and in the process, his right hand, while holding the knife, had been shoved across his body ending up over his heart. The force of the fall had been enough to sink the knife deep into his heart muscle, killing him instantly.

The bar owner sent for the sheriff and Uncle Rick and his friends gave statements which showed it was an accident. However, the sheriff insisted on keeping Uncle Rick in jail overnight for his own protection. He explained that he would send someone for Uncle Rick's father. Sal's friend offered to drive to the Howell place and explain to Uncle Rick's family about the unfortunate accident and bring them back to speak with the sheriff. He drove late into the night and arrived at the Howell farm well after midnight. Grandpa Howell sent Megan to get Papa, so the next morning, Papa and his brothers went with Grandpa Howell and Pastor Lawrence to Nashville to get Rick released.

The sheriff agreed that it was an unusual accident, determined it to be self-defense, and assured Grandpa Howell and Pastor Lawrence that he would testify if Rick was held over for trial. Rather than take a chance on a district judge bringing manslaughter charges against young Rick and ruining his otherwise spotless record with the law, the sheriff suggested to Grandpa Howell that if it were his son, he would have him join the armed forces and go into service for his country a few weeks early. He would, no doubt be drafted next month anyway. He explained to Grandpa Wingate that would be one sure fire way of keeping Uncle Rick out of a messy trial and possibly jail. With the war getting more desperate each day, America was clamoring to get young people trained to defend us and with the new draft laws, he was a sure bet to go in the next draft round.

Pastor Lawrence believed it was an accident and helped Rick get out of town. No charges were ever filed in the case, but Uncle Rick joined the army to serve his country. He was sorry for the accident and haunted by the needless death of a young man and the strong possibility that he might have gone to jail for manslaughter. Papa agreed that Rick would have been drafted anyway and this was just a precautionary measure.

Papa believed that although the death was an accident, Rick should have backed off and not accused the man of cheating him. In his own way, Uncle Rick was doing time for his crime by serving in the Army. It was kept very hush, hush and never discussed openly with anyone. Not even Pastor Lawrence discussed the accident. As Mama said, some things are better left unsaid, especially when you cannot change the outcome.

Papa's middle brother, Eddie, was in the Navy. He had been drafted, but was allowed to choose the branch of service. Eddie, his wife Nadine, and their son lived in Florida at the naval base so we hardly ever saw them. Both Uncle Rick and Uncle Eddie were in the service because of the War. Both came to visit Dry Valley and family before reporting for overseas duty about three months earlier.

I remember they were handsome in their uniforms, Uncle Eddie in his dress blues and Uncle Rick in his dress olive drab. Uncle Rick's uniform looked green to me, but they called it olive drab for some reason. They called themselves GIs and wore these flat hats to cover very short haircuts. I remember thinking Uncle Rick's hat was shaped like a nurse's cap. I asked Mama what GI meant and she said, "Government Issue, meaning they belonged to Uncle Sam now." I was a little confused at Mama's comment, but thought it best to keep other questions to myself.

Mama and Papa didn't discuss the war. Mama was thankful that Papa had been draft deferred because he had four children. She said there were other ways men could serve their country besides fighting—like farmers raising crops to help feed the nation.

We had a slew of other cousins, some older and some younger than Anna, Tom, David, and me. It was fun being with our cousins, aunts, and uncles. We children looked forward to boarding the wagon, sitting under a blanket snuggled low beneath the seat to keep warm, and riding the mile to Grandpa and Grandma Howell's. Papa put sideboards up on the wagon to help block the wind during the journey. With only Pearl pulling the wagon, the journey took longer than usual. It was my responsibility to keep the children quiet during the ride. Sometimes we played quiet games like "I Spy." We took turns spotting something along the road and seeing if the others could guess what we had spotted. We gave clues, like the color and where it was along the road. Usually, by the time the younger ones tired of the game, we had arrived at Grandpa and Grandma Howell's farm.

Mama baked most of the day on Tuesday of Thanksgiving week. She made two big, mouth-watering apple pies with a cinnamon smell that took your breath away. Mama had also baked a five-layer white coconut cake, with vanilla filling between the layers that oozed out when cut. She got the coconut from Mr. Parnell, the peddler, and hoarded it for special occasions. Mama made the best desserts in the whole world. Just knowing they were riding in the back of the wagon with us made us hungry.

The food was stored in a large wooden box near us in the wagon. Mama had packed some of her best towels around the dishes of food so they would not tip over during the ride. Every year she brought a gallon jug of her famous "Bread and Butter" pickles. Rounding her portion of the dinner off were large baked sweet potatoes and a squash casserole about four inches deep with honey, bread crumbs and butter lining the top. The topping made the squash disappear in a whistle once everyone got to the table. Even the men loved that squash casserole.

Mama sometimes brought the turkey and dressing, but this year, Papa's oldest sister, Jill brought it. Yesterday Mama had cooked a turkey anyway. We would have it over the next couple of days. After the turkey was eaten the first day, Mama liked to pull the leftover meat from the bone and make hash with it. To make the turkey hash, Mama added onion, grated potatoes with a little butter and several different spices. It was then baked in the oven until golden brown. Once it was removed from the oven, it made wonderful sandwiches with slices of her soda bread or cornbread, hot or cold.

Thanksgiving dinner was a time when everyone in the Howell family gave thanks to God for his blessings that year. It was a good harvest year and even though Katie had died, Papa's work was done. The barn was stacked with hay, corn, peanuts, and popcorn, not to mention the many jars of fruits and vegetables that Mama canned during the summer and fall garden harvest. Irish potatoes and sweet potatoes lined the burlap sacks hanging from the pulleys inside the storage rooms. Papa had killed a hog and a calf during "killing time" earlier in the fall so we would have meat all winter.

Wintertime was excellent for shooting dove, wild pheasant, rabbit, deer, and squirrel in season. Papa always enjoyed going hunting and sometimes took Tom with him. Tom was a bit young to carry a real gun or learn to shoot, but it was good for Papa to teach him safety in the woods. David was too young to go, but as soon as he turned five, he would be included in the hunting trips. I had gone hunting with Papa a couple of times and Anna went once. Papa taught me to shoot his rifle. We had a spot behind the barn to practice shooting safely so no one got hurt. Sometimes, I hit a tin can from a hundred paces away with Papa's rifle. Papa had a rule—we kids were never allowed to touch the guns when Papa was not around. I only practiced under his supervision and the other children were not old enough to hunt with real guns.

Friday after Thanksgiving brought our first snow of the season. It was beautiful coming down. Big wet flakes the size of quarters drifted slowly from the sky. The temperature was just right Papa said.

"Jan, we might get a blizzard," Papa said as he came in the back door of the kitchen, stomping his rubber boots on the small rug in the doorway, he then removed them, leaving only his socks on. He tried hard not to track mud onto the floor. We had finished supper and were almost ready for bed.

Mama smiled as she put the kettle on for a cup of hot cocoa for us youngsters and poured cups of hot coffee for herself and Papa. Mama got the cookie jar down and laid oatmeal cookies and large teacakes onto the plate for us to enjoy. She didn't need to encourage us to come to the table for a treat of cocoa and cookies. She and Papa enjoyed a cookie with their coffee as the snow continued to drift slowly from the sky.

"Papa, do you really think we will get a big snow?" Tom's big eyes sparkled with excitement.

"We just might," Papa said as he smiled at Tom. "Would you like that Tom?" He looked around at the rest of us as we drained the cocoa from our cups. "It might be an early Christmas present for us all!" he grinned again. "We could make a snowman in the front yard and put a big carrot for his nose." David perked up now and began to giggle. "I'm sure we could find an old hat for his head and a broom for him," Papa said picking David up and tossing him high in the air. David squealed as Papa caught him again.

"Ross, please be careful," Mama warned rising from her chair and pushing it back to its place under the table. "Now, we need to get a good night's sleep so we can all make that snowman tomorrow!" Mama reminded.

Thanksgiving with Papa's Family

Anna and I cleared away the cups and put the empty cookie plate in the sink. I quickly poured the water from the kettle, washed up the dishes and tidied the table without being told. Anna, following my lead, dried the dishes and put them away. Everything was finished so we could go to bed.

We quickly said our prayers that night. The house was chilly and Mama allowed us to do a quick prayer on our own without the Bible reading that normally accompanied them. She tucked the boys in first and then Anna and me. She cautioned the boys twice to keep their eyes shut, stop talking, and go to sleep. They obeyed. They wanted a big snow to cover the ground so we could roll a snowman together.

Around midnight the snow stopped. The moonlight streaming through our bedroom window flooded our room with light as I awakened from a sound peaceful sleep. The ground outside the window looked like marshmallow fluff or a white cloud. It was beautiful. I pulled the curtains back and peeked outside in the wee hours of the morning. I climbed back into bed and pulled the covers up around my neck and hoped the snow wouldn't melt before our family woke up. Tom, David, and Anna would be so happy to have snow. I couldn't believe Papa and Mama were going to help us roll a snowman. I wanted it to be morning right away!

The next day, we had six inches of snow. The ground was completely covered like a fluffy white blanket. You could see rabbit tracks on the ground beneath our window. It was as if they had been waiting for the snow to stop falling to come out. It was breathtakingly beautiful! The snow was all wet and stuck together, just perfect to make a great snowman. Mama and Papa kept their promise and soon the Howell's had a five-foot snowman on our front lawn. Mama dug out an old straw hat for his head, a moth-eaten old blue scarf that Papa wore years ago around his neck. We used pieces of cinder for his eyes and smaller tree twigs to make a line for his mouth. As promised, Papa pulled a large carrot from the vegetable cellar in the barn for his nose. We had all enjoyed working together on the snowman. The sunshine brightened up the skies and the snow quickly began to melt. By milking time that day, snow was dripping from the house, the barn and the smoke house and had already melted from the hickory trees lining the pasture fence. It would be gone by the end of tomorrow if the temperature continued to rise. At dusk that night, clouds were gathering in the west. We were hoping our snowman would survive the night. It was a quiet evening and everyone went to bed early.

    The rain began falling sometime after midnight while everyone was sleeping. All that was left of Mr. Snowman the next day was a wet straw hat and the old blue scarf. Mother Nature had not been kind to our family project.

CHAPTER 12

Finding
the Perfect Christmas Tree

THE RAIN CONTINUED to fall all day Sunday. After church, we children stayed inside and were under Mama's feet and on her nerves. She finally retired to her room with another headache. Papa read his book in his favorite chair and took catnaps all afternoon. Anna and I prepared the meals that day. She was getting rather good at peeling the potatoes and onions while I cooked the pork chops and the cornbread. We finished up the pinto beans and opened a jar of Mama's cream style corn. Tom had gone to the cellar in the barn to get the corn for us. Mama didn't come out of her room for supper so Papa took a tray in to her. Anna and I cleared the dishes, washed and put them away. I swept the kitchen floor while the others washed up and got ready for bed. Papa helped us with prayers and tucked us in that night. It was an unusual treat. He usually let Mama take care of the night routine.

Monday morning was school as usual and Mama seemed to be feeling better. I got up early just in case she needed help in the kitchen preparing breakfast. She had most of it cooked, but let me cook the eggs. I soft scrambled them and added just a few bits of bacon for taste. The others, including Papa, came through the door and took their seats just as we put the food on the table. Everyone ate heartily. Then, Anna and I were off to school.

That week passed very quickly and the next one too. Soon it was the middle of December. Christmas was only ten days away. I could hear Mama working long into the night. She did a lot of sewing in her room, but sometimes she would sit by the fire when working on blankets or darning socks or sweaters. She asked us girls to make a wish list for Christmas. However in a private conversation with Anna and me, she explained that we did not have a lot of money, so we could only ask for one thing. That item should be low in cost and if possible give two or more items on a list for her and Papa to consider. Tom and David still believed in Santa Claus. Mama asked us girls to play along with the idea and not spoil the boys' Christmas.

Two years before, I had gone to the cellar in the barn to bring some canned goods to the house the week before Christmas. I noticed a large cardboard box up in the hayloft almost covered with hay, but half sticking out. I had not seen the box before. I wondered where it came from and what was in it. Curiosity got the best of me. I climbed up and brushed the hay away from the top of the box. No clues indicated that it was anything more than a plain old cardboard box. We did not often have cardboard boxes lying around. My conscious told me to get the canned goods and leave the box where it was undisturbed. I pushed it back under the hay and covered it completely with the loose hay.

The next afternoon, Mama needed a can of beans brought from the barn. She once again asked me to fetch them for her because she needed them in a hurry and I was the oldest and the fastest one to complete the task. As I pulled the Mason jar of beans from the storage shelf, the thought of the box once again entered my mind. I set the jar down and quickly moved up the ladder to the hay loft. It only took a few minutes to find the fully covered box hiding under the bed of straw. I rubbed it, then put the straw back on top of the box and scampered down the ladder. I had only wasted a few minutes. Mama was ready for the beans when I came through the door.

"What took you so long?" she questioned. Looking sheepishly I shrugged my shoulders and murmured, "Sorry."

A few days passed and I put the box out of my thoughts. Chores and school work took up time as Mama worked more on her Christmas sewing projects. Monday afternoon after chores were done and homework was completed, Mama asked me to go to the barn and get a jar of blackberry jam for our breakfast the next day. Anna and the boys were busy with other things.

This time I went straight to the hayloft and found the box in a couple of minutes. It appeared to be exactly as I had left it all covered with hay and not visible from the naked eye.

"Lord, I can't help myself. Please forgive me," I said as I opened the lid of the box and peeked in.

Inside the box was a beautiful porcelain doll. Hidden further in the box were two pairs of boots for girls—for Anna and me. There were a couple of toys for boys and a set of cowboy guns, holsters, and caps to fire in the gun.

I rushed to put the gifts back into the box, find the jam and return to the kitchen before Mama got worried. As I pushed the box firmly under the loose hay and strewed more hay on top, I felt guilty that I had snooped and seen our Christmas presents.

I felt so guilty that I later confessed to Mama what I had done. She didn't punish me, but shook her head and said, "I'm so sorry, Lily. Christmas won't be the same for you ever again! But now you should concentrate on the true meaning of Christmas—the birth of Jesus Christ. You are growing into a fine young lady. Your Papa and I are very proud of you."

Of course, I told Anna. She was my confidant. Whatever I knew, she knew. But Mama was right. Christmas was not the same and not as much fun after that. We understood the meaning of celebrating it more, but some of the magic of being a child at Christmas was gone. The boys still believed

Finding the Perfect Christmas Tree

in Santa Claus and we tried really hard not to spoil it for them. Some parts of Christmas remained fun like before from just experiencing the wonderment in our little brothers' eyes, the questions on their faces, and the joy of Christmas morning. God was good.

My favorite part of Christmas was choosing and cutting the tree. For the last two years, I had gone with Papa to cut our Christmas tree. Last year, Papa let Anna come with us for the first time. I watched each year how Papa searched until he found a beautiful tree that exactly fit our needs. The space for the tree was limited so it had to meet certain criteria to be the right one. Papa had commented last year that we girls were getting old enough to choose the tree and relieve him of that duty. Later that day, Papa and Mama asked if we girls would like to help them out by finding a Christmas tree. The instructions they gave were that the tree should not be over five-feet tall, be very full, and it could either be a cedar or a loblolly pine.

Cedar trees are harder to decorate because the cedar pricks the skin when you put things on them. The loblolly pine tree has longer needles and stays green better than regular pines. The loblolly pine is the best tree, but the cedar tree fills the house with a clean cedar smell like no other tree. That cedar smell lets everyone know that Christmas is near. The pine tree also gives the house a woody pine aroma. The cedar tree doesn't shed needles like the pine trees, but after Christmas, the cedar tree is harder to take decorations off for storage because of those prickly branches. It was Anna's and my decision this year—which tree would we find and get?

With these things in mind, we set out on our adventure to find the perfect tree. We were excited but also a little anxious to have such a big responsibility. After all, Christmas was such a blessed event—we had to find the perfect tree. Mama, Papa, Tom, and David were all counting on us.

We walked through what seemed like acres of woods checking out various trees along the way. Then we saw it— the perfect Howell Christmas tree. It was growing in a small meadow with several smaller cedar trees growing around it. It was about five feet tall, fat at the bottom, with the middle of the tree thick and full with no bald spots. The top came up to a perfect point. It was a beautiful Loblolly pine. I reached out and broke a needle off—the smell burst forward. Anna agreed. This was the perfect tree for us. I marked the spot by breaking branches on the cedar trees surrounding the chosen pine.

We turned for home to get Papa, breaking into a run that sent rabbits and squirrels scampering for shelter. He had told us to find the tree and come get him. Papa would hitch the wagon, come and cut the tree for us. In the meantime, he and Mama retrieved boxes of Christmas decorations from the hayloft in the barn. They were stored there year after year. We stopped a few times along the trail to the house and carefully broke a branch to mark our way back to the tree we had chosen.

The weather was getting colder; the wind picked up and a few snow flurries began to fall. Anna and I were so excited. It felt like magic in the air. We giggled, held hands and made our way back as quickly as we could. Pleased with ourselves, we chattered about how we had been sent by Papa to find a perfect tree and our success. Perhaps there was a Santa Claus after all. We were tired and cold but excited when we reached the barnyard and then the kitchen door. We burst inside.

"Papa, Papa," Anna and I called at the same time.

"Well, did you find a tree?" Papa asked.

"We did," Anna exclaimed. "And it is beautiful!"

Papa turned to me. "Lily," he asked. "Where did you find it?"

"Just a little beyond the tree you cut last year, Papa." I said.

"Let me get my coat and we will go cut it," Papa said to the two of us just as Mama came into the room from the breezeway.

"Bundle up," she ordered. "It is getting colder outside. I noticed some snowflakes beginning to come down! We may be in for another snowfall tonight. And hurry," she added.

Papa took his overcoat from the rack just inside the kitchen door, pulled on his work boots, wrapped a woolen scarf around his neck and put his toboggan on his head. He took Anna's hand and mine and we started back through the pasture, along the fence line to the spot where we had marked our chosen tree. Papa wanted to make sure this was the perfect tree before he hitched Pearl to the wagon. The snowflakes were getting bigger as we came closer to the small area where the loblolly pine stood among the three cedar trees. The smile on Papa's face let us know we had made a perfect selection.

"Well, well!" Papa said. "This *is* a magnificent tree!" He took Anna's hands in his and twirled her around with glee. I laughed out loud to see Papa so happy. Then it was my turn—he caught me in his arms and swung me high in the air—snowflakes landed on my face, nose, and eye lashes as we celebrated our good fortune of finding the perfect tree.

We swiftly half walked, half ran back to the barn with Anna leading. I was close behind her and Papa brought up the rear. Papa went to the plowing shed and got the bridle and bit for Pearl. I removed the ax hanging on the opposite side of the tool shed. Papa handed the bridle and bit to Anna and went inside to get Pearl. Anna moved to the side of the barn hallway still holding Pearl's gear. Pearl was snorting and pawing a little as Papa took the gear from Anna and placed the bit inside her mouth, then the bridle over her head. He then walked her outside the barn to the shed housing the wagon. He backed Pearl up and hooked the lead lines to the front hitch of the wagon.

"Whoa, girl," he said softly to Pearl as she resisted a little. "Easy, now, Pearl," he continued to soothe her. I climbed into the wagon and took the lines Papa handed me. He quickly gave Anna a boost onto the wagon seat beside me. Then Papa boarded, placed the ax on the floor under our feet, took the lines from me and said, "Gettie up, girl."

Pearl pulled the wagon with us aboard into the pasture behind the barn. When we got to the back pasture fence, I quickly climbed down from the seat and opened the fence gate leading into the wooded thicket beyond. Papa drove the wagon up a few feet and I closed the pasture gate, fastening both the bottom and top wire loops so that the cows could not wander away. I quickly returned to the wagon seat. Once I was seated, Papa clicked the lines together and Pearl moved out slowly. Papa began humming "It Came Upon the Midnight Clear," his favorite Christmas carol. In no time, we were at the spot where the tree we had chosen grew. Papa stepped out of the wagon and handed the leads to Anna. Then he lifted me from the wagon and planted my feet on the ground beside the tree. He silently reached under the wagon seat and retrieved the ax.

The tall oaks, cedar, and pine trees of the woods stood quiet and serene. The calm of the winter afternoon was so quiet you could almost hear the snow falling. It brought tranquility to the meadows where birds fluttered about in search of food. As snowflakes settled on Papa's brow, he swung the ax up and around striking it full force against the tree base. The chop rang throughout the thicket. It took him five hard cuts to topple the tree. Two more solid chops with the ax and he had finished the job.

Anna gazed from the seat and I stood below watching as Papa gently lifted the tree onto the wagon bed. "I'll do a proper trim when we get it home," he remarked putting the ax back under the seat. "Climb up, Lily. Let's get out of this snow." He winked at Anna as he took Pearl's leads from her. I quickly climbed up and we were off. "Come on, Pearl. Let's go to the barn," Papa called. His voice broke the silence of the woods as he began to sing another verse of the Christmas carol. Pearl gave a loud bray as if she was singing along. Anna and I laughed and joined him in singing during the short wagon ride to the barn.

"Lily and Anna, I'll unhitch Pearl and feed her. You two run to the house and tell Mama to put the kettle on. I'll get the holder from the feed loft and fit this gorgeous tree into it. Hurry, but be careful, it's getting wet and slippery out here." Papa continued talking as he unhitched Pearl and led her to the stall.

Anna and I broke into a run. We hit the kitchen door with a bang. As it popped open, we fell into the room squealing and almost knocked Mama down. Tom and David came running into the kitchen to see what was causing the commotion.

Tom asked, "Where's the Christmas tree?"

Finding the Perfect Christmas Tree

"Papa's bringing it," Anna explained as she patted him on the head and picked David up and swung him onto her left hip. Anna showed strength as David was much too big for her to carry. "Papa wants you to put the kettle on," Anna said over her shoulder to Mama.

Mama just shook her head smiling. After putting the kettle on, she removed David from Anna's grip and helped us both remove our coats. Papa came through the door carrying the tree mounted into the old metal stand that had held all of our Christmas trees. The stand was a wedding present from one of his younger sisters, Sarah. Sarah had become Mama's best friend since Mama and Papa married.

He carefully placed the tree in the corner of the den and stood back to admire his handiwork. The boys laughed while Lad sat quietly on his quilt in the corner taking in the family excitement. David pointed and reached out his hand touching the pine branches that cascaded down from the upper parts of the tree. It was beautiful without decorations.

Mama poured hot cocoa for us children and coffee for herself and Papa. After cautioning us to be careful, she allowed us to take our half-filled cups to the den to watch as she and Papa decorated the tree. We dropped in sitting position on the floor beside old Lad, who sniffed the air and our cocoa, but settled once again. Mama led us in a round of Christmas carols we knew. First we sang "Jingle Bells," then "Silent Night." She and Papa finished off with more of his favorite—"It Came Upon the Midnight Clear."

The tree sparkled with the wooden ornaments that had been collected over the years and other special ornaments that Mama had made. Each year she added a special ornament that she sewed or made from cornhusks. This year Mama sewed a little rag girl and boy with button eyes and small clothes on their sock bodies. She had stitched them together so it looked like they were holding hands. Over the next few days before Christmas, we would string popcorn into long ropes and lay it around the tree. That was always a lot of fun for us kids as we instantly saw the fruits of our labor. It would also keep us busy and out of Mama's hair.

Snow kept falling into the night after we had gone to bed. It was difficult for the boys, Anna, and me to settle down. Putting up the Christmas tree was almost as good as Christmas morning. It was a family time that didn't require presents or money, but it was a time of joy. The evening was finished with prayers by Mama and Papa for a good harvest year and thanks for baby Jesus. The last thing that night, Mama told us was she had a big surprise for us. She and Papa would share it with us on Christmas Morning. Each of us slept that night dreaming about the surprise. What could it be? The boys hoped for special toys. Anna wanted new clothes and I wanted new shoes—perhaps even canvas shoes that were so popular. Only Christmas morning would bring an answer! Which ones would get their wishes? What could the surprise be?

CHAPTER 13

Christmas Surprises

THE NEXT NINE DAYS passed quickly. School was out for the Christmas season for Anna and me from December 20th until January 4th. Things were busy at home. Mama stayed in her room more during the holiday school break. In secret, she worked on the Christmas presents she was making for us. She sometimes felt sickly and large brown circles developed under her eyes. I asked her what I could do to help. She smiled and asked me to keep the house reasonably clean, our rooms picked-up properly, clothes stored in their place, all the floors swept and mopped, kitchen cleaned, and dishes washed, dried and put away. She asked that Anna and I keep the other kids as quiet as possible, fed, and happy. She said we could fix snacks for dinner and make supper at night. These things were a tall order for a nine and seven year old, but she said it would help her. We had done these types of chores for Mama just before David was born and we were even younger then.

Since Papa was finished with the fieldwork for winter, he was working for the other farmers again. Neighbors were eager to get his assistance on many projects. He left the house early in the mornings and returned after dark.

Christmas Eve finally arrived. The Christmas tree stood magnificently in the corner. The popcorn roping gave it that extra needed cheerfulness and finished touch. It had been fun watching the boys. They would string a kernel, then eat one then string one and eat another. We girls had also eaten our fill, but Papa allowed for that. He popped the corn and set a huge dishpan of white popped kernels on the floor in front of the four of us for two evenings in a row. We had created five long strands of corn roping. Anna and I were true to Mama's wishes and kept the house clean.

Everyone was excited, even old Lad and Skip when Skip was allowed to come inside for a few minutes, which was not often. The boys were beside themselves chattering away about what Santa might bring them tonight. We had to shush them several times. It was hard to play quietly, but especially hard on Christmas Eve, even after being reminded that Mama was ill. Anna asked me several times what I thought the surprise might be. But I really didn't have any idea and told her that we would know tomorrow.

Papa did not go to work that day. All the neighbors would be spending time with their families. Christmas Day was usually spent with Papa's family, but this Christmas, Mama was ill. We children would go to church with Papa, return, and spend Christmas at home. Perhaps some of his family would stop in later. Grandma and Grandpa Wingate, Mama's parents, were expected to come by this year to check on her.

This Christmas Eve, Papa killed the biggest rooster on our farm for Christmas dinner. Even farmer men knew how to kill and prepare a bird for Christmas dinner. Papa boiled a kettle of water and, after killing the bird and while it was still fresh, he took the kettle outside and poured the scalding water into a large pail. He then dipped the dead bird head first into the scalding water three times, leaving it just a few seconds each time. This method allowed the feather quills to loosen and they could be plucked out easily. He then plucked the feathers from the bird, dressed it by removing the insides and used fire to burn tiny feather quills that remained after plucking. After dressing the bird, Papa stored the bird in the cool smokehouse until Christmas morning. Then he would stuff it with a special stuffing made from the livers, gizzard, cranberries, chopped onion, sausage and sage and just a few cornbread crumbs mixed in. The final step was pouring the broth obtained from the boiled neck and heart, then stirring the stuffing batter, adding more broth until the texture was perfect. After stuffing the bird, Papa put it into a large pan and surrounded it with mounds of cornbread dressing before setting the pan in the oven. The bird and dressing would roast for about four hours. The large rooster would be the focal point of our meal.

Mama came out of her room before noon and greeted us all with hugs and Christmas Eve wishes. She looked better and patted Lad on the head, saying, "Good dog." She washed her hands and brewed a fresh pot of coffee, then began preparing dinner. While the soup boiled in the large kettle, she quickly mixed cornbread and placed it in the oven. Then she wrote a list of items on a piece of paper and handed it to Anna.

"Anna," she began, "after dinner, I want you, Tom, and David to fetch these items from the barn. You carry the items in the glass jars, but Tom and David can carry things that don't break like the potatoes, onions, apples, and nuts. It may require more than one trip. But I know you can do this for me." She turned back to the stove and stirred the soup.

"Lily," she said without looking up. "I am going to need your help making the pies and the cake for Christmas dinner. I think it's time you learned to bake more complicated things. You make fine delicious teacakes. What do you think?" She turned around and placed both hands on her hips and looked me in the eyes.

"Wonderful Mama! I want to learn to bake and cook like you do. What kind of cake and pies will we make?" I asked eagerly, clasping my hands together in anticipation.

After eating a hearty dinner of soup and cornbread, everyone was off to do the tasks they had been assigned.

Anna and the boys made two trips to the barn, but soon had everything on Mama's list. Anna cleaned the food filled jars with soap and water, as they wouldn't be needed until Christmas morning.

The afternoon was filled with smells of cinnamon, apples, sugar, and nuts coming from the kitchen. Mama and I first baked two large apple pies. The pies were cooling on the eating table. Our second project was a triple layer Black Walnut Cake. The cake was cooling and ready to be iced. The cake icing was made from six eggs whites. First, the whites were separated from the yellows and placed in a large glass bowl. Then beat with a fork. After several minutes of constantly beating they formed mounds that looked like the snow on Mount Rushmore's highest peak. After beating the egg whites to perfection, warm white sugar syrup was added a little at a time until the sweet delicate icing melted when it hit the tongue. Rich toasted black walnuts were sprinkled through the cake batter before baking. More walnuts were dusted on top of the icing between the layers and on top of the cake. Mama had allowed me to finish adding the walnuts so I felt the cake was my creation. Anna had never shown much interest in cooking, but watched while we finished icing the cake.

Papa read while Tom and David played some games with Lad lying in his corner, his eyes half shut. We heard an occasional laugh or squeal as Papa told some stories to them about Christmas when he was growing up.

It was cold, but dry. It had been a few days since it had rained. Before we knew it, it was time for evening chores. We wore light jackets while doing the barn work. While Mama rested on the couch, Papa milked the cows. Anna and I fed the other animals and gathered the eggs. Tom, with David's help, brought in wood for the fire. By working together, everything was done in record time. Following a light supper of milk and bread, we children washed up and the Howell family went to bed. It was a brisk cold winter night with stars shining in the sky, a night for dreams of sugarplums, especially in Tom and David's heads. The boys needed little encouragement since they were eagerly awaiting the arrival of Santa during the night.

The crisp cold night air with stars illuminated above made a perfect backdrop to the bright full moon lazily inching across the sky that gave way to a cold and breezy but sunny Christmas morning. The boys woke first. Rushing to the den, they were not disappointed. Lad was startled by their early entrance but settled back into semi-sleep in the corner on his quilt. As Lad got older, he was less bothered by children around him. He merely tuned them out and rested.

Nestled under the tree, the boys each found a stash with his name on it. In special army cloth bags, toy soldiers were carefully tucked inside. They had plastic army trucks and jeeps. They each found a new book, a shirt, vest, and jeans that Mama had sewn. They each also had new boots, bought at the store, and socks that Mama had knitted. Each stocking was filled with a big red delicious apple, a plump juicy orange, hickory nuts, black walnuts and a big fat stick of peppermint candy. The stockings were returned to the spot where the boys had left them the night before.

Their squeals of delight brought Anna and me to the floor in one leap from our bed. Even though we no longer believed, the excitement of Christmas morning was contagious. We scampered to the den, joined the boys, and soon we were pulling out gifts that had been crafted especially for us girls.

Anna giggled with delight as she held the new dress up in front of her and did a twirl around. "It's beautiful," she said. "I can't wait to wear it." She also found a new petticoat with ruffles to make the fullness of the dress show off her thin waist. The sleeves were long with puffs near the shoulders that showed the pretty delicate white flowers on the yellow material in a stunning way. Mama had outdone herself for Anna. I watched in delight to see Anna so happy. She also found a lovely yellow and white sweater that Mama had knitted to go with the dress. She had a new denim skirt and white blouse. Just what she had asked for—new clothes. Anna also found a pair of plastic rain boots to wear over her shoes when it rained. She had a new bonnet made of the same material as the dress and some pantaloons to wear underneath. She was all set for church or a special occasion.

After she finished opening everything, holding it up and twirling around with glee, Anna dropped on the floor beside me. "Well," she asked. "Aren't you going to open yours?"

At that moment, Lad nudged Anna and walked to the door. She immediately got up opened the door and let Lad outside into the crisp air. After saying good morning to Skip and giving him a quick hug and pat on his head, Anna closed the door and returned to me.

I dug inside the bag carrying my name and pulled out a bright green raincoat—full length with matching hood. Mama had made it beautiful—it had four toggle wooden buttons with loops made from the same material. It had a pink nylon lining inside. The coat itself was a lightweight parachute-like material that was almost water repellent. She had also stitched a book bag for me of the same material. It was beautiful. Tears filled my eyes as I pulled it on over my nightgown. I felt so grown up and pretty. Nestled deep in the bag was a pair of black and white oxford shoes and a green pair of socks that Mama had knitted. I also had a new denim skirt and a white blouse from Mama, some underwear and a new bra. Just the things I needed for school.

Anna gave me a hug and said, "The coat is beautiful and the shoes are really neat. I would like to have some like those."

"Thanks," I said. "When your feet grow into them, I'll share."

Anna and I left the boys playing with their new toys and went to prepare breakfast. We did this sometimes on the weekend when we were up before Mama and Papa. It was fun. I could not make biscuits, but I did fry mashed potato patties, eggs, and ham. That made a tasty breakfast. I put the coffee on to brew while Anna laid out the silver beside each plate. She got the butter and milk from the ice box. Just as we were about to call the boys, Mama and Papa came into the kitchen. They each gave us a hug and we thanked them for our gifts. Mama was pleased that we loved everything she had made for us. Papa smiled as we described each item to him. Mama poured their coffee. Anna poured milk for each of us children. Papa called the boys and soon we were all enjoying Christmas breakfast.

Papa asked us to get ready for church. He would hitch the wagon. Mama was not well enough to go. We were to come straight home afterwards. Grandma and Grandpa Wingate would be coming over around 1:00 pm and we would have Christmas dinner then. Mama's parents would stay for Christmas dinner. Papa's family, as far as we knew, would not visit us today. Mama assured us she would be fine and would wash the breakfast dishes while she prepared Christmas dinner, without our help. We were out the door, in our rooms, and ready in a split second.

Anna's dress was stunning as was my new raincoat. The boys wore their new jeans, shirts, and vest and Papa wore a new leather vest and shirt Mama had made him for

Christmas. She had spent all those hours in her room sewing and knitting gifts for our Christmas. Papa had gotten material for a new dress for Mama and matching bonnet. She would sew those later. He had bought her a new pair of dressy flat shoes for church. They were dark brown and could be worn with anything. Made from soft leather, the shoes looked comfortable and would last for years.

Mama said we girls looked beautiful and Papa and the boys were handsome in their new clothes. She gave us each a hug and the boys a pat on the head and asked them to behave in church. She assured us she did not need one of us girls to stay behind and would be fine until after the church service.

We were off in the wagon, huddled together in the back under the woolen blanket Mama had made just for our trips to church. Papa rode in the seat up top and whistled and sang all the way to church. The morning air was cold, but dry and bearable. We had dressed warm and were snuggled together in comfort. The ride was short and we were soon seated in the pew with Pastor Lawrence preaching the Christmas message. Bible verses read about the birth of Jesus and the plight of Mary and Joseph were interesting even if we heard them every Christmas. I still listened very carefully. Anna and I were the first out the back of the church when the service was over with Tom and David on our heels and Papa bringing up a lagging rear. He was chatting with some neighbors about some additional projects they wanted him to build for them during the winter months.

When we were outside in the bright sunshine, I couldn't believe my eyes. Not more than ten feet away stood Uncle Rick in his dress olive drab Army Corp greens. He smiled, bent down and held out his arms. I think we all saw him at the same time. We almost knocked him flat as we all hurled ourselves into his arms all at once. "Uncle Rick, Uncle Rick!" we all shouted. Everyone in church this morning gathered around to see Rick Howell. He was a sight for sore eyes.

Papa's voice broke as he hugged his little brother. "What are you doing here, Rick? This is a wonderful surprise. How are you?" Questions came so fast that Uncle Rick could not possibly answer them all. They hugged again, then he boarded the wagon and sat with Papa. He decided to ride home with us. We kids climbed under the blanket again in the back of the wagon and Papa shouted for Pearl to "Gettie up, girl." She started off smoothly, and we headed home.

Uncle Rick told Papa he was on medical leave from the army. He had been shot in the left shoulder and sent back for a period of six weeks to get well. After the surgery, his shoulder had become infected so he had to remain in the hospital for four additional weeks. He was actually home to see the family for a few days before he had to return to the battlefield in Germany. He and Aunt Patty Ann arrived yesterday and were staying with Papa's parents. They wanted to come over after Christmas dinner today and visit. He would be home for only three more days.

Papa decided to let us off at Ripple Creek. Uncle Rick would say hello to Mama and grab a cup of coffee. Papa would then drive Uncle Rick home before unhitching Pearl.

Mama had a better idea. Papa should take Pearl and the wagon and go with Rick to pick up Aunt Patty Ann. She allowed it was too cold for them to walk the three miles from the Howell Place to Ripple Creek. Papa could then return them to his parents late that afternoon. It was a good plan.

Mama and Papa visited with Rick just long enough to drink the coffee to warm them before they rode to the Howell farm.

Uncle Rick asked us kids to go play so they could visit undisturbed. We obeyed. He assured us that he and Aunt Patty Ann would be back in a few hours and that we could visit then.

Papa and Rick finished their coffee, said goodbye to Mama and returned to the wagon and Pearl. Papa handed the reins to Rick and suggested that he drive. They both laughed as Rick signaled to Pearl to go and she obeyed. Papa waved to Mama from the wagon seat.

It was a short ride to the Howell farm and the boys caught up on the war and what America was doing. Rick shared as much as he could with his brother without breaking army codes and military secrets. They enjoyed this special time together.

As they pulled into the Howell farm lane, they both noticed Pastor Lawrence and a Naval Officer descending the preacher's buggy and walking to the porch steps.

Uncle Rick was overcome, "Oh no! Dear God, have mercy." He moaned out loud to the sky as Papa's hand grasped his shoulder and squeezed hard.

They scampered from the wagon together and broke into a run for the porch just as their father opened the front door to the visitors. Grandma Howell, Papa's sisters, Patty Ann and his younger brothers all came through the door at the same time. Pastor Lawrence introduced the Naval Officer who came to attention and saluted Grandpa Howell. A quick introduction of the others on the porch was made and Uncle Rick saluted the officer, when introduced. The party went inside the house together. Once seated in the foyer, the Officer explained his reason for visiting:

"Your son, Seaman First Class Eddie Howell, is assigned to the USS Leary (DD-158, a destroyer class vessel). It saddens me to report to you," he said, as he pulled a paper from inside his jacket and read from it. "Yesterday, 24 December 1943, the American hunter-killer Task Group 21.13, formed around USS Card (CVE11) was spotted by a German reconnaissance aircraft. The aircraft accompanied by German wolfpack *Borkum U-boats* attacked our ships. The carrier had a narrow escape when three FAT torpedoes fired by U-415 (Neide) missed her at 04.43 hours. The same U-boat also missed the USS Decatur (DD 341) with a Gnat."

(Low gasps could be heard from the Howell females listening.)

The officer continued, "At 05.05 hours, U-275 fired a Gnat at USS Leary (DD 158) Commanded by Cdr. J. E. Keys, and hit her on the starboard side in the aft engine room. A second Gnat fired by U-382 missed the already sinking destroyer. She sank after a huge internal explosion within one minute about 585 miles west of Cape Finisterre. The survivors were picked up by USS Scheck (DD159) which found U-645 later the same day, evaded a torpedo, and sank the U-boat with depth charges."

Screams from Papa's sisters erupted and Grandma Howell fainted. Patty Ann swung into action, held Grandma's head in her lap while wiping her face with a cold wet cloth that Teresa supplied, and held, smelling salts under her nose until she opened her eyes. Patty Ann continued to hold her head in her lap and remained on the floor beside Grandma as the officer patiently waited until things were more under control, then continued,

"Seaman First Class Eddie Howell has not been listed among the survivors that were picked up by U.S. Navy ships. Accordingly. Seaman Howell has been officially determined by the U. S. Navy as being 'Missing in Action,'" The officer continued, "The reason Seaman Howell is listed as MIA rather than as "Presumed Dead" is that the German submarine U-275 was observed to be picking up a few survivors, but it had immediately ceased rescue activity and dived to safety as the U-boat spotted U. S. Navy ships approaching."

Speaking unofficially to Uncle Rick and Papa, the naval officer confided that if Seaman Eddie had been picked up alive, he would be a Prisoner of War of the Germans and that sooner or later the Germans might release names of POWs held by them to the neutral Swiss Government offices, but that could take weeks or even months before the US Government would know.

Screams and sobs then filled the room from Howell sisters who could not be consoled by their husbands who had sat soberly listening to the report. Grandma Howell sobbed almost uncontrollably while silent tears from Patty Ann dropped onto Grandma's dress. The younger brothers were in shock as were Papa and Uncle Rick.

Grandpa Howell was the strong one. He thanked the officer for his speedy report and said it was not news they wanted to hear on the radio. He also asked if Nadine had been told and the officer assured him she and the children would have received the news today from another naval officer. The commander of the Navy thought hearing the news from a fellow navy man would make it a little less difficult for the family and he was right, Grandpa assured him.

Grandpa Howell then asked Pastor Lawrence to say a prayer for Eddie to return to them safely and that the war end before other sons could be killed fighting for their country.

Pastor Lawrence asked everyone to pray silently with him.

"Lord, with humble hearts, we ask that you watch over our brother Eddie Howell wherever he is today and that you give him strength in body, heart, and mind to serve you and to return to us free from harm. God, our Father, we ask that you forgive us for our trespasses. Lord, keep us forever in your arms as we seek to slay the giants in the name of freedom. God bless this officer, Eddie's wife and family, and the Howell family, and help them to understand and grow closer to you with each fleeting day. In Jesus' name we pray. Amen."

The officer stayed for a cup of coffee and a piece of apple pie with the family before he left with Pastor Lawrence. Papa had to return home to break the news to Mama and us children. Uncle Rick and Aunt Ruth said they would borrow Grandpa's wagon and come over later in the day or early evening to spend some time with us children after things settled down at the Howell house. Mama might need a little time to adjust to the bad news and the Wingates would be there for Christmas dinner in the early afternoon.

As Papa stepped onto the wagon seat, Uncle Rick said. "He's not dead, Ross. I can feel his presence here now. He's not dead!" Papa shook Uncle Rick's hand gripping it extremely tight and called to Pearl to go home.

Papa turned the wagon for home worried about how he would break the news to Mama and the children. Tom and David were too little to understand death or "missing in action," but the girls were different. They would be frightened and heartbroken. Uncle Rick and Uncle Eddie were so special to them, finding time on home visits from the army or navy to spend time with just his family. Papa admired his younger brothers for fighting for freedom and sometimes thought he was neglecting his duty as a man by not fighting alongside of them. He never thought it was okay to be excused from war just 'cause you had children.'

He couldn't help but notice the dark cloudy sky above as tiny snowflakes landed faster and harder with bigger flakes mixed in. "We are in for a cold, winter night, girl," he said to Pearl as she continued a steady pace with condensation trails, much like smoke, flowing from her nose. He allowed her to take her time as he closed his eyes and prayed that God would keep his brother safe and return him to the family soon. He also asked that God give him words to explain the situation to Jan and the children so as to not destroy their happiness this Christmas.

About half a mile from Ripple Creek, a deer family grazed near the dirt road. The large six-point buck was a beautiful deep caramel colored creature with dark brown surrounding the deep brown eyes and tufts of white near his ears and under his belly following through the pointed tail. His partner, only about half his size, stood beside her mate showing off her deep chestnut brown coat with almost a black hood covering her small head and amber eyes peering out. She too had the white tufts and light gray under belly with the white extending through the tail. Two small fawns munching away on abundant grass pods sticking out of the ditch leaned closer into their mother as the wagon passed, but none of them bolted away. Papa thought to himself that God made beautiful creatures on his earth while a family of squirrels darted from tree to tree as if they were trying to keep up with Pearl. He pulled his collar closer and turned up the lane to Ripple Creek.

CHAPTER 14

Christmas Dinner

GRANDMA AND GRANDPA Wingate were already at Ripple Creek as Papa pulled the wagon near the barn, descended the seat, and unhitched Pearl. He unlatched her stall door; she was glad to be in from the cold and snow mixed with rain. Papa gave her a full portion of feed, poured fresh water in her bucket, and then headed for the house in a brisk walk. Skip stood, yawned, and wagged his tail as Papa took the steps to the porch two at a time. Papa gave him several gentle pats on top of the head, and Skip walked to the door behind him.

"Stay, boy," Papa said as he opened the kitchen door and stepped inside.

Mama had everything ready for Christmas dinner when Papa got home from the Howells'. She had stitched small white cloth napkins before Christmas and had placed them strategically beside our plates. The table looked pretty. Upon arrival, while waiting for Papa, Grandma and Grandpa Wingate showered us with gifts. As we children all surrounded Papa speaking at once about our gifts, Papa decided to wait until later to share the sad news about Uncle Eddie.

Tom and David each got a new flip that Grandpa Wingate had whittled from limbs off the large chestnut tree that stood like a monument in their front yard. Each flip was a perfect fork with a strong stalk bottom. To make each flip, Grandpa had used heavy rubber and anchored two pieces onto the top of the v-shaped fork. A large piece of leather was attached to the center of the pieces of rubber for a pullback mechanism. A rock could be held in the center of the leather part. When you aimed and pulled the rubber back, the rock became a projectile weapon. Grandpa made a leader holder for each flip fixed onto a rawhide neck string.

Tom and David already had a small flip. They practiced shooting things with rocks and Tom had killed a couple of birds with his old one. According to Grandpa Wingate, the power of this flip could kill a rabbit or squirrel from ten paces away. He reminded them that this flip was a weapon, not a toy, and should be taken seriously. Boys their ages were old enough to learn responsibility.

Anna and I got new colorful bands for our hair and Grandma Wingate had made beautiful lace hankies for Mama and us. She had crocheted a beautiful pink shawl for Mama and a small hat and gloves for Anna and me. They were practical and beautiful and unlike any we had seen. We loved them.

Grandpa Wingate had made Papa a neat leather tool belt to hold his ax, knife, and gun shells when he went hunting. It also had a place to hook a small lantern on the side. It buckled at the waist and Papa loved it. Grandpa had worked hours finishing the leather so the texture, color, and shine were stunning.

After opening Christmas presents and then sharing them again with Papa, we were all hungry. Mama served Christmas dinner hot from the stove. The golden browned rooster held its place of honor on a huge platter, surrounded by cornbread dressing and cranberry relish in a pottery pot placed near the center of the kitchen table. Rich mashed potatoes with lots of gravy, steaming biscuits and cornbread, bubbling cream style corn, hot pinto beans and deviled eggs, each in its own dish, surrounded the center dish. Bread and butter pickles from the jar and thinly sliced sweet onions rounded out the meal. The cinnamon apple pie and black walnut cake would make a wonderful ending to this Christmas feast. Grandpa Wingate gave thanks, and we all ate heartily.

Anna and I quickly and silently cleared the table while the adults enjoyed a second cup of coffee with their dessert. The boys asked to be excused, then took their toys and headed for their room to play soldiers. We girls placed the dishes in the large pan ready to be washed. Mama had taught us that adults needed privacy so we should excuse ourselves when we had visitors. Even if the adults were family, this rule still applied—unless she invited us to remain in the room. Today, she had not invited us to stay.

After we children were in the other room, Papa shared the news of Uncle Eddie being MIA. Gasps from the women, surprise, and sadness lingered over everyone. Grandpa gave Papa a big hug as did Grandma. Papa took Mama in his arms for a firm hug. Mama managed to keep her composure and thanked Papa for waiting to tell the children.

"They were so excited and having so much fun, I thought a few more hours of celebration would be what Eddie wanted for his nieces and nephews," Papa said as he and Mama stepped apart. We can tell them together later. Grandma and Grandpa Wingate stayed only about an hour after Christmas dinner. They needed to get home in time to do farm chores before nightfall. They told Mama and Papa that chores took a little longer than it use to when she and Papa lived with them. It was their way of letting them know they missed them and the work they used to do.

Just after they left, Uncle Rick and Aunt Ruth arrived in the Howell buggy, pulled by Grandpa Howell's horse, Dan. Papa got a small bucket of feed and some water for Dan and placed them on the ground. He would remain hitched to the buggy until after their visit.

"Weather has taken a nasty turn," Uncle Rick said and then continued, "We can't stay long. Don't want to leave the old man and woman too long, considering."

As he and Papa joined Patty Ann and Mama on the steps, Papa said, "I haven't told the children, yet. Jan's parents were here and they were having so much fun, I just didn't think it was the proper time." Uncle Rick patted his brother on the back.

"Ah-h, Ross. Why don't you wait until they are in bed or wait until morning?" Uncle Rick said. "Don't spoil their Christmas. Farm kids don't get many chances to celebrate, you know."

The four adults opened the door and entered the house together. Mama and Papa continued to visit with Uncle Rick and Aunt Patty Ann while we were in our room and unaware of their presence. Actually, Anna and I had taken a little nap and the boys continued playing with their soldiers, fighting battle after battle as quietly as little boys could. Finally around three o'clock, the door opened and Uncle Rick and Patty Ann came into our room. The boys both darted from behind the curtained partition and jumped full force onto our bed. Uncle Rick took them both in his arms and returned them to the floor. Each boy had him by a leg. It was a funny site to see Uncle Rick wrestled to the floor by two small boys, half squealing, half giggling, and kicking and flailing arms everywhere. Aunt Patty Ann came over and encircled us girls one in each arm. We were so happy to see our favorite Aunt and Uncle.

"How pretty you look," she smiled.

"Christmas clothes from Mama and Papa," I said.

"They are so stylish. Did she make them?" she quizzed with that twinkle in her eye. She most likely knew already that Mama made our clothes because we didn't have money to buy clothes.

Anna shook her head "yes" and Aunt Patty Ann smiled and gave us both a kiss on the top of our heads.

"How's school?" she asked no one in particular.

"Fine," we both chimed in.

"And what's your favorite subject, Lily?" She now turned to me.

"I like them all. But, I guess my favorite has to be reading," I replied as I twirled a curl of my hair around a finger.

"If you are a good reader, you can do anything. Everything builds on reading," she replied stroking my back as we sat on the bed.

"What about you, Anna?" she quizzed again. "What's your favorite?"

"Math," Anna replied with smiling eyes. "I enjoy figuring things out."

Aunt Patty Ann said, "Well, I am very impressed. Both of you like school and your Mom said you both make straight A's." She gave Anna's shoulder a quick pat.

Uncle Rick came up for air from wrestling with the boys. He glanced at his wife and then said, "Want to see what we brought you for Christmas?"

"Sure," we all squealed together.

"Well, let's go to the den. We left the bag there," Aunt Patty Ann offered. We all tried to get through the doorway at the same time while our favorite Aunt and Uncle laughed in delight at our enthusiasm. Anna and I finally stepped back and let the boys stumble through first. Uncle Rick took my hand while Aunt Patty Ann took Anna's. We followed the boys into the den. Mama and Papa quieted the boys by the time we arrived. Old Lad aroused from his sleeping spot from all the noise, whined a little and walked to the door. I instinctively opened the door for Lad to go outside.

A large burlap bag was sitting near the Christmas tree. Uncle Rick opened the bag as we sat waiting patiently on the floor. He began pulling brightly wrapped gifts from the bag. First, he gave Aunt Patty Ann a beautiful dark blue box. She immediately passed it to Papa. "This is for you, Ross," she smiled.

"Why, thank you. But you should save your money," Papa said turning a little red behind the ears. Next was a beautiful lemon colored box, even bigger than Papa's. She gave that to Mama.

"This is for you, Jan," she gave Mama a peck on the check.

Mama blushed and said, "I don't know what to say! Thank you."

Uncle Rick teased, "Let me see, I know we put more boxes than those in here, didn't we, Patty Ann?" This was one of the reasons why we loved him so. He was so funny and could keep us guessing forever.

"David, why don't you help me, by taking out that red box?" he said as David got up and with his mouth wide open, stuck his hands and head inside the bag and pulled out a medium size beautiful bright red package.

"This one?" he asked.

"Yes, that will do."

"But there's no name on it?" David said, looking for a name tag.

"Now, Tom, why don't you come over here and help us by taking out the green box?" Uncle Rick continued playing the game. Tom was on his feet immediately after hearing his name. He put hands and head in the bag and pulled out a dark green box about the same size of the red one.

"This one doesn't have a name, either," Tom said. Tom sat back on the floor as David slipped onto the couch between Mama and Papa with those big eyes shining.

"Anna," Uncle Rick continued, "Why don't you come over and see if you can find a striped box for me?" Anna needed no additional prompting. She reached her arm and hand into the bag and pulled out a beautiful white, green, and blue striped box decorated with a large green ribbon tied around the center.

"Lily, it's your turn," Uncle Rick smiled adding. "It's hard being the oldest, isn't it? It requires patience, but like your father, you have patience. You know, Lily, your father is my oldest brother."

I smiled and moved to the bag and gently pulled out a large pink and white box with a white and pink cloth ribbon neatly tied together on top. It was beautiful and definitely worth the wait. I slid back near Aunt Patty Ann. The box felt kind of heavy as my mind immediately began thinking of what it might hold inside.

There were no more packages in the bag. We all sat there boxes in hand ready to open, when Mama said, "Patty Ann, please take the two packages left under the tree. One has Rick's name on it and the other is for you."

Aunt Patty Ann did as Mama asked. She found knitted socks for Uncle Rick and a crocheted hat and mittens for herself. Mama had made hers in black with a small white thread going through the cuff of the mittens and the brim of the hat. She looked very sophisticated as she placed the hat on her head and pulled on the mittens. Uncle Rick said, "Well, what are you waiting for?"

We all ripped into the packages at the same time. The boys had each gotten a toy army rifle replica much like the one Uncle Rick used in combat. Theirs were made from wood and not real. Papa had gotten an army cap, also like his brother's, and a Swiss army knife that could be used for many things. Mama had received a beautiful yellow bed jacket to be worn over her nightgown. It was fuzzy material and would keep her warm on chilly nights. Anna had received a journal bound in real leather and some bows and hair clasps. She did not own a journal so she loved the gift. Aunt Patty Ann had given me a similar journal two years before and I still used it. I save it for recording special stuff.

I got a new book from the Nancy Drew Mystery collection. This made three books that I owned. Anna and I shared them but kept them up high on a shelf in the closet pantry so the boys could not get to them. I read them over and over, again and again. It was the best gift. After hugs and kisses, we went to the kitchen for dessert. The adults had coffee and we children had milk with our pie or cake.

There was plenty so we had a choice of which dessert we wanted. It was fun. After that, Mama asked us kids to get our chores done before dark. The weather was turning colder while snow and sleet sputtered down. We left the adults visiting in the kitchen, dressed in our chore clothes and headed for the barn.

The four of us worked hard and the chores were completed just in time to say goodbye to Uncle Rick and Aunt Patty Ann. We wouldn't get a chance to see him again before he shipped out to Germany. I tried to keep from crying as he held me tight and gave me a kiss, but tears welled up in my eyes. I still didn't fully understand the seriousness of the war and the danger it presented for my favorite Uncle. I just knew it broke my heart to tell him and

Aunt Patty Ann goodbye. They settled into the buggy. Aunt Patty Ann pulled the blanket around her to keep the weather at bay as they pulled away.

"Goodbye, goodbye." We all waved.

Mama and Papa changed into chore clothes. While they milked and fed cows and Pearl, Anna and I got supper ready. We had supper on the table when they returned from the barn. Supper tonight was left over vegetables and dressing from the Christmas dinner. With eating dessert earlier, not much was needed to satisfy even the hungriest mouths. Papa said the blessing, including a special prayer for his brothers fighting the war, and we ate. After finishing the main meal, Mama announced,

"There's still some dessert. Would anyone like some?" Papa declined and we went for small portions. Children never passed up dessert.

"Now get ready for bed," Mama suggested. "I'll get these dishes done and come in to say goodnight."

"Mama," Anna questioned, "You never told us about the surprise. Did you forget?"

Papa looked up from the table, but did not seem disturbed by Anna's question. Mama smiled, "No, we didn't forget. We were just waiting for the right moment. Papa got up and moved to stand just to the side and slightly behind Mama.

"We do have a special surprise to tell you about, but your Papa and I have decided to save that until a more appropriate time," Mama began. Papa picked up then continuing, "You know when I took your Uncle Rick to Grandpa's after church and thought I would only be gone a few minutes and that Aunt Patty Ann would ride back with us?"

He asked as we shook our heads together. "Well, something happened and the family got some bad news while I was there." Papa had our attention now—all four of us were standing quiet as could be, waiting.

"Your Uncle Eddie is a seaman, so he serves his country on a ship out in the Atlantic Ocean. The ship he was serving on got sunk yesterday by a German U-boat," Papa began.

"Uncle Eddie is dead?" I asked, tears welling in my eyes.

"Lily, we don't know that he was killed. There is some evidence of survivors."

Papa continued now as Anna sobbed, then Tom, then David. I tried to hold back the tears, but they streamed from my eyes while I struggled to muffle the sobs. Papa's voice sounded far away now.

"We are praying that Eddie survived, but for now he is 'Missing in Action.'"

"Who told you this, Papa?" I questioned with tears streaming and my voice quivering, unwilling to accept this tragic news.

"A naval officer came to give the news to Papa Howell and Mama Howell himself," Papa said. "He was there with Pastor Lawrence when your Uncle Rick and I arrived. So, Lily, we must take him at his word."

At that point Mama and Papa were bombarded with crying, hysterical children. Papa picked up both boys as Mama put one arm around Anna and the other around me. The six of us went into our bedroom together, followed by Skip and Lad close on our heels. The dogs did not know what was going on, but did not like us children crying. Skip and Lad whined and got as close as possible to the boys' bed as Papa tucked them in, quietly consoling each one. Mama got us girls settled down. She told us to keep Uncle Eddie in our prayers each night and that God would protect him and if possible might bring him home to us again someday. It would require a lot of faith, hope, patience, and love with many, many prayers, but she had faith in our praying for him each night. After she kissed the boys, Papa and Mama knelt in the middle of our bedroom that Christmas night and thanked God for giving the world His son, Jesus Christ, that we may all live in faith, peace, and love. He asked God to watch over Eddie and, if it was God's will, to bring Eddie home again someday. Amen.

Both boys, at the same time, asked if Skip and Lad could sleep in our bedroom tonight so they would be safe. Papa patted Tom's side of the bed first and Lad jumped onto the foot and lay down. Next, he patted a spot on the foot of David's side of the bed and called "Skip" who jumped up and lay down. Our parents gave each of us a kiss and left the room together, pleading for us to stay quiet and get a good night's sleep. The snow fell gently outside our window but each of us fell asleep in our own sorrow about Uncle Eddie being reported MIA.

We were too sad to be happy about the snow.

Chapter 15

The Surprise

Next morning, about six inches of snow covered the ground. However the clouds had lifted and it was clear to the west. The cold temperature would keep the snow from melting for a few days. It was just enough cover to give the appearance of a snow white blanket spread across the earth.

I was up early and went to the kitchen to find Mama and Papa already drinking coffee. "Morning," They each acknowledge my arrival and, I, acknowledged their presence as Mama took hot biscuits from the oven and cracked the eggs directly into the bacon pan. Hot bacon sat on the table. I washed my hands and sat the appropriate dishes on the table, then took my place near Papa, who reached over and gave my hair a gentle toss.

"Papa," I began. "Do you think Uncle Eddie has a chance of *not* being dead?"

"Lily, honey, why of course he does!" Papa reassured me. "They know some ships picked up men in the water after the ships went down. More than one ship was sunk and your uncle's name was not on the "killed in action" list, so he has a good fifty per cent chance."

"When you know for sure, will you tell us and not shelter us from the truth?" I asked.

"I promise I will," Papa said thinking to himself that his daughter had grown up mighty fast. Mama, for the first time in front of Papa, placed a steaming cup of coffee in front of me. I automatically added about half milk before raising it to my lips as Anna, Tom, David, and Skip with Lad trailing behind all came through the kitchen door.

Papa got up, opened the back door to the porch and motioned for Lad and Skip to go outside. They obeyed. Skip was an outside dog except for special times, and Lad knew he did not belong in the kitchen.

Mama placed the fresh breakfast onto the table before us. Papa said grace and we ate again. Breakfast was the most important meal of the day for getting farmers ready for hard work. It was also my favorite meal because you could eat even if you were not hungry. The smell of eggs, bacon, sausage, grits, oatmeal and biscuits would make anyone's mouth water uncontrollably.

"Mama, can we find out the surprise now?" Tom asked this time. Mama looked to Papa who shook his head in agreement.

"Papa and I have struggled with when to tell you," Mama began. "David, you are growing into such a big boy. Tom, you are getting big enough to help Papa do things like hunt, fish, and small chores. Anna, you are growing more every day. You are old enough and big enough now to cook and wash clothes with little guidance. Lily, you are so grown up. You can cook, clean this house as good, or better than me, and take care of your brothers and sister. Why there's not much you can't do." Mama's face was serious now.

Papa nodded in agreement with each thing she said. I don't think I ever heard Mama talk so serious before last night and the news of Uncle Eddie. My heart pounded loud within my chest. I hoped no-one could hear it. My imagination took off.

My first thought was Mama's ill. She must be going to die. She is getting us ready. Anna and I will need to take over and take care of the boys and Papa. My mind raced so fast, that I hardly heard the conclusion of Mama's message. "We are going to have another baby. It is due in a few months," she finished.

Tom and Anna clapped. Tom wanted another brother and Anna wanted a baby sister.

David was too young to fully understand. "I am the baby," he said.

"Lily?" Mama brought me back to earth. "Are you alright?" she asked. "You look a little dazed," she continued.

"Yes, Mama," I said trying to take everything in while keeping my fears in check. This family could not handle more bad news. The news of Uncle Eddie's MIA was almost too much to comprehend.

"Which would you like, Lily?" Mama was asking me.

"I don't really care," I said trying to sound cheerful. "Either one," I corrected. "It will be fun to have a baby again," I said trying to convince myself.

"Alright, then, off to play," Papa said as he gave each one of us a smack on the behind as we left the kitchen. "Tom, David, play inside the barn. It's too cold to be outside," Papa added.

"Can we play with our new guns from Uncle Rick?" They asked not to anyone particular and not expecting an answer as they scampered for the bedroom.

Anna and I removed the dishes from the table and began the washing up. The boys returned and put coats on before heading to the barn for their cowboy soldiers game.

I swept the kitchen floor, while Anna made the beds in our bedroom. She then moved to the living room and straightened the chairs, removed the ashes from the fireplace and laid a fresh fire. I swept the bedroom floor and joined Anna cleaning the living room finishing with sweeping that floor too. Mama and Papa had disappeared into their bedroom and closed the door. We could hear them talking behind the door but their voices were low and garbled and we could not make out the words.

We changed into work clothes and did not wait to be told to gather the eggs, feed the chickens, and mind the boys while they played in the barn. I took my new book and Anna took her new journal to the barn with us. We could spend some quiet time together while the boys played their games. The crisp wind cut into us as we did the outside chores quickly then retreated to the warmness of the hay in the loft.

The morning and afternoon passed quickly. After dinner of a bowl of Mama's soup made from leftover Christmas dinner, we were sent back to the barn for the afternoon. Papa came to the barn in the late afternoon and said Mama had a severe headache and asked if we girls would mind making supper. He said we had eaten so much yesterday that milk and bread should be enough. We still had dessert for us children to have a taste.

Anna and I did our nightly farm chores before going inside. Papa stayed in the barn with the boys and allowed them to assist him in milking Bessie and the other cows and feeding Pearl.

By the time they came inside, Anna and I had the table set, the cornbread cooked, and the desserts set out. I took the milk pail from Papa and strained the fresh milk into two clean gallon containers which he stored in the pans of water under the house. I kept enough fresh milk for our cornbread dinner that night. Papa later carried a bowl of milk with bread to Mama, who was still not feeling well. He said the strain of the last two days had been a little much for her in her pregnant condition.

Anna and I assured Papa that we would clean up from dinner and get the boys to bed. Anna and I would tell them stories until they fell asleep. He retired to the living room and we could see the candle burning and Papa reading his Bible. The boys had played hard so after one story by each of us, they were ready for sleep. We said prayers with them and then tucked them in for the night.

Later that night, I lay awake in the stillness of the night for a long time. Uncontrollable tears welled up in my eyes and dripped onto the pillow below. I was sad about the news of Uncle Eddie being MIA. And I felt guilty! I couldn't stop thinking of the fear that gripped me when I thought Mama was ill. The fear had been overwhelming. Where would we be if anything ever happened to Mama or Papa? I felt guilty and ashamed of my selfishness, but couldn't dismiss the fact that I felt that way. I prayed that God would forgive me for not wanting another little brother or sister. I remembered in church just a couple of weeks ago, in Thessalonians 1:16: "*God instructs us 'Be joyful always; pray continually; give thanks in all circumstances, for this is God's will for you in Christ Jesus.'*" I had been omitting reading my Bible lately and praying only my bedtime prayers. "I will do better on both of those," I vowed out loud to God.

Sleep evaded me long into the night. I prayed quietly for God's forgiveness and atonement for feeling selfish this

Christmas. Just, please God, bring Uncle Eddie home! I vowed to help Mama more without being asked. I thanked God for His gifts of my family and the new baby. Soon my tears dried and peaceful sleep came.

Part IV – New Year, New Hopes

CHAPTER 16

Mathew Paul Howell

CHRISTMAS VACATION from school zoomed by like a whirlwind. Classes resumed as the winter weather brought on ice and snow. School was cut short more days for bad weather in 1944 than ever in the history of Dry Valley School.

Farm chores still had to be done even in bad weather. It was too cold to tarry outside so the chores had to be done at rapid speed. We hurriedly fed the chickens and gathered the eggs with socks or mittens over our hands to keep our fingers from freezing. Papa spent more time than usual inside because of the cold temperatures, and Mama seemed frozen each time she came from milking our cows. Icicles formed on the eaves of the house and barn and hung from the edges—some as long as three feet. Temperatures stayed below freezing for days on end. The pasture was dotted with spots of frost each morning that looked like patches of snow from a distance. The cows and Pearl stayed inside the barn or in the closest pasture. Papa increased their hay portion of food, and he gave Pearl an extra bucket of corn about every third feeding. He wanted Pearl's energy to stay high in case we had a family emergency and he had to ride her in the colder weather.

Mama found us children under her feet with the weather being so cold and confining us to the house. She sent us to the barn to play when she had had enough of the boys' rough housing or pulling pesky pranks. We played in the hayloft and in the barn hallway. With the animals lingering in the hallway, the hayloft was the best place. Anna and I took our books to the hayloft to read. The boys took some of their toy soldiers, cars, and their flips that Grandpa Wingate gave them. They made a game out of shooting their flips at mice and occasionally a house wren that was perched on a high rafter near the barn's tin roof. We usually managed to stay in the hayloft a couple of hours before getting chilled and returning to the house. This usually gave Mama the break from us she needed to keep her sanity.

The most memorable events in the winter of 1943-44 were changes that became the focus of Americans with families serving in the military overseas. Papa bought a battery powered radio. Each night he and Mama would sit by the fire and listen for progress reports on the war in Europe. Papa prayed for an update on whether Uncle Eddie was dead or alive. The voices of news correspondents Edward R. Murrow and Lowell Thomas filled the household with instantaneous, coast-to-coast communication about the war and united the American population in a way never before possible. On Saturday evenings we children were allowed to listen to The Grand Ole Opry, live from Nashville, Tennessee.

General Dwight Eisenhower, commander of the American and Allied forces in Europe, had troops gathered in southern England anticipating a cross-Channel invasion to stop Hitler's army. Papa and Mama seemed very worried about Uncle Rick and had no further news about Uncle Eddie. He was still considered "Missing in Action." Uncle Rick was under General Eisenhower's command in the European/American forces while Uncle Eddie's ship was sunk in the Atlantic in December 1943 by a German U-boat. Several weeks after the ship sank, it was reported that her commanding officer, Commander Ron E. Kyes was lost in the battle. American forces were spread thin, but spirits were high and we fought beside Allied forces to stop the slaughter.

Papa kept reassuring us children that as far as Uncle Eddie goes, "No news is good news."

Our family still believed that Uncle Eddie was alive and somewhere in Europe, either being protected by whomever picked him up in the water or in a German consecration camp.

"Either way, when the war is over," Papa said, "our men will come home."

I often heard Mama and Papa speculating about when the war might be over. A black market had cropped up in some of the larger cities throughout America and people were illegally buying and selling food and commodities that were on ration. People with money could obtain just about any type of product they wanted from black market peddlers. Poor people often sold their allotment of commodities to get extra cash. Despite this, Papa thought President Roosevelt was doing a good job of keeping the black market under control. Papa said there were always a few people who would break the rules, no matter what. Generally, the American people accepted price controls and rationing as a necessary price for winning the war. Wartime was a good time for farmers. Hog production was at an all time high while products such as vegetables, fruits, and milk were also up. If you raised it, it would be bought. This resulted in better and more food production than Americans had enjoyed in recent pre-war years.

I overheard Papa discussing the war with Mr. Walsh one afternoon. They were saying that even though meat was rationed, consumers ate more meat during wartime than in peacetime. According to the newspaper, net farm income rose. Agricultural prices and land values were on the increase allowing farmers to pay off some overdue loans, save money, and achieve the highest living standards ever experienced by the agricultural sector of the economy. Papa said for the first time, "If things continue on the upswing, I won't have to ask the bank for 'seed money' this spring." He and Mama had saved since Christmas and with no foreseeable tragedy, they were in much better shape than last year. Mr. Walsh said his family was in the same situation. God had blessed the farmers of Dry Valley this year.

Papa believed that we would win the war. He was sure it was God's will that freedom ring and that both of his brothers would return home. Mr. Walsh had brothers serving in the war just like Papa. All in all, they had a lot in common.

February brought much of the same weather, sleet, snow and lots of time inside for us children. Mama stayed in her room more often now and it was all Anna and I could do to keep the house clean, watch our little brothers, wash and iron everyone's clothes, make the meals, and still get our homework done at night. Several nights, we both fell asleep at the kitchen table and Papa would wake us up to go to bed. Each morning brought the same routine. Anna and I fixed breakfast, fed the boys, gathered the eggs, and fed the chickens before running out the door for school. Papa helped by milking Mama's cows, feeding the mules and the other cattle, and washing up the breakfast dishes. We soaked the dried beans overnight and Papa started cooking them each morning, so we could have supper that evening.

We hardly saw Mama. This pregnancy was taking its toll on her. She stayed in her room more and more and Papa took trays in to her. I went in on the week-ends to clean their room. She looked very pale lying in bed. Sometimes she would sit in a chair and work on knitting baby things while I changed the sheets and swept the floor. I would then help her return to bed again. Papa had gotten Mrs. Bowman twice already. Mama almost lost the baby both times and was extremely weak. The last time, Mrs. Bowman had a hard time stopping Mama's premature bleeding. It was not time for the baby and Mama was not strong enough to survive giving birth at that time. Mrs. Bowman brewed special teas and had Mama drink them to build her blood. She came by every three days to check on us children and on Mama.

February crept by, hanging on like a lingering fog over a meadow with a cloudy sky above. Papa said one day at the end of the month, "That groundhog surely saw his shadow with all the bad weather." We were all beginning to get a little tired and a bit testy.

Mrs. Bowman stayed overnight the third time Papa went for her in early March. The winter weather had not let up. March was roaring in like a lion as the old folks say, but not only did it pack a strong breeze, the sleet and snow continued to fall in the valley.

Mrs. Bowman stayed with Mama for a little while, examined her belly and private parts and then sent Papa that afternoon to fetch Dr. Hayes. About eight o'clock that night, Papa and Dr. Hayes came through the door. Doc's 1943 Ford had stalled out in the water filled creek bottom with Papa and Pearl bringing him the rest of the way to the farm. The weather was miserable outside so Doc and Papa were both soaked.

Mrs. Bowman took the doctor's coat while he warmed himself beside the fireplace for just for a moment before taking his medicine bag and going in to see Mama. He asked Papa to wait outside with us children but asked Mrs. Bowman to bring him up to date about Mama's condition.

Papa asked Anna and me to get the boys to bed. Anna agreed to read to them until they fell asleep. With Papa's permission, we let Skip inside and he stayed on the floor beside the boys' bed. Lad was on his quilt in the living room near the fireplace. The cold wind whistled through the trees outside our bedroom window as rain mixed with snow continued to pelt the house.

Around midnight, Doctor Hayes came out to speak with Papa. I waited near the fireplace, sitting in the chair near Lad's quilt, where the old dog lay sleeping. I could keep wood on the fire easily from this position. As the warm fire blazing in the fireplace cast orange shadows on the wall from the dim light of the oil lamp, I prayed to God that Papa would let me stay. I wanted to hear about Mama from the doctor, himself.

Anna had fallen asleep while reading and was still with the boys, all three of them in the boys' bed. Papa glanced my way, but did not ask me to leave.

"Ross, Jan's condition is grave. Mrs. Bowman tells me she has been bed-ridden for about two months and almost miscarried two times." He looked deep into Papa's eyes while he stood beside his chair.

"That right, Doc. She has had a hard time since before Christmas." Papa shook his head as he spoke.

"How many children, Ross?" Dr. Hayes asked.

"Four. We have two girls and two boys," Papa said his voice breaking a bit.

"Well, here's the situation, Ross. The baby is breech, so I am going to need to use forceps to turn the body around so it can be born. A breech birth can be tricky, but if the baby and Jan cooperate, it should be okay with minimal bruising to the child and less damage to Jan."

Papa shook his head that he understood. Dr. Hayes continued,

"We have no choice. We have to do it. The problem is Jan is very weak from the loss of blood and being in the bed for so long. It will be touch and go. She won't have the strength to push much or for long periods of time. We need to pray for a quick birth."

Dr. Hayes looked over my way and said, "Are you the eldest?"

"Yes sir," I said as I moved from my chair and came to my Papa's side. He unconsciously placed his arm around my waist.

"Pray to God that he gives your Mama strength to pop this baby out quickly, okay!" he said as he patted Papa on the shoulder.

"Now," he said and paused, looking at me. "Lily."

"Sir," I said, without needing a prompt.

"Get me a full kettle of boiling water. And, when we are finished, I want a cup of good black coffee for your Papa, Mrs. Bowman, and me." Dr. Hayes smiled and I leaped at the opportunity to serve him and to help my Mama. I went to retrieve the hot water from the kitchen that Mrs. Bowman had heating on the stove in preparation for the birth. It was boiling.

Doc then turned to Papa and said, "Mrs. Bowman is a good midwife and she will help me. You just stay calm and pray. With God's help it won't take too long."

I got fresh bed linens and white towels from the pantry and swung them over my shoulder. Then, I carried the hot kettle into the room to Dr. Hayes and Mrs. Bowman. Mama was awake and very weakly said, "Thank you, Lily."

I stoked the fire, threw on another log while watching Papa read his Bible and silently mouthing the words of his prayers as we waited. Time slowly crept by as that log burned down and I threw another log on the fire. I went to the kitchen and began brewing a fresh pot of coffee, praying continually to keep my mind off what might be happening in the bedroom. Early in the morning hours, Mama screamed. I was on my feet as was Papa, then we heard the shrill cry of the newborn, then quietness.

Mrs. Bowman cleaned the baby up first. She removed the soiled sheets from the bed, handed them to me from inside the bedroom door and asked me to help her remake the bed. I left the soiled sheets on the floor and entered the bedroom.

Dr. Hayes was listening to Mama's heartbeat then checking her pulse as we rolled her to one side to change the bed sheets. Then, he and Mrs. Bowman rolled Mama to the clean side while I pulled and straightened the fresh sheets where she had been lying. She had a large towel under her backside with her gown covering most of her upper body but I could see small spots of blood slowly seeping through the towel. Mrs. Bowman passed the baby into my arms and asked me to allow my new little brother to suckle my pinky finger for a few minutes while she and Doc finished. She then gently pushed me with the baby in my arms through the door onto the breezeway and I darted into the fireplace room where Papa paced back and forth waiting. He pulled the small blanket back and looked at the infant while the baby sucked hard on my pinky finger. "Mrs. Bowman said it's a boy!" I offered although he looked very worried and not very excited about anything.

A few minutes later, Dr. Hayes stuck his head out and asked Papa to step in. Mrs. Bowman joined me and the baby a few minutes later, and the three of us went to the kitchen to make some sugar water for the baby. She showed me how to dip my finger into the warm liquid and then place it into the small baby's mouth. The baby would suck and suck and then cry and cry. Mrs. Bowman took the baby from me and headed back into Mama's room with the cup of sugar water in hand and the infant wrapped tightly with his head covered because the night air was cold. She did not want to take a chance that the baby might get sick from chill.

I poured three cups of coffee and placed them on the wooden tray Aunt Megan had given Mama last Christmas. Alongside the cups, I pour a creamer full of fresh milk and put the sugar bowl on the tray in the center of the cups. I gathered three spoons, lifted the tray, and walked back to the fireplace room where Papa and Dr. Hayes sat in chairs close together. I offered them coffee, which they both took. Dr. Hayes thanked me with his warm smile. Words were not necessary as I heard him tell Papa that Mama would be fine in a few weeks, but it would require some help from everyone, including the children and him. Dr. Hayes turned to me and then asked,

"Lily, are you a good student?" He flashed that gentle smile again.

Papa answered for me, "She's an excellent student—makes straight A's."

"Good," Dr. Hayes said. "I am going to give you a note for your teacher, Lily. I think she will allow you to miss a couple of months of school and make the work up later. Your mother is going to need you at home with her for at least two months, maybe longer." Then he turned to Papa and asked,

"What are the ages of your other children?"

Papa replied, "Anna's almost eight, Tom soon will be six and David is three and a half. Why do you ask?"

The doctor replied, "Ross, times are hard and I know you are just starting out farming and work long hours. If Lily cannot do all the work at home, I will write a note for Anna to be excused from classes too. I know the school will respect my medical recommendations and allow the girls to make up the work. If you want to give Lily a try first, you should hold Anna's note until you need it. I will leave the date blank, so you can fill it in, if that occurs. Perhaps Jan is stronger than I think and will bounce back much quicker and neither girl will be out of school long." With this said, he rolled his shirt sleeves down, pulled on his jacket, and went back in the room with Mama and Mrs. Bowman. Dr. Hayes and Mrs. Bowman both stepped from the bedroom and the midwife motioned for Papa and me to come in and whispered,

"She's pretty weak, Ross, so only stay a minute. Lily, she asked to see you too, so don't tire her out." Papa and I went into the bedroom together while Mrs. Bowman picked up her cup of coffee and she and Dr. Hayes sat on the chairs taking a nice warm sip. After tasting the black coffee, Mrs. Bowman added one sugar and milk to her cup, stirred it briefly and took a second sip.

They chit-chatted for a few minutes and Dr. Hayes finished the birth certificate with information Mama had supplied before the long delivery had begun. If it was a boy, the name would be Mathew Paul Howell. He was born March 4, 1944 at 2:15 am and was 19 inches long and weighed 8 lbs 2 ounces. He was a fine baby with Papa's long toes, dark hair, and blue eyes. He had a good set of lungs too, they laughed as they heard the cries from the bedroom and assumed that Mama had moved him to her other breast for feeding.

The doctor asked Mrs. Bowman to stop by every few days over the next two weeks to check on Mama and baby and to see how I was holding up with the work load. It was important to make sure Mama was sticking to her promise to allow the family to do everything but care for the baby with some possible mending, knitting or sewing after several weeks.

Papa and I came back into the room and Dr. Hayes told Papa that Paul was another fine boy to help him run the farm. Papa pulled his coat from the rack and put it on as he moved with Dr. Hayes toward the door. "Gosh, Ross," Dr. Hayes smiled, "Pretty soon you and Jan will have your own baseball team, if you keep going!" He laughed as he picked up his bag from beside the door and gave Papa a slap on the back.

Mrs. Bowman stayed with Mama and me while Papa returned Dr. Hayes to his car in the creek bottom. Mrs. Bowman and I gathered blankets from the pantry and made a bed for her on the floor near Lad's. I told her I could sleep with Anna and the boys so Papa could have our bed. That way Mama could get some rest. I removed the soiled bed linens and placed them on the floor in the pantry until the rain stopped. Then, I could wash them.

Papa came back into the room from delivering Doc to his car, which had started on the first crank. He was able to drive it out of the shallow water. Papa watched until he drove out of sight, then rode back to the farm, got Pearl settled for the night, and came inside. He left the lantern lit for Mrs. Bowman and me while we took a quick trip down the hill to the outhouse. Papa went in to say goodnight to Mama and Paul.

Once Mrs. Bowman and I returned, Papa took the lantern and blew it out. We all turned in for the night.

A few hours later, Anna and the boys woke me by squirming in the bed.

"What are you doing in our bed? Tom asked me looking rather upset. "I don't have enough room." He kicked his feet into my back.

"Please don't wake David up," I pleaded with Tom. "Anna fell asleep reading to you and I came to bed much later and crawled in with you because Papa needed a place to sleep. He's in our bed," I whispered trying not to appear tired or grumpy.

"But why?" Tom didn't sound pleased.

"If you will be real quiet and come to the kitchen with me, I'll tell you," I whispered again as I pulled a sweater over my nightgown and pulled slippers on to keep my feet warm.

Tom rolled out of the bed and put his shoes on without socks. He then followed me through the breezeway and into the kitchen. Burr-r, it was cold but dry. We managed to leave everyone else sleeping. Mrs. Bowman had already started a fire in the stove and coffee was perking on the burner. A pot of hot water sat on the other burner. "Tom, would you like some hot cocoa?" I asked knowing that it would only take a minute to make a cup of cocoa for him with the water hot and I could grab a cup of coffee for myself. I put some cocoa powder and sugar in the bottom of the cup, stirred in enough hot water to mix well, and then added milk to fill the cup. I poured myself a cup of coffee and added half milk. The two of us took a noisy slurp at the same time. Tom laughed and I did too.

Tom looked at me and asked again, "Where's Mama? Why is Papa in your bed and you and Anna in our bed?"

"Mrs. Bowman stayed on a pallet in our parent's bedroom. Dr. Hayes went home earlier this morning after Mama got better. Papa needed a bed and we could all fit in yours, so there you have it," I said as he finished his cup of cocoa and I took another drink of my coffee.

"I want to see Mama." He surprised me with this statement.

"We will have to ask Mrs. Bowman, first," I said as Tom started for the door. I decided not to fight this one and followed behind him. Lad met us at the door and came outside as we went in. Mrs. Bowman came out of Mama's bedroom to meet us.

"Morning Tom, morning Lily," she greeted us.

"I want to see Mama," Tom said pouching his lips out.

"She's resting now," Mrs. Bowman said adding, "She is very tired but I know she will want to see you all when she wakes up. Did Lily tell you, you have a new baby brother?"

"Wow! Just what I wanted!" Tom clapped his hands.

"I didn't tell him. 'Cause I figured he would want to see the baby too, so I thought I would hold off as long as possible," I said to Mrs. Bowman.

"Good thinking," she agreed. "After everyone is up and has eaten breakfast and your mother wakes up, then we will let you all see mother and baby. How's that?" She asked Tom as he swayed side to side.

About an hour later, we all crowded around the bed to see the new baby. Mama was half asleep and very tired. But, Mrs. Bowman picked Paul up and let each of us hold him for a few minutes. Then she placed him on Mama's chest and he snuggled close. He was not red this morning and had a head full of black hair that was almost long enough to braid. You couldn't help but love him as he sucked at nothing at all and his tiny hand latched onto your finger when you touched his small fist. "Go on now," Mrs. Bowman suggested.

"Your Mama needs her rest." She smiled as she shooed us from the room. She later came out herself with the remaining soiled towels and laundry that needed washing. I took them from her and would do the wash later.

The household was busy over the next few weeks with the daily routine of the new baby settling in. Paul devoured all of

Mama's attention. When she wasn't feeding or changing him, they were both asleep.

Anna returned to school but I took over Mama's work. At first it did not seem to be a lot more work than when Mama was feeling ill. Papa milked Mama's cows and did her share of the farm chores. Anna helped me in the afternoons after school. We took turns caring for the boys and baby and did the outside chores, made supper, and let Mama continue to rest. Tom took over my chicken feeding and egg gathering duties with Anna. Laundry increased a lot with baby clothes and loads of diapers, which took a lot of time. Mama suggested that I integrate the baby clothes into our white clothes. He had more diapers, shirts, blankets, etc. but they were small. Every Saturday was taken up with laundry. During the week I sometimes hand washed diapers and blankets and hung them on a rope strung across the pantry.

CHAPTER 17

Wash Day / Flying Jenny

MAMA WASHED OUR clothes using creek water from the pond during the months that rainfall was plentiful. She would have us kids gather wood for the fire and pile it around a big iron wash pot. Then she heated water for boiling the white clothes—bed linens, the baby clothes, blouses and shirts, underwear—everything white was boiled with lye and bluing to keep them snow white. Mama would shave her all-purpose soap and add it to the boiling water. With a long stirring handle made from a hardwood tree branch, she would stir the clothes and boil them for about twenty minutes, then she would transfer the clothes to a second iron wash pot with cold water. Here she used a rub board and scrubbed out any remaining stains. She used a large bar of her all-purpose soap and strong hands to accomplish this part of the wash. We had super white, clean clothes. She would transfer the clothes back to the first wash pot that had been refilled with water for rinsing. Then she would hang them on an aluminum wire line for drying using wooden clothes pegs to hold them in place. The same routine was followed with the rest of the laundry without the boiling step. She used cold water for washing colored clothes. Washing took the biggest part of a day for our family, but Mama made it fun for us.

Papa and Mama had created a playground near the cattle pond where Mama did laundry in the spring and early summer when rainfall was plentiful. Papa cut down a large birch tree that was located several feet into the woods but grew near the pond and close to Mama's wash area. The tree left a grand old stump standing about three feet off the ground. He created a seesaw on the stump, but it was different from your average home made seesaw. It was two rides in one. The ride was created by Papa loosely mounting a smooth board onto the stump. The board was made from half of the fallen tree. The joining was done by placing a large metal plow screw into the tree trunk with a washer on each side between the screw and the board. It would allow the board to move freely either up and down or side to side. It was called a "Flying Jenny" because you could use it as a seesaw or as a merry-go-round, depending on how you moved the board.

As a seesaw, four children could ride at one time, two on each end to balance. This part of the ride allowed one or two children, depending on their weight, to balance on each end of the long board fitted across the stump. Holders were placed far enough from the end of the board to allow the largest child to either hold on or to allow the youngest child to hold while the older child sat behind and held on with arms around the smaller child. Pieces of rawhide served as harnesses for the smaller riders. The rawhide was tied around the child's waist to keep the child from falling off when the ride was in motion. The ride would go up and down and was powered by feet of the older children. The child with the longest legs squatted down on the board and raised the other end up to the sky. By pushing off with your legs, the opposite end would rise and your end would be high in the air, hence the name seesaw. It was designed with an eight-foot board that allowed the opposite end to be raised about five feet. High enough to command a loud scream from the smaller children and a good lift off for the older ones. The seesaw was a lot of fun. Sometimes the neighbor kids would play with us on it when their families came for water from the spring well.

Most farms had a seesaw for their children to play on. But Ripple Creek was the only farm with a "Flying Jenny". Papa designed and made the jenny himself by using a giant water wheel platform mounted to the stump. Papa had inserted a large bolt that allowed the board to turn counter clockwise. The water wheel platform was very hard to find. Grandpa Howell bought the water wheel from a traveling man who bought and sold farm machinery. Grandpa gave it to Papa. He tucked it away in the barn until he found the perfect use for it. Papa had once seen a Flying Jenny at the state fair. The design stuck in his mind until he began making our seesaw/Flying Jenny.

Papa decided to see if he could duplicate the design he had seen. It was a big hit with all the kids in the neighborhood. The jenny part of the ride was designed for two children to run as fast as they could while hanging onto to the side of the board by using the holders. A jenny captain was appointed between the two children riding the jenny. Once both of them were running as fast as they could, the captain signaled to let his partner know when to simultaneously swing themselves up onto the board. Force of gravity and weight would continue to pull the jenny around for several fast turns—as you hung on for dear life—and a few slow ones like a merry-go-round. To continue the game, the process was repeated, sometimes for hours, until participants got tired. It was one of our favorite things to do while Mama did the wash.

We had gathered the wood for today's wash. Mama got the fire burning and the water boiling. She put the bleach and soap into the big pot and stirred the pot of clothes as if they were beans cooking on the stove. Her long stirring pole, made from a young oak sapling tree with the bark removed, gave her space to stand away from the fire at a safe distance so she wouldn't burn herself.

Baby Paul slept peacefully on the quilt while Skip lay next to him keeping watch. Being almost four months old, baby

Paul did a lot of sleeping, a lot of eating, and a lot of pooping. However, he was beginning to be more fun and would laugh and coo when anyone talked to him. He would also squeal and giggle when you tickled him. He could roll over and could push himself up on his knees, but he could not crawl. Mama said he was an advanced little boy for his age. His blue eyes sparkled when you placed a toy in those tiny chubby hands. The toy immediately then went into his mouth. You couldn't help but love him. It was hard to imagine our life without baby Paul. It was hard for me to believe that I selfishly had not wanted another baby in our lives. Babies required a lot of work but were so much fun.

When baby Paul got fussy, Mama stopped stirring the pot. She let me stir while she fed and changed him. If he wasn't hungry and only needed changing, then I did it without disturbing Mama. If he started crying while she was rubbing clothes on the rub-board she would let me finish rubbing the white clothes while she fed Paul. Mama asked me if I'd like to try my hand at the rub-board. It was the first time I had tried to use a rub-board. It was hard work. I learned why Mama was always extra tired on wash day. All of Mama's chores were hard and time consuming, but I think washing clothes was the hardest one she had. That's why her hands were always red, rough, and raw particularly in the winter when she did the wash outside in the cold weather. In the winter, Mama's hands chapped so badly they sometimes bled from putting them in hot soapy water filled with bleach and lye and then in cold water to rinse the clothes. You could tell how painful they were, but Mama never complained.

While I helped Mama, Anna, Tom, and David played on the seesaw. Tom and David rode one end while Anna balanced them by riding the other end. Tom and David had both grown taller over the past year; but David had gained some weight as well. They wanted to seesaw without Anna. She patiently stood back on the end David was riding in case she needed to catch him should he fall. She was pleasantly surprised to see that he was almost as tall as his older brother. David was a bit heavier than Tom, but Tom was still a few inches taller than David.

After about half an hour of supervising the two of them, Anna felt it was safe to leave the boys on their own to seesaw and came over to help me and Mama with Paul and the laundry. Mama and I had finished washing the whites and the colored clothes were now in the wash pot. Anna plopped down on the quilt and began playing with baby Paul. Mama leaned back on the quilt and closed her eyes. We both knew she was tired. Paul fell asleep as did Mama. Anna and I stayed quiet, each of us in our own little world with our private thoughts as the boys continued to chit chat and squeal occasionally from the seesaw.

It was a beautiful day with the lazy old sun moving ever so slowly across the July sky. A nice breeze floated gently, ruffling the clothes on the line and swirling the smoke away from the wash pot. The fire was dying out so it was time to finish the dark clothes. They would have lots of time to dry before nightfall, if we got them on the line quickly.

"Anna," I whispered as I slowly got up from my sitting position on the quilt. "Why don't you help me with the dark clothes while Mama naps. We can surprise her when she wakes up."

Anna shook her head yes and rose immediately. Together we began to remove the clothes from the first pot to the rubboard. Anna had never used the board before, so I showed her how to remove any stains that were still on the clothing. She caught on quickly. She wanted to rub so I rinsed, rung them out as dry as possible, then hung them across the aluminum wire to dry. It was mostly the boys' short pants and Papa's work pants and shirts. Anna and I each had a jean skirt and a pair of jeans in the wash. Mama had a couple of house dresses and a jean skirt in the wash also. We were finished in no time flat.

With the laundry finished, Anna and I took the soiled water and doused the fire under the wash pot as Mama normally did. We then emptied the other water and turned the pots over on a couple of stakes that were driven into the ground to hold the pots in place until we needed them again.

"What now?" Anna smiled as we both glanced over at the seesaw where Tom and David continued to go up and down.

"It should be about time for dinner," I said. "We could get everything out of the basket and set up while Mama is napping." Anna shook her head in agreement. Mama always packed a good dinner for us on wash days. Biscuits, left over fried chicken or pork chops, carrots, green onions, cucumbers, and some cookies would round out the dinner. We had melamine plates, glasses, and cloth napkins. It was one time we would skip milk as it would spoil in the hot sun. Kool-Aid was a special treat for us kids on wash days. Mama kept the Kool-Aid in a gallon jug, fastened it to a twine string tied to a large stake, and submerged it in the edge of the pond until someone was thirsty.

Anna and I together removed the picnic quilt from the top of the basket and spread it onto a flat area near the quilt where Mama, baby Paul, and Skip lay napping. Skip lifted his head, but did not make a sound or move as we began to spread out the food in the center of the quilt. Anna went to the edge of the pond and removed the Kool-Aid from the cooling spot in the edge of the pond. Tom and David continued to seesaw nearby. I spread the large towel from the bottom of the basket over the food to keep flies and insects from it. Then Anna and I sat down to wait for Mama and baby Paul to wake up.

A few minutes went by. Soon Tom and David spotted Anna and me sitting on the ground with the food spread on the quilt. They were off the seesaw as quickly as a bird could shake its tail feathers and scampered down the rise from the play area to the flat area near the pond where we had set up.

"Can we eat dinner?" David asked as they jumped onto the edge of the quilt. Tom was right beside him.

"Go wash your hands in the pond," Anna commanded as Mama stirred on the quilt nearby. The boys darted off to the edge of the pond without arguing. Mama opened her eyes and sat upright. Baby Paul was still sleeping, but Skip raised his head and began wagging his tail.

"I must have dozed off," Mama said as she slowly got up from the quilt. She looked around and saw that we had completed the wash.

"What a wonderful surprise," she smiled looking at us.

"Anna helped me finish the wash," I said.

"Yeah," Anna began. "Lily taught me how to rub clothes on the board." She smiled at the accomplishment. "It was really neat to see the stains come out."

"Good," Mama replied. "Thanks to both of you—and you put out dinner." She looked at the food on the quilt and the Kool-Aid sitting on the edge. "How long did I sleep?"

"Only about half an hour," I replied. "You were tired."

"How about I let you all go for a swim after dinner?" Mama asked just as the boys came back from washing up at the pond.

"Wow!" David squealed. "I get to seesaw without help and go swimming all in the same day. I like wash days!"

We all laughed to see David so happy. We seated ourselves on the edge of the quilt. Mama said our dinner prayer and we began to eat the feast Mama had prepared for us. The food tasted so good.

After we all ate our fill and fed Lad and Skip, Anna and I carefully put everything back inside the picnic basket. We then folded the towel and quilt and placed them on top.

Baby Paul began wiggling and squirming on the quilt. Checking his diaper, I found that it was wet and changed him. He was happy again as I lifted him into my arms and began to point out birds and leaves on the trees. Baby Paul cooed like he understood every word I said.

The boys were near the pond tossing rocks into the water. Mama cautioned them to watch for snakes in the tall grass nearby. Anna went over and began playing with them, challenging them to a game of rock tossing. Mama came over to the quilt and sat beside me and baby Paul. She looked really tired. The breeze gently rustled the leaves in the trees, but it was still hot. Looking at the sun, Mama commented it must be about two o'clock in the afternoon.

Some dark clouds were gathering in the western part of the sky.

"Looks like rain," Mama commented. "I hope the laundry gets dry before it comes."

"Mama, why don't you lie back and rest your eyes, I'll watch baby Paul. You look tired," I coaxed as I rubbed Paul on the back and he cooed as if to second my suggestion. I then positioned Paul over my shoulder and began swaying back and forth, rocking him gently.

"Just for a minute," Mama said. "Then you can go swimming with the others and I'll take the wash down."

Mama went on as she closed her eyes. She fell asleep immediately. I watched a few minutes as her breathing became regular. Baby Paul fell asleep on my shoulder and soon I had him nestled on the quilt close to Mama. Skip took his place on the quilt on the other side of Paul. I slowly moved from the quilt and looked up into the sky to survey the clouds. I saw some puffy cumulus clouds gathering in the western part of the sky. We had studied cumulus, stratus, and cirrus clouds in science so I could detect what they mean. The cotton candy looking ones were cumulus and the other stratus clouds were like thick blankets over parts of the sky. Looking to the eastern part of the sky, another batch of nimbostratus clouds gathered with long "mane's tails" rolling over and over. These clouds meant rain was approaching from a distance. Although the thunder heads or cumulonimbus clouds had not started to rumble to warn us of the approaching bad weather, it would only be a matter of time before they arrived. I prayed silently for the wash to get dry as I moved from the quilt to check how damp the clothes were. I removed the driest ones from the line and folded them for the basket. Only a few heavier pieces remained when Mama woke. She stood up, looked up into the sky and came to help me. Mama called to Anna and the boys over her shoulder to dry off and get ready to run for the house. A rain storm was headed our way.

Mama had not studied the clouds in school but had a keen instinct and knew it was going to rain. Anna and Tom came and began to help us. David sat down on the quilt beside Paul. Some of the clothes were still damp and would need to be hung up inside the house once we had them safely in out of the rain. Lad sat on his hunkers watching the cloudy sky while Skip walked back and forth beside the quilt as if he were protecting the younger children from the clouds.

Together we made it back up the hill and inside the house before the rain drops began falling. They began falling gently from the sky and then came down in large sheets of rain. The cloud would lighten up and the rain would stop briefly, but then it came down hard again.

Papa came through the kitchen door and took the towel from the rack inside. "Boy, we are getting a soaker," he snorted, blowing his nose at the same time he talked. "I put the mules in the barn, but I will need to go put everything away later when the rain slacks off. Nothing left to do in the fields, but I can work on arranging some of the tools and supplies in the barn if the rain continues more than today. It will be time well spent."

"We barely made it to the house with the wash," Mama said. "The clouds came up very quickly. Anna, would you and Lily mind hanging the clothes that are still damp on the line in your bedroom? They should be dry by tomorrow."

"Okay, Mama," Anna replied as I had already moved the basket of wet clothes to our bedroom for that purpose. Both boys followed us into the bedroom. They sat on the floor and began playing with toy cars and trucks. Anna and I worked quickly to get the wash strung on the line to dry.

Mama and Papa drank coffee while Papa ate his dinner. The boys grew tired of the cars/trucks game after a short period of time, crawled onto their bed, and fell sound asleep. Anna and I both rested on our pillows and read for a short time before we too fell into a deep sleep.

Mama came and woke us around four o'clock. She suggested that we do our chores outside as soon as possible. Since we had such a wonderful picnic while washing, she would make a fresh pan of cornbread and we could have a supper of bread and milk tonight. That suited us fine. She aroused the boys and they kept her company in the kitchen while Papa and us girls did the evening chores. It was an early evening for the Howell clan. The rain made it just right for a good night's sleep.

CHAPTER 18

Spring Time

I MANAGED THE HOUSE while taking care of Tom and David. Papa was busy with spring planting and was behind in his work. He took some of the money he and Mama saved and purchased a new mule, a second double plow to produce a wider row, another harness for the two mules, and two baby calves to add to Mama's milk cows. The new mule would let him use double plows again. Papa prepared the fields for planting new crops in a record breaking four week romp. During this time, he had worked sunrise to sundown, six days a week, falling into bed late at night too tired for anything else.

Papa was a good three weeks behind in planting and the growing season was in full bloom. After he talked with Mama one morning, he sent Anna's note to Mrs. Parnell. Anna would stay home from school and she would take over Mama's duties that she could manage and I would begin working in the fields alongside of Papa. Papa thought girls didn't need much education. We could read, write, and work math. What more did girls need? Papa did not see a problem in pulling us from school. I overheard some of their conversation from the bedroom while cleaning the living room. Papa said, in hindsight, he should not have spent the money except on the mule, the other stuff could have waited. He would not be able to recoup his money if he sold the things he had bought now because everyone had their equipment for the year. If he did not have a good crop, we would not be able to pay the bank in the fall. Mama agreed for Papa to take Anna out of school.

Mrs. Parnell dropped by after school at the end of the second week and left books, paper, and pencils for Anna and me to continue our school work.

On Sundays, Papa continued to listen to the radio for war news, read his Bible, and prayed to God for the country and peace. Each day, the routine was the same. Papa and I left the house at sunup with both mules hooked to the plows and bags of seedlings to be planted. Some days we took biscuits and ham for dinner and did not come home until sundown. We drank water from the closest point of Ripple Creek near whatever field we happened to be working in. The weather was good. Showers occurred during the night hours and never too much to keep Papa and me from working in the fields. Some mornings I was so tired that I prayed for rain. God was smiling on the farmers in Dry Valley. Sunday became my favorite day. I helped Anna with the house work and cleaning on Sundays, which was almost a vacation day for me. Papa continued to keep Sunday as a day of rest and church going. Mama managed the strength to attend church for the first time about a month after giving birth to Paul.

By late-April, Papa had the field crops laid by, corn growing in the fields in rows free of weeds, and tiny cotton plants growing a little each day. The garden vegetables were flourishing in the ground, with beans beginning to climb the birch poles Papa and I had placed beside each plant. Although we planted about a week later than most everyone, our plants were thriving.

Papa realized how valuable I was to him as a field hand. I worked hard and learned quickly. He taught me to check the fences and together we mended them as needed. Tom and David were growing in height and responsibility. They had raised two new calves by bottle until weaning time, while Anna worked in the house and I worked in the fields.

We had seventeen new baby calves at Ripple Creek that spring. Papa had increased our cattle herd during the winter months, and all the new cows had delivered fine babies. Even our two sows had delivered large litters of baby pigs. We had a total of eighteen baby pigs and so many new baby chickens, it was impossible to count them all. Springtime was good at Ripple Creek. Work was never finished. Some days, Papa, Anna, Tom, and me wished we could make three of ourselves. Even David fed the chickens and the calves and helped Tom slop the pigs, but the increase in the amount of work was staggering. It left very little time to make up schoolwork now that we no longer attended school. Anna and I began to use the lamp in our room less and less to complete schoolwork before going to sleep. We dragged ourselves into bed at night and slept through to morning.

Five o'clock in the morning came early. I got dressed and woke Anna at fifteen minutes past five. I brewed coffee in the morning and took a cup to Mama and Papa, drinking half a cup myself before tackling other chores. Since the spring crops were growing, I took most of the barn work over again. I fed the baby calves and pigs and checked on the other animals and put out fresh hay for them.

Anna was right behind me. Her morning chore was to gather the eggs. She usually finished gathering the eggs as I completed feeding the animals. We then rushed back to the house and prepared breakfast for everyone. One morning, as I poured my coffee, I poured a second cup, added half milk and set it in front of Anna. Her eyes widened as she smelled the coffee in a deep inhaled breath before putting the cup to her lips and drinking the caramel liquid.

"Good, isn't it?" I asked, remembering Mama's words to me.

We always had breakfast together as a family before Papa and I headed to the fields and Anna began the household chores. Some days, I stayed behind to help Anna with the housework before going to the field in the afternoons with Papa. Our spring harvest was looking good.

The last weeks before the end of the school year, the farm children were let out at noon so they could help their parents in getting the spring crops in. Sons of the local farmers were needed at home. School would be out for summer at the end of the second week in May. Mrs. Parnell dropped by the house after school one afternoon to check on Mama, new baby Paul, Anna, and our progress on the schoolwork. She visited with Tom and David too. Tom would be in school in the fall with us girls, but David had two years to go. We gave her the work that we did during the first few weeks at home before the chores took up all of our time. She looked it over and told Mama that she could pass both of us to the next level. After hugs all around, Mrs. Parnell said goodbye.

Papa and Mama were happy. The first of the summer crops were ready for harvesting and a letter arrived from Uncle Rick. He wrote stories of sitting in his fox hole and listening to the sound of night. However, spirits were high and he and his friends wanted the war to end so they could come home to family. There was no word from or about Uncle Eddie. His wife and family chose to stay in Florida where she had a job.

Tom and David had both grown about a foot and little Paul was a chubby four months old who had a good disposition. He hardly ever cried and was happy whenever anyone held him. All in all, he was a very good baby. Mama's health was getting better. Three months free of the stress of household chores, managing family, and field work had provided her with opportunity to work on her stamina. Tom and David had surprised her by taking charge of watching Paul when she put wash on the line or needed to do an errand outside. They were willing to help with little brother.

Papa and I had a bumper crop of beans, peas, turnip greens, collard greens, cabbage, onions, and radishes. We loaded the wagon up with fresh vegetables each Friday morning and Papa headed for Dry Valley to the farmers' market. Papa came back with an empty wagon each week and money jingling in his pocket. Papa gave us each twenty-five cents a week to spend with Mr. Parnell the peddler. We felt rich. Sometimes we bought ice cream and sometimes a bag of penny candy and had money left over. The choice was ours. I saved most of my money and before the summer was over, I had $3.00 tucked away in a money jar stored under my bed. Mr. Parnell was coming that day and I wanted to buy a special rattler for baby Paul. After all, I did not need the money, so I opened the jar and emptied the coins in my apron pocket while waiting for the peddler's truck.

Mama asked me to rearrange the hay bales in the crib room of the barn so she would know how many cans would fit and how much space she would have for the new crop. She would then know how much she should plan to sell to Mr. Parnell. I forgot all about the coins in my pocket and was a bit annoyed at this sudden project. I stomped to the barn and began the chore.

Tom and David showed up and offered to help. They had been in the woods practicing shooting with their flips and saw me in the barn.

"Sure thing, I would love the help," I accepted. They helped me move the canned goods out into the center of the barn one jar at a time. We went to work and had the jars removed to the barn floor in no time. We did not have a lot of goods remaining from last harvest so it did not take long. I then restacked the hay bales as they were too heavy for Tom and David and let them hand the food jars back to me and I restacked them, so we could see what we needed before taking the jar down. However, moving the bales of hay was heavy work and almost too much for me. I did not realize that David was standing in the door when I attempted to move a large hay bale from the upper stack to the floor of the food crib. I used the hay tongs and grasped the bale of hay with all my strength and pulled it full force. It was too heavy and fell to the floor knocking David out the door onto the barn floor. David hit his head against a post used to step-up to the floor of the crib as he fell.

I screamed and David shrieked in pain as blood trickled down the side of his head and toward his eyes. Tom and I both jumped to the floor and I sat down and pulled David into my lap. Tom took his handkerchief from his pocket and handed it to me. "Get some water—get me Pearl's drinking bucket," I said to Tom as David opened his eyes and started crying. Tom got the bucket and I quieted David.

"Shush now. You have a shiner but you are okay. This will feel cool but will not sting," I continued as I wet the handkerchief in the water then squeezed small amounts onto the cut.

"Mama's gonna be mad," David said concerned for us.

"Nay, she won't," I said, not convinced myself. "It was an accident and we didn't break anything except your head." At that, David laughed! Tom and I joined in. I sat in the dirt with David's head in my lap while Tom stood over us giggling and laughing.

David scrambled to his feet. I got up from the ground, brushed my backside with my hands, and got back into the food crib to finish the work. The boys leaned against the side of the barn while I opened the bale of hay and scattered it about the crib to provide cushioning for the canned food. We quickly returned the canned jars back to their proper place. I counted thirty cans of food remaining. The boys and I headed for the house just as Mr. Parnell pulled up in his truck. We raced to meet him as Anna came outside just in time to board the truck.

Mr. Parnell had the perfect gift for baby Paul, a blue rattler with a silver rocking horse painted on the side. It cost a whole dollar. I would have money left over. I took nothing for myself, but took the rattler and put my hand deep into my apron pocket to retrieve the $3.00 I had saved. I pulled the coins out to find I only had $.75 in total. I had lost the coins while working in the hayloft and during the excitement of David's accident. I told Mr. Parnell what happened and he said he would give me credit for the other twenty-five cents until I earned it from Papa. I thanked him, took the rattler and left the truck with my siblings.

Papa sold twelve of the calves and sixteen pigs from the litters. Prices of both pork and beef were the highest they had been in five years. Papa told me he wished he had a hundred calves and two hundred pigs to sell. If he had those, he could pay off the balance of the mortgage and add another room to our house. Instead, he was happy for the blessing he had and paid the mortgage on the farm. The addition to the house could wait a while longer. Besides, baby Paul slept with Mama and Papa so we didn't really need another room.

One rainy afternoon in mid July, Mr. Walsh came by to see Papa. Anna, Tom, David, and I were all playing in the hayloft. Mr. Walsh rode his horse into the barn's open doorway. He wore a waterproof cape. Papa dashed from the kitchen to greet him. "Hello, Ross," Mr. Walsh called.

Papa nodded and replied, "What brings you out in this storm, John?" as he removed his slicker and shook the drops off. Mr. Walsh stepped down from his horse, removed his cape, shook it hard, and placed it on a large hook on the barn wall. Then he lit a cigarette, and offered Papa one. Papa and Mr. Walsh lit up before the conversation began again.

"I'm just so tired of being cooped up every afternoon with all the rain. I had to get out for a while. Hope you don't mind me coming over," Mr. Walsh said as he took a drag on the cigarette.

I put my finger to my lips, motioning for Anna, Tom, and David to be quiet as I crept a bit closer to the opening in the hayloft. I crouched on my knees then lay flat on the hayloft floor. The others followed my direction and soon we were all silently lying near the opening in the hayloft. From this position, we could hear the conversation almost as clear as being in the barn with them.

"John, you are welcome anytime," Papa replied. "Do you think the rain is ever going to stop?"

"I don't know, but we really need to get back into the fields. I am about a good week behind now," Mr. Walsh commented. "Martha and I have saved some money, so I think I might buy one of those new tractors to get caught up when the rain stops."

Papa replied, "I have been reading about them. They say you can plow a field five times faster with a John Deere then with four good mules. That would really be a blessing to get the work done that fast. I can't afford it, but if you can, I think you should buy one. With the rationing of gasoline for farmers somewhat relaxed, you could finish your work in a fifth of the time it takes now. Plus you have so much more land than a small farmer like me. You've got to keep up with the times, don't you think, John?"

"Thanks, Ross. I guess I just wanted another opinion on the matter before I made the leap. I tried talking with Martha about it, but she doesn't understand farm work. We have farm hands that do our outside work that Jan and the kids do for you. She didn't say no, but she wasn't much help either. I guess I just needed to hear it from a hard working friend, like you," Mr. Walsh replied as the rain began to slow to a drizzle.

"I'll be going up to Huntsville tomorrow afternoon to see a Farm-All and a John Deere," Mr. Walsh replied as he pulled his cape back on over his clothes. "If it's raining, would you like to ride with me? It would take about four hours out of the afternoon. Can't do much in the rain anyway and you could pick up some literature on them for yourself. I'll be taking my car, so we can stay dry. Besides, I could use your level head to help me make up my mind, Ross. I would appreciate it if you could come."

"I guess it wouldn't hurt to go with you. Let me check with Jan to make sure she doesn't need me to help with the kids. Stop by on your way and I'll be ready. You are right, not much can be done in the rain. Lily restacked the hayloft and got the barn ready for new canning this fall. All my plows are sharpened and the mules are shoed so there is nothing more that has to be done right away. You bet. I would love to ride along and see these new farm machines. What time are you thinking?" Papa shook Mr. Walsh's extended hand, then gave him a slap on the back. Scratching his head, Papa watched as his neighbor mounted his horse as a light drizzle continued.

"How about ten o'clock, if it's raining. That will give us enough time to get back and do evening chores before dark," Mr. Walsh said as he moved his horse out of the barn and started down the road. The sky cleared and the drizzle stopped, leaving everything drenched.

Just as Mr. Walsh got to the end of our lane, Tom scampered down from the hayloft with the rest of us following. "Papa," he blurted out. "Are you going to buy us a tractor?"

"What have you kids been doing? Eavesdropping on my conversation with John Walsh?" Papa grinned. "Nah, son, I can't afford a tractor. Besides I have two hard working mules and Lily. They'll get the work done for us, if it ever stops raining." He ruffled Tom's hair and we all started for the house.

Papa and Mr. Walsh made their trip to Huntsville and Mr. Walsh bought a bright green John Deere tractor for his farm. He also got a nifty plow, a hay combine, and a contraption called a sprayer that looked like a big spider with six legs. Mr. Walsh told Papa that in the fall, if Papa would plant his rows three feet apart rather than the normal two, he would help Papa with the tractor when his own work was finished. Papa was so excited for Mr. Walsh's good fortune to have money to purchase new farm equipment to make his work easier, more efficient and five times faster.

The next Sunday, our church had its summer harvest festival, the yearly event held at the end of school to celebrate summer crops and give thanks to the Lord for his blessings. This festival was smaller than the fall celebration, but it was still fun for everyone. Neighbors had a chance to visit with friends they had not seen often during the winter months. Children and young adults had a chance to play games and hang out and visit with friends. Everyone in our community was at the church that day. The church harvest festivals were rivaled only by the county fair, which came to Dry Valley each fall.

Each family brought several dishes of food, mostly new vegetables from the crops we were celebrating. After Sunday church service, large tables were placed under the trees. Fresh vegetables from the early crops were my favorite. Large platters of fried chicken, roasted pork chops and pork tenderloin, braised pot roast and New York strips with brown gravy overflowed other platters on the massive main table. Another table had Kool-Aid, sweet tea, coffee, milk, and water to drink. Another table had desserts, breads and silverware, glasses, plates, and cloth napkins.

Some families brought folding chairs, but most just brought quilts to spread on the grass to sit while eating. After Pastor Lawrence prayed over the food and asked for God's guidance and continued blessings, children were allowed to eat with friends, if they chose, and families moved about to visit with others during their main meal or to have a drink and dessert after the meal. Everyone enjoyed the fellowship.

After the summer harvest, the weather became more unpredictable. Dark clouds gathered in the afternoons many days bringing heavy thunderstorms with torrential rains. Most of the summer crops had been gathered, but the land needed to be replanted for a full fall harvest. Crop rotation allowed the farmers to get two full crops in per year. Papa and our neighbors were beginning to get worried if the rain would cut their fall growing season short.

Each afternoon Papa would seat himself near the fireplace and read from his Bible. He would then gather us together and discuss the verses he had read and close with prayer. My favorite during this time was Psalm 25:4: *"Show me your ways, O Lord, teach me your paths, guide me in your truth and teach me, for you are God my Savior, and my hope is in you all day long."* I loved the Psalms section of the Bible. To me it was poetry in motion pointing out ways to live our lives. Papa was more serious these days and we children were quieter. We were cooped up in the house or sent to the barn during the rainy part of the day.

As the rains continued, the creek bottom at the end of the lane leading to Ripple Creek began to flood with the water rising a little more each day. It was difficult for wagons and horses or mules to cross. Some of the crops were flooded in the fields. With water standing between the rows, hot sun could literally cook the plants where they stood in the water.

Papa continued to read and to pray saying many times that we needed Noah's ark to survive the flood.

CHAPTER 19

Mr. Jeremiah

GRADUALLY THE CLOUDS cleared and the sunshine was bright over the valley. The rains had stopped. Some crops suffered damage but for the most part they survived the rain. Surviving plants grew bigger and better. Field corn grew sweeter. Melons were bigger and juicier, tomatoes bigger, beans longer, onions sweeter, carrots and radishes plumper, squash and other vegetables grew hardier. The rains came and stopped at the right time allowing sufficient time to complete the work in the fields. We were blessed, according to Papa and Pastor Lawrence, not only as farmers but as a nation while the war continued in Europe and other parts of the world. Our soldiers were winning, but slowly. Still no word from Uncle Eddie so Papa's family no longer spoke of the celebration they would have when he returned home as hopes for that homecoming dimmed when days passed with no news.

Days turned into weeks and weeks went by quicker than a jack rabbit chased by Skip. Lad, however, had slowed down during the rainy months; he was getting old and feeble, hardly leaving his pallet near the fire in the damp weather.

One day in late summer, Papa was pulling weeds from the sweet corn in the field closest to Mr. Jeremiah's house. He had taken his dinner to work that day since I was helping Anna in the house and would not join him until early afternoon. Since the rainy season, the weeds were growing higher than the corn in some of the fields. It was a slow process to remove each weed by hand, but Papa, with my help, was up to the task. His sweet corn crop was the best in years and it was not the time to let the straggly weeds squeeze out the fresh corn plants. The other fields were laid-by just biding the growing time and waiting for harvest. Late summer was in full swing with hot weather and unbearably high humidity. Southerners called this time of the year, "the dog days of summer."

Papa worked hard that morning, stopped to rest and eat his dinner around noon. He noticed that Mr. Jeremiah was not sitting in the big rocker on his front porch. He decided to investigate. He took his dinner pail and went to the front of the Smith home. He called, "Hello." Not getting an answer, he knocked on the front door. The two big rockers on the front porch were vacant. A big Persian cat sat lazily in the sun close to the end of the porch. She opened a lazy eye and after stretching came over and rubbed against Papa's leg.

Mr. Jeremiah 305

He stooped down and scratched her behind the ears. Cats like to be scratched. Still no answer right away, so Papa knocked a little louder. Then he called out "Mr. Jeremiah, are you in there? It's Ross Howell. Just want to say 'hello.'" Papa heard the shuffle of his feet across the floor as Mr. Jeremiah came to the door. He opened it and smiled at Papa.

"Hello, Ross," he said in a weak voice as he stood before Papa, barefoot with just his pants and undershirt on.

"Good to see you," he continued as Papa removed his hat.

Papa stepped back from the door and asked, "Are you okay, Jeremiah? You don't look so good." Papa waited his reply as Mr. Jeremiah came onto the porch and sat down in the nearest rocking chair. He motioned for Papa to take a seat in the other chair.

As Papa sat in the chair and dropped his hat on the floor beside it, Mr. Jeremiah continued, "I haven't been well for a few days now. Rena and May went to Dr. Hayes to get some medicine. Rena thinks I had a light stroke." His voice trailed off to just above a whisper. "The rainy weather has got to my arthritic joints and without sunshine, the house gets very small for May, Rena and me," he rambled a bit.

"And this heat, it is almost unbearable. It's just about got me down. Dr. Hayes said a while back at my age, I probably have a weak heart." He looked at Papa with sad eyes. Papa noticed several days' stubble growth on his chin signaling he had not been doing well. Jeremiah was always well shaven and had on clean clothes when he sat in the rocker on the porch.

"Jeremiah, you should have Rena let us know when you are ill. Jan will be upset that she didn't have an opportunity to make some of her "chicken soup" for you. It's guaranteed to either cure or kill you," Papa joked and smiled at his elderly friend patting him on the back.

Jeremiah smiled back as he leaned against the back of the chair. "You know, it came on all of a sudden," the old man said in a low voice. "I was fine one day and down the next. Didn't have any kind of symptoms. I have high blood pressure and take pills for it, but I ran out of the pills a couple weeks ago. With the weather so bad, we couldn't get more right away."

"Next time that happens, you let me know and I will go get the pills for you," Papa said.

"Thank you, my boy," Jeremiah said softly. "Now you eat your dinner. Your field looks really good. The corn is growing higher than it has in years. Should be a bumper crop!" Jeremiah made small talk while Papa took one biscuit and offered him the second one.

"Might help you to eat a bit," Papa urged as he handed the biscuit filled with ham over to Jeremiah. As Mr. Jeremiah took a bite of the biscuit, Papa added, "Got to keep your strength up so you can beat whatever is ailing you."

Mr. Jeremiah 307

"How long have the girls been gone?" Papa inquired as they finished off several teacakes Mama had put inside the dinner pail.

"Just a couple of hours," Jeremiah said. "They will be getting back pretty soon. Don't worry about me. Go on back to pulling those weeds. You have worked too hard to let them take over your corn. I'll be fine, Ross. I am feeling stronger and better already." He smiled tiredly as Papa stepped down from the porch.

"Ross," Jeremiah smiled at Papa. "Thank you. You are a good friend." Papa blushed at the sincere appreciation in his voice.

"Please have Rena or May come and get me if you or they need anything," Papa said as he once again picked up his hat and sat it on his head.

"Anything at all, Jeremiah."

Papa walked over to the old man's chair, shook his hand and then stepped down from the porch and walked back into the corn rows just as I came up and joined him pulling weeds. The rows were tall enough to hide me and almost tall enough to hide Papa as we pulled the weeds taking two rows at a time. We should finish this field by noontime tomorrow. Papa glanced at the Smith house on each turn.

The girls returned around 2:30 that afternoon. Mr. Jeremiah was still sitting on the porch at 3:30 when Papa and I stopped weeding for the day. Papa waved to him and

Jeremiah waved back. We headed for the barn walking side by side as I walked briskly to keep up with Papa's long legs.

The story told was that after Papa and I left the field, Mr. Jeremiah had a heart attack, spilling out of his chair and onto the floor. He lay on the porch barely breathing, unable to call out, until granddaughter Rena came through the door and found him on the floor. She rushed to her grandfather and took his pulse which was faint, but steady. May followed Rena onto the porch looking for her father. May followed Rena's instructions and got a clean wash cloth and a pan of cool water for Rena. Rena wet the cloth and washed her grandfather's face until he came around. She then cradled his head in her lap and sent May to our farm to get help while she kept her grandfather Jeremiah calm and still.

Miss May found me, Papa, Anna, Tom, and David all in the barn working on evening chores. She was excited and scared but managed to tell Papa her father was dying. Papa hitched Pearl to the wagon, May started running along side of the wagon. Papa stopped the wagon and May stopped shaking her hands and crying soft sobs. Papa motioned for her to join him on the wagon seat—she started to run again, then turned back and ran back to him wanting him to follow her.

"May," Papa called gruffly, "Get in!"

She finally understood and stepped up onto the wagon as Papa pulled away and took the shortcut through the new corn field to their place. Mama came to the back door hearing the noise. I quickly told her about Mr. Jeremiah and she instructed me,

"Lily, go help your father."

I ran as fast as I could through the pasture and through the rows of corn to the Smith place arriving just as Papa was unhitching Pearl from the wagon.

Mr. Jeremiah was still on the porch, but Papa, Rena, and I were able to lift him. May held the door open and we got him through the door onto his bed. Rena pulled the sheet up and spread blankets over him to keep the chill away until Papa could fetch Dr. Hayes. Papa rode away on Pearl. May positioned herself on the floor near her father clasping his hand and rubbing it across her face again and again. She sang a low soft song to him but I could not make out the words.

I wanted to cry, but didn't. I needed to be strong and help Miss Rena.

"Lily," Rena motioned for me to join her in their small kitchen area. "Thank you for helping," she said sensing that I was on the brink of tears. "Will you have a cup of coffee with me while we wait for the doctor?" she asked and moved to pour the coffee into two white cups as she set the milk near mine. I shook my head afraid to say anything, thinking my voice might crack and I would lose my courage. I had never seen anyone as sick as Mr. Jeremiah. Not even Mama was that sick after giving birth to baby Paul. He was so weak and so thin.

Miss Rena went to check her grandfather's pulse several times and washed his face with the cool cloth. She lifted his head and with my help had him drink a strong tea that she brewed on the stove. He managed to swallow an aspirin for her but he was very weak and tired. May refused to let go of his hand and continued to sit on the floor beside the bed and hum as she stroked his hand with hers.

Miss Rena asked me if I was hungry. I found my voice and said no, but thanked her for the offer.

In an hour or so, Mama knocked at the door. She had two quarts of her homemade soup from the food crib for the Smith family and a large pone of fresh cornbread. She gave Rena a hug suggesting that her friend warm the soup for their dinner. Next, Mama spoke to Mr. Jeremiah letting him know she was praying for him, but he was too weak to acknowledge her. Lastly, she gave Miss May a loving pat on her shoulder but made no effort to get her away from her place on the floor beside her father. I stood on the sidelines watching my Mama interact with the Smith family. I was so proud to be her daughter.

Mama joined Rena and me in the kitchen, and Rena poured a cup of coffee for her. I added milk for Mama before she drank from the cup. She said she could only stay a moment, she had left the baby, Tom, and David in Anna's, Lad's and Skip's care and didn't want to leave them too long. She explained that Anna was good for a short while with all the children, but could lose her patience with them if left for long periods of time.

Rena explained what happened to Mr. Jeremiah and that Papa had gone to get Dr. Hayes. Mama suggested that I stay with them just in case they needed an extra pair of hands or someone to come and get her until the doctor arrived. I agreed and my nerves settled somewhat. Mama finished her coffee and left, while we waited for Papa and Dr. Hayes to arrive.

We heard moaning from the bedroom. Miss Rena rushed to her grandfather's side. He gradually opened his eyes, becoming conscious, but he was very weak. Just then Dr. Hayes and Papa appeared at the door. Without waiting to be invited, they came into the room. Dr. Hayes tipped his hat, opened his bag, and began to examine Mr. Jeremiah. Papa asked me to wait on the porch with him. He picked up a bucket of rain water from the nearest eave of the house and took it over to Pearl who was very hot. She drank a long drink before raising her head up. He then moved her to the shady side of the porch and tied the rope gently to the post frame, so she could eat the grass below.

About thirty minutes later, Dr. Hayes stepped outside. He confirmed to Papa that Jeremiah had a heart attack. He didn't know the extent of the damage but he appeared to be over the worst part. He gave Rena two medications to keep him calm and help him sleep for the next few days until his strength returned. Then she should monitor him closely until he recovered fully.

"Ross, he will be on bed rest for five days, then only short walks, nothing too strenuous. I want Jeremiah to take an aspirin a day until he comes in the clinic for a full check-up." Dr. Hayes said.

"Rena," Papa said as she joined us on the porch. "I'll be happy to take Jeremiah in to see Doc. Just let me know when you are ready and Pearl and I will bring the wagon."

Dr. Hayes said he best get going and left. Miss May came out and said her father was asking for Papa. Papa stayed with Mr. Jeremiah just a short time, but prayed for him before leaving. While Papa was talking with her grandfather, Rena heated the soup and offered to share dinner with Papa and me. Papa declined, but said we would be in tomorrow to check on them and Mr. Jeremiah. In the meantime, if they needed anything to send May to fetch us.

That night, Papa and Mama had a discussion.

"Jan," Papa said. "That was a close call for Jeremiah today. I think he is much sicker than I or Dr. Hayes knows. He's an old man. I am worried that he is going to die. What will happen to May and Rena if Jeremiah dies?"

Mama gave Papa a hug. She was proud to see his concern for his old friend and her friends. She caressed his back and said, "Dying is a step we must do alone, Ross. God is in perfect control. We can be there to help Rena and May when they need us. We are offering help to them now. Outside of that, there is nothing else we can do. You and Lily will check on them tomorrow afternoon and make sure they have food and other things. Ask Lily to bring their wash down and we will do it for them. Do you think that will help?" Mama folded her darning to put it away as she and Papa talked.

"That will be good, Jan. We told Rena we would check on them when we finish weeding the corn field. Who knows, he might be sitting in that old rocker just waiting for me to stop by tomorrow." Papa sounded more enthusiastic now.

They both went to bed earlier that evening to get prepared for the big day of laundry and weeding work for Papa and me. With just the one cornfield left, he was anxious for us to complete the task.

CHAPTER 20

The Swimming Hole

Papa had gone to the field alone today, allowing me a day to help Mama and Anna because it was wash day. Mama was having another one of her down days. She had been tired now for three days running. I knew Papa was concerned too. He asked me to wash the lion's share of the clothes and encourage her to take a long nap while I did. I promised Papa I would. She drank the sassafras tea but still had no energy. Knowing Mama's history with tiredness, I prayed softly that she wasn't pregnant again.

Only a few black clouds roamed the sky. Other clouds looked like cotton candy filling the air. Clouds fascinated me. On a clear day, it looked as if you could reach up and pluck one from the sky. We also had studies on other things about the atmosphere—how the pressure can change quickly and some causes of tornadoes and other storms. I found science to be very fascinating. I didn't like the part about cutting up frogs and dissecting worms. Not that I was squeamish, mind you. I realized how much I missed school, science, and the other classes. I missed the children and Mrs. Parnell. Perhaps Anna and I would get to return to classes soon.

Farm girls grew up tough—not afraid of the sight of blood. We were expected to kill chickens for Sunday dinner and to hunt and shoot just like the boys, especially if you were the first-born. Some boys thought I was a great tomboy, so much so that they called me one as a nickname. They didn't like it when I beat them at boy games such as tug of war or flip shooting. Papa said I had good muscles in my arms and legs and I was a dead eye when it came to the flip. Boys were not eager to challenge me to a game involving either.

While Anna and the boys continued their game, Mama and baby Paul continued their nap on the quilt. I checked the white clothes on the line and took down and folded those that were dry. I placed them carefully in Mama's wash basket. A couple of pieces needed a little more time in the sun as did the dark clothes. If the rain held off a couple more hours, the clothes would be dry. I said a little silent prayer for the clothes to dry quickly as the wind blew a cool breeze across the meadow. The leaves seemed to whisper softly as they rustled in the breeze.

The wind continued to blow gently helping dry the clothes. The cattle were grazing on the west side of the barn.

Papa had taken his dinner to the field as he often did on wash day in late summer, so we only needed to return to the house in time to complete evening chores and cook supper when he returned at dusk.

I checked the white clothes again. They were dry. I folded them and put them carefully in Mama's basket with the others. The lighter weight dark clothes were also dry. I removed them from the line and folded the shirts carefully so they would only require minimum ironing. Same thing with Mama's house dresses, my clothes and Anna's clothes. The boys' shorts were dry so I repeated the process. The only things still damp were the jeans and Papa's work clothes. If the rain continued to hold off a little longer, the clothes would all get dry.

Anna and the boys had given up rock skipping and moved to tadpole racing. Tom's large tadpole was winning the race thus far. I grinned to see the competitive spirit in my siblings. Anna hung in there. She did not want her little brothers to beat her at anything. Playing games with your brothers was a good time to be competitive and not use lady-like manners. Let the fastest tadpole win! David was the youngest, but in a tadpole race, it didn't matter what age you were. It was how you coaxed that small tadpole to move faster than the others and David could hold his own. It may have been the way he placed his small hand in the water just behind the tiny creature, but that tadpole shot out in front and across the finish line leaving the other two half a tail behind. David screamed like he had just won the first prize at the 4-H fair.

David's loud scream brought Mama up from the pallet on her knees. I patted David on the back as Mama got up and walked down to the pond.

"What happened?" Mama asked, realizing that nothing was wrong.

"David just won his first tadpole race!" I giggled as David continued to jump up and down and chide the others. Anna and Tom now joined in and congratulated David. They were being really good sports.

"Okay, kids," Mama spoke to us all. "We had better get you in that water, if you still want to swim. We have some rain clouds over in the west so we may not have much longer to play. David, Tom, Anna, and Lily, you all know the rules. Don't go beyond the willow tree in the center of the pond. Girls, keep your eyes on your brothers. I'll get the rest of the laundry off the line and gather things up. Swim in your underpants." Mama began walking over to the clothesline as she talked over her shoulder.

We all stripped down to our underpants, following Mama's instructions. Anna was the first in the pond. Tom second, with David and I bringing up the rear. David was a natural swimmer and took to the water like a duck. Papa taught him to swim when he was six months old. He could now swim the full length of the pond using the breast stroke or underwater with his eyes closed. He could dive from the

The Swimming Hole

make-shift diving board which was merely an old fallen tree extending about four feet over the pond. He had no fear of the water. Tom was a good swimmer too, but David could beat Tom. Anna and I were not good swimmers. I was really frightened of the water and refused to put my head under. When Mama tried to teach me, I had a panic attack and nearly drowned during my lesson. I could float on my back and tread water. Anna was not much better than me. We usually played around the edge and stayed close to the cow-made beach without sand, created by the cattle constantly walking in to drink. It was solid and firm enough to serve as a shoreline so we pretended it was our beach.

It had not rained for a couple of days and the water in the pond was clear. It was only muddy where the boys and Anna had walked into the pond from the beach area. I liked to sit on the make-shift diving board sometimes and watch the others. I went for my favorite spot today. You could see moss growing and fish swimming from the top of the board. Occasionally, you could see goldfish and schools of stripe minnows or perch and other small fish swimming around. At other times small bullfrogs would swim up and sit on a lily pad, flicking their tongues out catching insects and flies that got a little too close. The pond had lots of water lilies which sported giant, spectacular flowers that attracted dragon flies with beautiful colored wings that perched on the lily flowers or in nearby branches. Nature was beautiful and the pond was a good place to watch it unfold. My favorites this time of the year were the small snapping turtles. As babies, they were so cute with that little mouth quickly snapping on a small stick when you tested them. As an adult the snapping turtles grew large and could become irritated easily. Their jaws were powerful and their bite deadly. Snappers, as they were called, bit anything that got in their way. The old people said "a snapping turtle would not turn loose of his prey until sundown." Mama and Papa warned us to leave the adult snapping turtles alone and to stay out of their way.

Mama finished the laundry, packed everything up and stacked the baskets neatly together. She was sitting on the quilt, feeding baby Paul while Skip continued to be at their side. Anna, Tom, and David were enjoying a game of water tag, being careful not to go beyond the middle of the pond where the large weeping willow marked their boundary. The swimmers darted in and out, this way and that, squealing and laughing. David and Tom kept dashing under the water while Anna swam on the top. The water was just deep enough to keep the pond clear and not stir up the muddy bottom. They were having so much fun darting in and out. I crawled off the fallen log diving board, got out of the water and walked back up the hill toward Mama, baby Paul, and Skip. Lad did not come with us much anymore. He was feeling his old age and could not keep up easily.

As I approached the quilt and got dressed, Skip walked down to the pond and drank water from the edge. He did not return to the quilt, but instead sat down on his haunches beside the pond, watching our swimmers with guarding eyes. I sat down on the quilt near Mama watching baby Paul as he suckled on her nipple pulling as if he was very hungry. Mama changed him from her right breast to her left. He fretted until she placed the left nipple into his mouth. He again began sucking while his small hand rested on Mama's breast. She whispered to him softly as he settled down. I enjoyed watching Mama feed the baby. Her tenderness came through in the soft whispers she made to calm baby Paul.

Although my back was to the pond, I could hear the swimmers continue in their fun. The game had moved from swimming tag to jumping into the water from the make-shift diving board. The water was less deep at this particular spot in the pond. The depth ranged from eighteen inches of water at the beach area to close to seven feet in the center of the pond. The deep water in the middle was why Mama forbade us to swim beyond the willow tree. When Papa was with us, he allowed the boys to swim the entire length of the pond with him. At the willow tree boundary, the pond was a maximum of six feet deep. Papa could stand on his tip toes at this point and still have his nose out of the water.

Mama was more cautious. She was a good swimmer, but did not like to swim in the pond. We talked her into swimming with us occasionally. In the summer on wash days, she got into the shallow end just to cool off. This summer she had only gotten in one time. It was harder for her since baby Paul was so young. Today was no different. Baby Paul was hungry and fretting so Mama would not get into the pond. I was growing somewhat bored with the entire day and stretched out on the quilt. The sun went behind a cloud as the dark clouds seem to come closer, but were still far above us and off to the west. The cool breeze had died down and it was getting hotter again.

I closed my eyes and imagined how it must feel to fly in an airplane up in the cotton candy clouds. I imagined how beautiful it must be to be able to be close enough to almost reach out and touch them. I drifted on in my imagination and daydreamed and dozed as I lay on the quilt beside Mama and baby Paul.

Meanwhile, the game of jumping from the makeshift diving board was still going on. Mama never allowed us to actually dive from the tree. It could be dangerous. The water was too shallow and mud had settled on the bottom of the pond. The mud was a mixture of black soil and red clay which made it very thick and compact. It was also sticky.

Because the tree had fallen, cattle did not water at this particular spot. Instead they walked into the beach area and walked out about two feet into the pond to drink. The cattle watering kept the mud in the beach area packed down and firm. It was a safe point for us to enter the pond for a nice swim on a hot day like today.

The jumping, squealing, and jockeying for first jump continued for several minutes more. Quiet rotation after the farthest jump had long passed. Now three children were

The Swimming Hole 323

scampering up and jumping into the water with lightening speed. They also pushed one another from the board. Mama was comforting baby Paul and not paying much attention to those in the water while I dozed on the quilt beside her. Skip watched the children and began pacing back and forth on the bank. Skip was not easily agitated by the children's noise. He whined and fretted pacing back and forth and wagging his tail constantly. Still the game went on.

Tom gave Anna a shove that sent her flying out about two feet from the tree. He immediately jumped in after her. David was on the tree alone while his brother and sister raced and pulled each other back from the bank. They were bobbing in and out of the water and not paying attention to David.

David was giggling watching the two of them in the water. He yelled, "Look at me!" and gave a long dive head first into the water. Neither Anna nor Tom saw him as he plunged head first deep into the sticky mud below.

Skip saw him and started barking wildly, running back and forth on the bank, looking up at Mama and me on the quilt. We heard the barking and then the splash as Skip jumped into the water and headed for the two small feet sticking up in the mud. Skip began pulling as hard as he could on David's underpants.

Mama instantly pushed baby Paul into my arms waking me from my dozing state. "Lily," she yelled and was up from the quilt and headed for the pond. Mama jumped into the water fast and fully clothed. She took both of David's feet and pulled him free from the mud. He spat and gasped for breath as Anna and Tom frantically swam for Mama and David. Mama had David out of the water in a few seconds. She lay him on the bank, removed her blouse and had Anna wet it in the pond water. David continued to spit mud but was breathing okay. Mama washed the mud from his eyes and face as he began to cry. She had him blow his nose hard several times to help remove the slivers of mud that still lingered inside. She hugged him close and assured him he was okay.

"What happened?" Anna and Tom wanted to know getting out of the water and sitting on the bank.

"While you two were clowning around, your brother dove in head first and stuck up in the mud!" Mama shouted angrily. "That's why you aren't allowed to dive from the tree," she continued.

By this time, baby Paul and I had made it to the side of the pond where Mama was still working cleaning up David.

"I'm sorry, Mama," Anna said first with tears building in her eyes and spilling over onto her cheeks.

"I'm sorry too," Tom echoed as he started to cry. Big tears rolled down his checks and onto the ground.

"It's okay. It's nobody fault." Her anger subsided. "David knows he is not supposed to dive from the tree, don't you Sweetie," Mama asked David as he whimpered and buried his face in her wet slip. "This is why! It is very dangerous because of the mud. You won't do that ever again, will you David?" Mama asked.

"I want you all to promise me that you won't ever try to dive from the tree and that you will watch out for each other when you swim. Otherwise you won't be able to swim unless your Father or I swim with you. Promise me," Mama coached while she managed a smile for her three distraught children.

"Hey, what's going on?" we heard Papa call as he came down through the pasture and saw us all gathered on the bank. He walked up still dressed in his field work clothes.

"Thank God for Skip!" Mama began. She told Papa the story of what had happened and how Skip had gotten her attention just in time. If David had been in the water a few seconds more, he would have drowned.

We must have been a sight. Mama dressed in her skirt and slip, wet from head to toe, holding David in her arms with Anna, Tom, and David all crying. Me and baby Paul were walking up and down while a very wet Skip stayed close to Mama and David. Papa had just finished pulling the grass from the cornfield near the Smith house. He thought since it was washday and still early enough, he would join us for a family swim. He gave everyone hugs and Mama a kiss in front of us kids, saying he was thankful that everything turned out okay. After everyone calmed down, Papa first helped me and Anna take the laundry to the house. When we returned to the pond, Tom carried baby Paul and Mama held David close to her heart with Papa beside them. Anna, me, and Skip walked side by side at the end of the Howell family line as we returned to the house together. It had been an exciting day of work, fun and near tragedy, but we had been blessed and everyone was okay. Somehow Papa forgot about the swim.

CHAPTER 21

Let Him Live

THE LAST SUMMER weeks rolled by and harvest time was upon Dry Valley. Papa, Mama, us children, and the mules were in the fields first, pulling corn for the market and for the feed in the winter. Mama was feeling much better now and was beginning to take on a full load of work again.

Cotton fields were fluffy white with cotton bursting forth from the bolls just waiting to be picked and taken to the gin. It was the second crop to be gathered after the corn was in the barn or had been sold. School was delayed for six weeks each fall to allow farm children to help their parents gather the crops. With such an abundant harvest this year, it might be necessary to close school for another week later. Tom started school this year.

Papa was so busy in the fields that he had not seen Mr. Walsh since he got his tractor. One of the merchants from town ordered a load of corn from Papa. He took the mules and delivered the corn. Mr. Walsh was coming out of the farm supply store as Papa hitched the mules to the post outside. Papa saw Mr. Walsh's car parked near the store and hoped he could see him and inquire about his progress with the tractor. Papa extended his hand and John Walsh shook it firmly and inquired about Mama and the family.

"Can't complain," said Papa. "Everyone is healthy and the crops are better than I've seen in years. How about you? How's the tractor working out?"

John Walsh smiled. "I agree with you. The crops are the best I've had in possibly five years. The John Deere is a dream machine. It's easy to handle, covers far more ground, and only requires a little diesel fuel to run it. No horse shoeing, no currying, no buckets of feed, and no hitching and unhitching from the plow twice a day. I just leave the plow attached until I finish."

Papa grinned to see his friend so caught up in his tractor experience.

"Has the rain delayed your getting into the field with the tractor?" Papa asked.

"No more than usual with the mules. My farm has a pretty good rainwater runoff system and a sandy, black soil base, so it dries out rather quickly. Maybe a few hours' delay, but you make that up in a day," Mr. Walsh replied as he stepped closer to Pearl and gave her a scratch behind the ears.

"Ross, how's the new mule getting along with Pearl?" he asked as he continued to scratch Pearl.

"Bertie's great and Pearl just goes with the flow," Papa replied. "I was lucky to find her. I heard about her from Parnell. Her owner was sick and could no longer manage her, so he gave me a good price."

"Ross, what's your secret with mules?" Mr. Walsh asked with a quizzical look. "A few years ago, I tried to bring in a new mule to go with my two. I never could get my pair of mules to accept her. They literally tried to kill the new mule. You must know some secret," he smiled, waiting for Papa's reply.

"Thanks to you and Hal Bennett for letting me use your mules to get my work done, Pearl kind of got accustomed to working with other mules. I think too that she really was lonely without Katie. I took it slow and left Bertie in the pasture for a couple of days and only let Pearl out when I could observe them together. After the first day and the usual pawing and neighing, they were okay together."

Mr. Walsh shook his head in disbelief. "I still think you know a secret there. Come over and see the Deere work one day soon." Mr. Walsh shook Pap's hand again and began walking away, saying over his shoulder, "I'll let you try her out." With that, he opened his car door, pulled his hat from his head, placed it on the front seat with him, sat under the steering wheel, and started the engine. Papa waved goodbye saying, "I will real soon."

Days grew shorter as temperatures began to change and fall was in full swing in Dry Valley. The corn was in the barn and most of the cotton was picked. Papa had already taken five bales of cotton to the gin in town. We had another two or so in the field to harvest. Mr. Walsh had finished his harvest and asked Papa if he wanted to use his farm workers to harvest the final bales. Papa had never employed outside workers to do his cotton picking before. He was able to make a deal with the workers to harvest the remaining bales at a sixty/forty split of the money. They would pick the cotton, Papa would use Pearl and Bertie and our wagon, take it to the gin, obtain the best price available for the cotton, then split the money with Papa keeping sixty percent and the workers getting forty. Papa thought that was a good deal. It would free Papa up to begin turning the corn stalks under for soil enrichment and give him a leg up on fall field preparation. The workers were fast cotton pickers and the remaining cotton was ginned the following week.

By using the farm workers, Papa was assured that his children would not need to work in the fields after the school term began. Papa and Mama did the lion's share of operating the farm with us children helping only with planting, harvesting, and doing daily chores when Mama was healthy.

Papa spent the next couple of weeks preparing his fields to rest through the winter months. Then he had some time on his hands and decided to go visit John Walsh's farm to see him operate his John Deere. Papa came into the house shortly after dinner.

"Jan, I think I'll ride Pearl over to John Walsh's place. He asked me to come see the tractor at work and this is the first opportunity I've had."

"Will you be back for supper?" Mama asked looking up from the shirt she was mending.

"Sure, it should not take that long. I should be back in time to help the girls with outside chores," he said as he stopped and gave Mama a kiss on the top of her head.

"Can I go?" asked David as he walked up close to Papa.

Papa looked to Mama as if to say, *"Help me here!"*

Mama came to the rescue. "Not today, David. Papa and Mr. Walsh have some grown up business to discuss, so you'd better stay with me. Besides, who would watch Paul until Tom and the girls get home if you leave me? I have sewing to do. Maybe you can go next time? Give my regards to Martha, Ross."

Papa smiled and left the room. He took a light jacket and his hat from its peg inside the kitchen door and headed for the barn to saddle up Pearl.

The Walsh's farm was a short ride away for Pearl who seemed eager to be out with Papa. She was so frisky that Papa had to hold her reins tight, otherwise she would have run all the way.

Papa noticed the beauty of the fall colored leaves as he and Pearl rode down our lane and turned north onto the main road. He thought of nature and how the dying leaves signified the beginning of a new season when a covey of quail flew up a few feet in front of Pearl. More in tuned to his surroundings now, he noticed a couple of grey squirrels working and hiding nuts away for the winter. He saw a rabbit, a wild pheasant, and several chipmunks as he traveled along the roadway. Once inside the Walsh's farm lane, two of Mr. Walsh's prize guinea fowls darted across in front of him. The gray speckled guinea was larger than a frying hen but smaller than a turkey and was a gift from Martha Walsh's brother. The guinea meat was said to be a delicacy with the meat having a delicate taste and a darker color than duck. The birds had thrived on the farm. Papa reminded himself to check on purchasing a male and a brooder guinea from Martha for Christmas. Mama might like to add guineas to her laying stock, and he could surprise her.

Papa was touched by the beauty of the Walsh farm each time he visited. The house, built in the center of a wooded knoll, was large and rambling. Two barns were whitewashed and trimmed with black shutters on the same style as the house. One of the barns housed John Walsh's prize quarter horses and the other his cattle and mules. Mr. Walsh's family had owned this property for several generations with each new Walsh owner improving on the beauty of the setting. Although the Walsh family came from money, Papa found John to be a dear friend without a pretentious bone in his body. His Christian faith showed through daily in how he lived his life and raised his children. Mr. Walsh always stepped up when needed by the community or friends. He was a pillar of the community who remained quiet in his assistance.

As Papa tied Pearl to the fence post, he thought how blessed he was to have John Walsh as a friend. Papa removed his hat and walked the short distance to the front door of the home. Carrying the hat in one hand, he knocked on the door with a firm but light rap. In a few seconds Martha Walsh came to the door.

"Hello, Ross," she greeted him.

"Martha," Papa returned the greeting. "John invited me by to watch him work on the tractor," he said.

Martha opened the door and stepped through onto the porch. "What fun!" she said. Then she cupped her hand over her eyes and walked to the side of the front porch. "He's plowing in the east section," she said looking into the sun. "See the dust?" She pointed to a rise of dust about a quarter mile away. You could see the tractor as it rumbled along. "You might want to ride your mule over. It's a ways to walk," she suggested.

"Good idea," Papa said. "Jan asked me to be sure to give you her regards," Papa continued.

"How is Jan and those beautiful children?" Martha asked.

"They are fine. Girls and Tom are at school with Nathan. David is a handful." He smiled as he said it. But she knew exactly what he meant having two boys of her own. Boys were all energy and constantly being boys.

"John will be thrilled you came. He loves that tractor. I call it his "big toy," she said smiling again.

"I can't wait to see him working it. He said I could try it out so I just might take him up on driving it," Papa said as he began descending the steps to go get Pearl.

"See you later then, Ross," Martha said as she turned to go back into the house.

Papa unhitched Pearl, allowed her to drink from the stock water trough, mounted her and they turned for the east section field. The dust cloud became larger the closer Papa got to the field.

Papa stopped Pearl at the edge of the field, stepped down from the saddle, loosely tying Pearl to the branch of a nearby oak tree. Mr. Walsh was plowing the field headed away from Papa and was not aware that anyone was near. The tractor ran smoothly as it moved along the ground leaving a long tunnel of dirt in its path. The furrow was about ten inches across, much wider than Papa's plow could make. Papa immediately understood how he got more work done with this machine. He marveled while watching John Walsh plow the field. Mr. Walsh proceeded to plow to the end of the row, turned the tractor, and began the drive back looking over his shoulder watching the plow as it turned the soil. He still did not see Papa. Papa stood watching in silence as the tractor continued doing its work.

The east section field was slanted on a down sloping hillside and unlevel. Papa noticed the tractor was sitting tilted at an angle that was off-balanced as Mr. Walsh continued to drive toward him. What happened next, Papa could not explain. Before his eyes, the tractor jack-knifed and flipped upside down, plow and tractor, with Mr. Walsh trapped somewhere in between. Papa was stunned for a moment, not believing what he saw.

Recovering from shock, Papa broke into a full sprint across the field to find Mr. Walsh lying underneath the seat of the tractor with the machine and plow both on top of him. The only protection Mr. Walsh had was the seat he was sitting in. The chair-like seat was protecting him from the full force of the weight of the tractor crushing his body.

Papa said out loud, "Oh God." For a moment he stood paralyzed beside the upside down tractor and plow. Then adrenaline kicked in and without thinking Papa began to act. First he called out to his friend,

"John! John!" as he knelt on the ground beside the contraption but John could not hear him. "John!" he called again as he noticed the diesel fuel dripping from somewhere inside the tractor motor housing. John *still* did not answer. Papa found the key in a slot in the upside down machine and turned it off, shutting the engine down.

As he knelt beside his unconscious friend, Papa prayed, "Help us Lord! "Please God, let him live!" The ground was cool with a clean smell of the fresh turned soil signifying a new beginning. The furrow was a makeshift pillow for John's head keeping it slightly raised above his body underneath the machine. Papa gathering his wits, whistled for Pearl. With two quick jerks of her head, Pearl broke the line hooked to the tree limb and came to Papa. He had trained her well. Papa unhooked his canteen from her saddle horn. After listening for Mr. Walsh's heartbeat, he soaked his handkerchief in water from the canteen and poured a little directly onto his friend's face, being careful to avoid his nose area. His eyes flickered open a little but closed again. He was alive but badly hurt. Papa could feel it in his bones. He prayed again to God and Mr. Walsh opened his eyes again only for a second.

"John, old pal, you gave me the shock of my life," Papa said. "Where does it hurt?" But he was unconscious again without answering.

Papa gently moved his hands along Mr. Walsh's arms and shoulders then moved them down to the lower body. Once his hands touched the stomach and thighs, Mr. Walsh groaned in agony. Papa continued to scan his body with slow gentle moves of his hands. Moves along his left leg and knee brought screams of pain and then unconsciousness.

"John. Listen to me," Papa said crouched near his friend still trapped under the tractor-plow combination. "You are hurt real bad and I can't get you out," Papa said trying to sound reassuring. "I need to get some help. Lie still until I get back. I will be right back and get you out. I promise! You are going to be okay. Don't move. Just trust and wait for me."

With this promise to Mr. Walsh, Papa mounted Pearl again and this time pushed her into an open run for the Walsh barn and house. When he got within a few hundred feet, he called out loudly,

"Martha, Martha!"

Martha came onto the front porch immediately, apron still on from her sewing.

"What's wrong, Ross?" She bounded down the steps full of concern.

Papa didn't bother to hitch Pearl to the post this time. He ran to meet Martha as she crossed the grass onto the driveway area. Papa gripped her shoulder and said.

"John had an accident on the tractor, but he's alive."

"No, no, no," Martha cried and the tears formed behind the expression of fear that she could not hide. She clinched her hands, then, used one hand to cover her mouth as if to muffle a scream.

"You must have faith, Martha," Papa consoled. Seeing uncertainty and fright in her face, he continued, "Stay with me, now. You must be brave. God is with us. I need you to get Doc Hayes. Can you drive the car?" Martha shook her head that she could drive as she shifted back and forth from foot to foot.

Sam Bowman and his son Mark had worked for the Walsh family for two harvesting seasons and lived at the back of the south pasture in a small house Mr. Walsh built to house his farm hands. Sam's wife, Lucy, was the local midwife and had assisted families with the births of most of the children in the area. Hearing Ross call Martha and seeing him ride Pearl so fast brought Sam and Mark to Papa and Martha's side.

Papa took a few seconds and explained what happened and that Mr. Walsh was still under the tractor. He reassured them by adding that Mr. Walsh had a strong heart beat and had opened his eyes. Papa thought he might have several broken bones and needed Sam and Mark to help get him out.

With this said, Sam and Mark headed for the tool shed and hooked two of the Walsh mules to the smaller wagon. The wheels were rubber which would make the ride for John smoother when they brought him home from the field.

Papa got Martha settled down by assuring her over and over that John was alive and God was in control. She retrieved her purse from the house and seated herself inside the car. John had taught her to drive about three months back at the beginning of the spring harvest season just in case she had an emergency with one of the children and needed to get a doctor while he was in the fields. Little did they know at that time that she would need to make that drive, not for a child—but for John.

By this time, Lucy had walked up to see what the commotion was about. She assured Martha that she would wait for the children to get home from school and cook the evening meal—just watch over the place until she returned. More importantly she would pray for John and Martha's journey to fetch Doc Hayes.

She backed the car out and started the drive into town. She should be back as soon as possible provided Doc Hayes could come right away.

Armed with shovels, pick axes, a sledge hammer and ropes, Sam and Mark pulled alongside of Pearl and waited for Papa to refill the water canteen. The men had gotten fresh towels and blankets from the birthing room of the barn and loaded in a half bale of straw to form a make-shift bed to put John on. The straw would help cushion the ride back from the field. Papa stepped into the saddle and led the way to the east section field with the wagon close behind.

The scene of the accident was as Papa had left it. John lay under the overturned tractor with the plow dangling upside down, still hitched to the back of the machine. John was silent as Papa, Sam, and Mark knelt beside him. Papa called his name,

"John." No movement. "John." Louder this time, but still no movement or sign of life. Papa wet the handkerchief again from the canteen water and wiped John's brow. He groaned slightly. Papa repeated the wipe while the other two men began unloading the tools for the dig.

"John," Papa said. "Don't try to speak, just listen. Sam, Mark, and I are going to remove some dirt from underneath you, so we can get you out from under the tractor. You are stuck and the tractor is on top of you. This will only take a few minutes, then we will have you free. Be brave, my friend."

John moaned again as Ross put the top back on the canteen, stood up, took a strong clean blanket Mark handed him and placed it on the ground as close to John as possible. They would use it as a sling to put John into the wagon once they removed him from the trap the tractor had created.

Sam asked Papa how he wanted them to proceed to remove the dirt from underneath John. Papa used his hands to guide them to remove the dirt directly from under the body, using first the pick ax to loosen the dirt and then the shovels to remove it. By using axes they could determine the exact area the dirt came from and keep the mound of earth holding the tractor itself intact. Removing only the soil underneath John to form a trench would lower the injured man and allow them to free him from the trap. Sam and Mark agreed with Papa. Mark would remove the dirt with the shovel and Papa and Sam would use the pick axes for the dig —Ross digging from the lower side and Sam from the top side.

It did not take long, once the digging and shoveling began. They lowered the soil several inches and watched as his body inched little by little from touching the tractor frame. Finally, they had removed enough soil to create sufficient space to ease John from the trap.

Papa took Mr. Walsh by the shoulders and pulled gently as John screamed in pain but Papa did not let go. Another pull from Papa with Sam assisting and Mr. Walsh was free from the trap and halfway onto the blanket. John moaned low in his throat, which was a good sign. He still lived.

Mark made a padded straw bed covered with a blanket in the bed of the wagon keeping another blanket to cover Mr. Walsh. The two men gripped an end of the blanket sling and lifted the injured Mr. Walsh from the ground onto the wagon tailgate. They stepped up onto the wagon floor and finished the job with one lift.

Mark placed a fresh towel he had rolled up under John's head then knelt and inspected the injuries. The left leg and knee area were beginning to swell but he was not bleeding except where a few small cuts and scrapes had dried blood on them.

"He may have some internal injuries and I'm pretty sure this leg is broken, the knee cap may be broken too," Papa said pointing to the swelling that was noticeable even through his pant leg. He pulled his hunting knife from his belt and cut John's pant leg from the bottom up checking the leg further. No bones sticking out but swelling was evident. Papa ripped the remaining cloth up past the knee area and looked to Sam for affirmation of his diagnosis. Sam shook his head in agreement.

"He has been blessed by God today," Sam said to no one particular. "He's still alive."

"Let's get him to the house." Papa jumped down from the wagon as Mark seated himself in the wagon bed beside John, and Sam stepped to the driver's bench as the mules turned their heads as if they knew what was coming next. Papa rode Pearl while Sam and Mark handled the wagon. Mr. Walsh moaned and groaned each time the wagon hit a stone or a bump in the road. It was not an easy ride from the field.

Martha drove the car into the lane with Doc Hayes' car directly behind her. Ross hitched Pearl to the hitching post as Sam and Mark opened the back of the wagon. The three men were waiting for the swiftly coming cars. Papa removed his hat and placed it on his saddle horn.

Martha and Doc Hayes emerged from the two vehicles and both approached the wagon with concern on their faces. Nodding greetings to Ross, Sam, and Mark, Doc did not waste any time. He boarded the wagon with Martha on his heels. He knelt on one side of John near the damaged leg while Martha stroked John's face with her hand.

"John," she called in her softest voice but John did not stir. She rubbed his cheek a little firmer and called his name again. John still did not stir.

"Doc," Martha asked looking sadly her eyes not leaving her husband's face. "Will John live?"

Doc Hayes was immersed in his examination but he heard the question Martha asked and gave a plausible answer based on what he saw at first.

"He's got a nasty broken leg, possibly some broken ribs, possibly a punctured lung. That I can determine from the bruising and swelling. He may have some other internal injuries that I can't see. He is unconscious and most likely in shock. We need to get him into the house so I can take a better look." Doc tilted his head to see Martha as she continued to look at her husband's face.

"We need a miracle to pull him through," Doc said. "The next twenty-four hours are critical." He motioned for Papa, Sam, and Mark to come near.

"Men," Doc said. "Let's pull the wagon close to the porch and use the sling you made of the blanket to get John into the house. That is the easiest and fastest way. Martha, take all the covers off the bed including the pillows, just leave the bottom sheet and we will bring John in. Hurry now, I need to examine him and dress his wounds as soon as I can. Martha, I also need lots of hot water."

The men did not wait for further direction. Papa stepped onto the wagon seat and Sam with Mark walked along side as he drove the mules pulling the wagon to the front porch leaving just enough room to not scrape the paint.

They stopped the wagon and all three moved to the wagon bed waiting for the room to be prepared. Doc Hayes went inside carrying his instrument bag and motioned for them to bring in John. Papa and Sam lifted the sling again as they had in the field while Mark held the door open for them to pass through. John made no sounds this time as unconsciousness settled over his body and he remained in shock and comatose.

Martha went back and forth from the kitchen to the bedroom several times carrying more hot water to Doc

Hayes. Lucy brewed coffee and brought cups out for Sam and Papa. Mark had gone to the barn to do the evening feeding and other chores for the Walsh family. The afternoon sun drifted behind clouds and moved low in the sky, signifying the change from mid-day to late-afternoon to sunset.

Papa thanked Sam for Lucy's good care of Jan and baby Paul earlier in the year. The men chatted about the harvest, crop yields, price of cotton, state of the economy, the war and the tractor. Sam knew how to operate it, had actually plowed a few rows. They could cover twice the ground in a short amount of time by using both the tractor and the mules. Finally, Doc Hayes appeared in the kitchen with his bag in his hand. He sipped a cup of black coffee as Sam and Papa rose from their chair.

"John's a very lucky man to still be alive," Doc began. "I've put a wood splint around his leg, but it is broken. Feels like a firm break and I was able to pop the bone back into place. The knee cap got pushed off its socket from the blow when he hit the ground. It popped right back. I'll put a plaster cast on the leg and over the knee as soon as I can get the materials for it from town."

Both men hung on each word.

"I'm sure he has three or four broken ribs that I could feel, so I taped the entire rib cage, just to be safe. He is still unconscious. This could mean several things. 1) He could have hit his head, but there is no knot. 2) The extreme pain may have simply sent his system into shock and he needs some time to come out of it, or 3) He may have some internal bleeding that we don't know about with some organ damage. We have to wait and be patient. If he survives the next twenty-four hours he has a good chance. If it is internal, he won't survive." Doc looked at both men in a pleading way as he picked up his bag and continued talking while placing his empty cup on the small table in the living room.

"Be vigilant in your prayers for God's help. John sure needs it now." After saying this, Doc Hayes walked through the door and to his car with Papa and Sam close on his heels.

"Thanks, Doc," Papa said shaking his hand through the window. Doc waved to Sam and turned the motor starting the engine. They stood back as the car descended the driveway and onto the road toward town.

Sam excused himself to go help Mark with the chores, but not before Papa squeezed his hand in a firm shake, thanked him for being there for his friend and for his help today. Papa watched for a few minutes as Sam headed for the barn, then turned, walked the distance back to the house and stepped onto the front porch, knocked on the door, then opened it. Lucy Bowman came to greet him but no sign of Martha. Something cooking smelled really good as Papa's stomach reminded him it had been a long time since dinner and it was beyond his supper time.

"How's he doing?" Papa asked.

"No change," Lucy replied.

"How's Martha?" Ross quizzed.

"She's just sitting beside the bed holding his hand and praying. Do you want to step back?" Lucy asked.

"No, Lucy. I won't disturb them. Just let Martha know that I am going home for a while to check on Jan and the kids and that I will be back later," Papa said as he walked a couple of paces backwards before turning to leave.

"Lucy, I really enjoyed talking with Sam and Mark today. You have two fine men there. John might not be alive if it wasn't for them helping us."

"Thank you for those kind words," Lucy blushed.

Papa left the house, put his hat firmly on his head, mounted Pearl and headed for home. As he started to turn south down the road to his farm, he changed his mind and turned Pearl north and headed for Luke Lawrence's farm and the church.

The sun was almost completely set by the time Papa road Pearl up the short stretch between the main road and the Lawrence farm. Pastor Lawrence was sitting in a rocker on the front porch. He closed his Bible, laid it on the porch, and walked down the steps to greet Papa with an outstretched hand.

"Ross, what brings you out this time of evening?" the preacher asked.

Papa related the story to Pastor Lawrence from beginning through Doc Hayes' diagnosis, placing particular emphasis to Doc's request to be vigilant in prayer and that the next twenty-four hours were critical in John Walsh's life.

"Where are you headed now, Ross?" Pastor asked.

"I need to go home and check on Jan and the children. I told her I would only be gone a short while—that was a little after 1:00 pm today. I know she will be worried."

"Can you and Jan meet me and some of the parishioners in a couple of hours at the Walsh's? Sally and I will take the wagon and pick up as many as can come. We will hold a candlelight vigil on their front porch and pray for John's recovery. Strength in numbers will make our prayers stronger in God's eyes as we pray in a united effort." Pastor Lawrence was eager to help.

"You bet," Papa replied. "We can leave Lily in charge of the other children for a short time, especially since they will be sleeping." He again stepped into the saddle stirrups, mounted Pearl, and turned to leave.

"Thanks, Pastor," Papa said as he reached down and gripped Luke Lawrence's outstretched hand, knowing in his heart that this was the right thing to do.

Papa rode Pearl into the barnyard and dismounted. He walked her into the stall, unhooked the bridle and bit and gave her a bucket of feed and a fresh bucket of water. He laid the bridle and bit across the top of the stall as he planned to use them again in a little while when he and Mama went to the Walsh place. He quickly fed Bertie, gave her a gentle pat on the neck and checked her water. She still had half a bucket.

The children had finished their supper and dishes were washed and dried by the time he came into the house. Mama had waited to eat with him. She walked into the kitchen with Paul half sleeping on her hip asking, "What took you so long?"

Seeing the tired and concerned look on his face, she knew that something had happened. Papa shared the events of the afternoon with Mama, covering the accident with the tractor and Doc Hayes's diagnosis of Mr. Walsh's injuries. They finished their supper as he discussed his trip to see Pastor Lawrence before coming home. She said she would get the children tucked in bed and leave Lily in charge. She could be ready to join the others at the prayer vigil in half an hour.

I had questions but knew that Mama would fill in details either later tonight or in the morning if it was too late when she and Papa got home. Mama had privately told me that Mr. Walsh had suffered a fall and that Doc Hayes patched him up but Pastor Lawrence wanted the parishioners to pray as a group at the Walsh house tonight. The boys were already sleeping and Anna was almost asleep, having said prayers and completed homework early in the evening. Mama gave me permission to bring Skip into the den with Lad to keep me company until she and Papa returned. Baby Paul was fast asleep in Mama and Papa's bed and should sleep all night.

Papa went to hitch Pearl and Bertie to the wagon while Mama spoke with me giving last minute instructions and assurances that everything would be okay. I closed the door behind Mama as she took her jacket from the coat peg and went out into the night air. Skip sniffed my hand then followed me into the den area. He lay at my feet with his head across his paw waiting for me to settle in. Old Lad dozed on his rug near the hearth. I leaned my head back, thanked God for my parents, my family, my friends and for Mr. Walsh, asking that God heal his injuries while blessing his family.

Papa handed Mama a quilt to place over her skirt as she pulled the jacket close to her neck. The air was chilly but invigorating and it was a lovely night. It had been several months, perhaps years, since she and Papa were out alone at night. She couldn't help but watch the moon and remember the first time Papa drove the Howell wagon to her father's place with she and her brother John as guests of his sisters, Megan and Jill. The crispness of the air and the scenery reminded her of that evening. She patted Papa's hand and moved a little closer as they drove the short distance in silence, both deep in their own thoughts.

Pastor Lawrence had managed to find three other couples to join their impromptu prayer vigil, plus the Bowman family who were already at the farm house. Martha came outside and said John was still unconscious, but breathing normally and was cool to the touch. Doc Hayes had just finished the plaster cast on the leg and had joined them for the prayer service on the porch. Mrs. Hayes had ridden back with Doc to assist in making the cast.

Martha had provided a candle for each couple. They handed Papa one for him and Mama when they walked onto the porch. Mama gave Martha a quick hug and expressed soft condolences. The Walsh children were there in the background seated close to the house. The burning candles illuminated the sky as Pastor Lawrence began:

"Friends, neighbors, and children of God, we are gathered here to lay before God our petitions in prayer for John Walsh. Our Christian brother is in need of your healing powers. Lord, we ask that you will bless him and his family. That you touch his broken body, Lord, and make it whole again. We lift up Martha and the children, Lord, and ask for strength in understanding your ways, for strength in the days ahead and firmness in faith to sustain them. We thank you for Doc Hayes and our community. We pray and give glory to you, Lord, in each and all things we do. Now Lord, as the Bible teaches, so let it be as stated in Matthew 21:22: '...Whatever things you ask in prayer, believing, you will receive.' Lord, we close in thanksgiving for your love and forgiveness of our sins, we humbly pray. Amen."

The group together echoed the "Amen."

Tomorrow would be a new day. Their prayer was that it be a better day for the Walsh family.

As Papa turned the mules for home that night, he and Mama kept silent, both deep within their own thoughts. Mama knew Papa was deeply hurting for his friend and wanted to silently express her love and support. Papa held the mule's reins loosely in his hands. Mama slid her hands over his and gave Papa a gentle squeeze. Pearl sensed that some tragedy was unfolding and needed no commands from Papa as she guided Bertie in the pace and the way home.

Papa swayed side to side with the gentle gait of the wagon being pulled by the mules as he reviewed in his mind the ups and downs of their life at Ripple Creek. He recalled his fatigue and frustration at the threat of being unable to compete the fall crop lay-by after Katie died and the miracle of timely community assistance arriving. He relived Mama's hardships of child birthing and the wonder and joy of welcoming new babies into their family. He remembered the courage of Lad as he protected the family and the sacrifice of the young Skip in taking the bite of the snake to save Tom's life.

He was reminded once again that the Lord is merciful and that by that mercy, Skip survived the ordeal. He thought about more recent tragedies and the uncertainty of the fate awaiting his brother, Eddie—was he dead or alive? And he thought of his old friend and neighbor, Jeremiah. Papa thought of his own shortcomings and his feeling of helplessness in being unable to save his friend, John Walsh. His mind wandered to the ebb and flow of the events in life itself and the thought reminded him of a swimmer treading water in order to simply stay afloat. Papa smiled as he acknowledged to himself that, with God's help, his small family was learning to tread water—though life was a challenge, they were still afloat on Ripple Creek.

As they turned into Ripple Creek Farm lane, Pearl and Bertie headed for the barn fence just outside the kitchen door. I had lit the oil lamp and its faint yellowish glow became visible through the window at the front of the house. That glow reminded Papa of the candle light vigil that had just taken place on the Walsh's front porch. Papa was overtaken by a sense of frustration at his own helplessness, yet in this time of testing trial he reminded himself of Jesus' agony in the garden of Gethsemane. Papa turned to Mama and quoted softly but clearly from St. Matthew 26:39: *"And going forward a little, he fell prostrate and prayed, saying Father, if it is possible, let this cup pass away from me; yet not as I will, but as thou willest."*

Yes, Papa would accept the ultimate will of the Father, but he also knew that the Father was approachable via prayer and supplications. Then Papa threw back his head, stared upward toward the heavens, and cried out loudly into the night, "Merciful God, please let him live!"

END

About the Author

BEULAH SHELTON COYNE, better known as Dr. B, grew up on a small working farm in the Deep South. Through her historical fiction writing, she draws on her own personal experiences, and tells a story of a special family and its struggles to keep TREADING WATER ON RIPPLE CREEK FARM.

She holds a Ph.D. from the University of Lancaster, U.K., an M.B.A. from Nova Southeastern University, and a B.S. from the University of Alabama. Her Dissertation, *Caregiving: A Gender-Neutral Glass Ceiling?* was a finalist in the American Society for Training and Development Dissertation of the Year Award.

Her book *Human Resources, Care-Giving, Career Progression and Gender* (Oxford, UK: Routledge, 2004) was co-authored with E. Coyne and M. Lee. Coyne has also taught research courses, including Demystifying the Research Maze during Beeson's Pastors School (2007).